SLEEP ON IT

Kellye Bel Alston
Sleep On It

Printed in the United States of America

Published by Spines
ISBN: 979-8-90223-149-3

SLEEP ON IT

KELLYE BEL ALSTON

This book is dedicated to my beautiful, sweet Mother-in-Love, Beverly "Babs" Alston. Thank you for being a wonderful second mom to me, a loving mother to my husband, and a devoted grandmother and great grandmother to our children! Thank you for always encouraging me to write and for just being sweet, kind and supportive. While heaven rejoices to have you there, we will love and miss you terribly until we see you again. Please give our love to all our loved ones, especially those we recently lost, Uncle George, brother, Jim Lampley, and our sweet pup, Lucy!

Love,

Kellye

ACKNOWLEDGMENTS

First and foremost, I give honor and thanks to God. Nothing good is possible without You. Great is Your mercy, Your faithfulness, Your grace, Your provisions, Your love and kindness. I praise Your Holy name!

Writing a book and balancing life is always challenging. I am deeply grateful to have such a supportive, God-fearing man in my corner, my husband, Patrick. Thank you for encouraging me to share my gift of writing. You will never know how much it means to me to hear you speak so proudly of my stories. You are quite simply, the best husband, dad, granddad, and person. Our children and I are so blessed to have you as the head of our family.

I am deeply blessed to be the mother of four incredible daughters and three beautiful grandchildren, each of you inspires me in ways I could've never imagined. You are the light of my life and the heart behind everything I do. I pray that I have inspired you to seek God first, be kind to others, and to yourself. My hope is that you love each other like Celie and Nettie, and try to get the most out of this thing called life. I pray that whatever you choose to do, that you prosper in health, live cheerfully with gratitude, and that all may be well with you. Your happiness is my greatest joy. You are my greatest gifts from God. To me you're perfect.

I want to thank all of my sisters, whether by blood or a sister from another mister, for loving without competition, hate, or jealousy, just that genuine I love you, I'm proud of you, and I believe in you kind of energy.

I thank my God-sent friend, National Best-Selling Author, Gracie Hill. You first became my prayer partner, and that connection led to a beautiful professional relationship. I believe you are the greatest editor, and your work speaks for itself.

And finally, a very special thanks to my parents. I miss you, Daddy. Thank you for sharing your love and knowledge of God, which continues to sustain me every day. Thanks for your laughter and most of all, thanks for always believing in me and for reminding me how proud you were of me, even when I stumbled.

Mama, your voice and your laughter are like music to my soul. I treasure every conversation and every word of wisdom you've shared. Your grace, strength and unwavering love have shaped me in ways I can hardly express. Because of you, I've come to understand that no one loves like a mother. Her love is constant, selfless, and truly unmatched.

Thank you all, and may you be blessed immensely!

Kellye Bel Davis Alston

CHAPTER ONE

Pam's breath escaped her as she ran down a dark alley. The broken glass that pierced the bottom of her left foot wedged itself deeper and deeper into the sole of her foot with each fearful stride. She jerked her head over her right shoulder to check behind her. Oh my God. He's going to catch me. Lord, please help me. Pain shot up her leg from her foot. She was almost dragging the leg behind her. Quicksand couldn't feel harder to push through.

Pam's strength was draining from her body like blood oozing from a wound. One, two, three bullets whisked over her head. A fourth bullet pierced her leg, bore through the muscle, into the bone, and forced her to the ground. Like a wounded animal, she howled as the pain claimed her body and blood gushed from the hole in her leg.

"That's right, man. Take that thief down. Let's cut her hands off, too, before we kill her."

Heavy footsteps echoed ominously within inches of her death seemed imminent. Her sight faded as the tall man with a broad chest and glasses loomed above her.

"Help me, please! Somebody, help me!" Pam's desperate cries echoed in her ears, yet they felt distant, as if they were coming from far away. Panic surged through her as she caught glimpses of shadows closing in around her. "I'm so sorry. I'll give it back, I promise! Please, don't do this!" she pleaded, her voice trembling with fear and desperation, hoping for a shred of mercy in the menacing darkness. She felt the cold, steel barrel of the gun pressed hard into her forehead. The sound of the bullet that dropped into the chamber took her breath. The sound of the gunshot was the last thing she heard, and the bullet piercing her brain stole her life instantly.

She sucked in a deep breath that filled her lungs and heaved her body straight up from the bed. A coughing attack made her body jerk, and a burning flood of tears forced her eyelids open. She reached down to feel for the hole in her leg the bullet tore through. Both hands flew to her forehead. Only sweat, no blood, covered her hands. It was a dream. A horrible dream.

Pam slid out of bed, stumbled across the plush carpeted floor into the bathroom, and turned on the faucet. She buried her face in the pool of cold water that settled into her hands. Now, staring at her reflection in the mirror, water dripping down her face, and with the fog of the dream lifting, Pam was sure she was alive.

For the next three hours, she cleaned her bedroom and bathroom, organized three closets, and washed two loads of laundry. A weary Pam glanced at the digital clock beside her bed as she dumped the basket of clothes onto her bed. It was now 4:00 a.m. She still refused to go back to sleep after being shot to death in a nightmare that felt too real. She walked over to the closet to consider what she might pack. "I may as well get started on that task, too," she told herself.

Angie stood in the doorway of Pam's bedroom. Her bottom lip trembled as tears slid down her cheeks. She swallowed the lump of emotion lodged in her throat and spat out, "This just isn't fair."

"What's not fair, Angie?" Pam asked.

"Mom, I just don't understand why you're going halfway around the world. It's the middle of the school year. That Dudley guy doesn't have kids. Why can't he go? I think this whole thing is absurd. How could you be so selfish? Jayden is only twelve years old. He needs you here with him." Angie swatted away her tears with the back of her hand, folded in her bottom lip with her teeth, and bit down hard.

Pam sucked in a deep breath and stepped away from the closet of clothes she was searching through. Quickly, she closed the distance between her and Angie. With only two feet between her and her daughter, Pam lashed out with her verbal defense.

"Listen, girl, who do you think you're talking to with that funky, disrespectful tone? I have sacrificed for you and your brothers all your lives to ensure that you, Nelson, and Jayden had everything you needed. You better remember who I am."

Pam drew in a sharp breath, the vein in her neck pulsing visibly. She let out a loud, airy exhale—an attempt to release her anger along with it. "Now, I have an opportunity to do something that's going to make me a lot of money, and I'm helping a friend. Think of all the shopping we can do when I get back." Pam tugged on the collar of her daughter's blouse. "I know you'll like that. Anyway, I'll only be in Japan for six months. Now, get yourself over here and fold these towels."

Angie shook her head. "Mom, I just cannot believe you will leave us here alone. Everything is about money with you?"

"You're right. Everything is about money because it takes money to live. Something you don't have the slightest concern about since I take care of all your financial needs." Pam's voice was strong, and her piercing gaze bore directly into Angie's eyes, causing her to glance away for a few seconds.

"It's not the end of the world. You know I'd take you with me if I could. But it's way too expensive and not necessary. I'm not packing up you and your brother to go away with me for only a few short months. You're almost twenty-two years old. You can handle this. You're in school, and you have a full life. You can't just put everything on hold to follow me around on a work assignment," Pam declared, searching through her closet again.

"I need you to look after your brother. You know, take him to his practices and feed him. You can do this if you're willing. I know you can. It's not too much to ask, considering the payoff."

"I know I can do it. That's not the point," Angie tossed back at her mother. "Jayden needs you, his mother, not me. And not some payoff."

Pam snatched a red blouse from the closet and tossed it onto the bed. "Jayden will be fine, Angie. So will you. I'll be back before you know it. Now, I'm done talking about this. You're starting to sound like your grandmother."

"Well, Mom, that just tells me that I'm not the only one who thinks this is a dumb idea. I hope we don't all live to regret it."

"You got one more time to let something smart come out of your slick mouth to me, and you are going to have a problem with me that you cannot handle," Pam's warning echoed in the room, the tension thick as she grabbed clothes hangers, rattling them from one side of the closet to the other.

Angie folded in her lips and pressed down hard as she quietly folded the towels on her mother's bed.

Later that afternoon, Angie watched the big raindrops crash into the windowpane and slide down the glass. "Jayden and I are on the brink of a crash ourselves. And that is my mother's fault," Angie said aloud as she snatched up the magazine from her dresser and hurled it across the room into the door. Her frustration pushed her to call her friend. Someone had to listen to her feelings. Her mother sure wasn't.

Angie plopped down onto her bed and pressed three on her speed dial while she chewed off the fingernail on her index finger.

"What's up, girl?" Sonya answered with a loud, chipper voice.

"Girl, I am so furious with my mom I could let out a blood-curdling scream." Angie's feet drummed the mattress in frustration, and she kicked the comforter onto the floor.

"You and your mother at it again?"

"Yeah, she's doing something stupid again." Angie spent the next few minutes sharing the details of her mother's upcoming excursion to Japan. "I wonder how her latest boy toy, Marcus, will handle her leaving the country?"

"What? Miss Pam got a new man. Is he fine and sexy?" Sonya wanted to know.

"Please, she keeps a new man. She's only dated him for three months, and that started a few days after she dumped the guy before him." Angie rolled over and gazed up at the ceiling with a deep frown.

"You don't like the guy?"

"He's okay. I think he's too young for her. But maybe not; my mom likes guys she can control. I've only seen him a couple of times. He is nice looking, though."

Angie and Sonya talked for another thirty minutes. Finally, Angie had calmed down and was ready to shake off concerns about her mother leaving. At least long enough to finish up a paper for class.

"Okay, girl, I got to go. Thanks for letting me spout off about my mom.

You know I love her. She's the best. But sometimes, she just drives me crazy."

Angie sat down at her desk and hit the power button on her laptop.

She tried to focus. But her fears overpowered the words she tried to type. How could she and Jayden live alone while her mother was out of the country? Her older brother, Nelson, had recently got married and moved to Amarillo, Texas. He was six hours away, and her mother would be a world away.

CHAPTER TWO

Pam sat at her kitchen table, making a list of things to do before she headed to Japan. She would get on a plane soon to promote and deliver her new employer's weight loss device that had better work. Dudley swore it would be worth millions of dollars. It had better be worth her traveling halfway around the world. Pam stabbed the notepad with her ink pen as she considered the long sixteen-hour flight.

The shrill of the cell phone singing out from inside her purse broke her level of frustration. Pam saw Dudley's name flash across the screen. She quickly punched the button to accept his call.

"I hope you're ready to make this money." Dudley dived right into the conversation.

"Yes, and I want every penny of the half a million dollars you promised me." Pam popped up from her chair, moved to the sink, and peered out the window.

"You just need to be ready to get on the plane and protect my device. It's going to make us both rich." His heavy voice stirred up excitement, drawing a wide smile across her lips.

"I've got everything set up in Japan. My contacts are ready to meet you and test the device. This cutting-edge technology will sweep the market and blow other weight loss gadgets out of the competition.

"Okay, I guess me staying in Japan for six months while the testing, marketing, and final contracts are worked out is definitely worth half a million dollars. I am all in."

"Absolutely! Meet me in my office in an hour. We'll go over the final details of your trip, and I'll give you the device."

"You got it. I'll see you then." Pam ended the call and gazed out of the window. When I get back home with all that money, my children will understand why I had to leave them.

Her thoughts flowed back over all Dudley had told her about the device. According to him, the market for the product was huge in Japan. It could more than double in profit if it gained the proper recognition in the United States. There had been some issues with promoting the device in the States because of the strict testing guidelines. However, it received terrific reviews from Japan and other countries. It was a hard sell in the U.S., even though it has the highest rate for obesity statistics. There had to be solid proof that this device would provide positive results for problem areas of the body.

The components and engineering needed to make the device work perfectly could be found and installed only in Japan. Dudley was sure he had orchestrated the perfect plan to make the deal go smoothly. That plan would be implemented in Japan, and then the device would be brought back to the United States and not only change lives but result in huge profits. Dudley's voice seemed to whisper in Pam's ear. "The success or failure of this whole thing is on you. We both need this to work. Don't F- - k it up."

Pam met Dudley at his office as scheduled. They talked for almost an hour. She knew who to contact after all the details had been discussed and reviewed. Most importantly, she was not to let the device out of her sight until she handed it over to the man who would make all their money issues disappear.

She glanced into her rearview mirror at Dudley as she coasted out of the parking lot. Pam snickered at his image. He's a good salesman. He should be the one going off to Japan.

Dudley had attempted to ease her doubts about the trip and gave her a crisp hundred-dollar bill for a manicure and pedicure, telling her, "Pamper yourself before you leave. You deserve it."

The trip would be an uncertain adventure in the hopes of financial security. This wasn't the first time Pam had done something unusual in hopes of a big payday. She had been a single mother for most of her children's lives. She divorced her older children's father before the kids left elementary school and met her twelve-year-old son's father four years later. By the time the boy entered kindergarten, the relationship between his parents had fizzled out. In fact, they'd grown to hate each other and couldn't stand to be in the same room. Pam proudly dated Douglas Carr because of his family's long legacy of successful politicians. Doug was running for Mayor when they met. They were both so sure that Doug would easily win the Mayoral election because of his father's reputation as the state governor. When Doug's family got wind that Pam was expecting, they reluctantly rushed the couple to the altar. As much as they hated the idea, they thought it would help if Doug appeared to be a family man. Regret and disappointment set the tone for the duration of their marriage. Surprisingly, Doug lost by a landslide, and Pam never let him live it down.

After years of embarrassing public arguments and fights that had morphed into irreconcilable differences, they mutually decided to divorce. Pam was determined that something had to change in her life. This will work. I just have to be confident, and the product will sell itself. That would be her mantra. She rehearsed it over and over the rest of the drive home.

CHAPTER THREE

Angie figured she needed to get used to the fact that no matter what she thought, Pam was going to Japan, and she should settle into the idea of being her brother's primary caretaker. She knew her boyfriend, Jacoby, would help out whenever possible. He was someone Angie had come to rely on. They'd dated for well over a year. He lived with his parents and two younger sisters whom she loved. After spilling her guts to them about her current circumstances, they'd all assured her they would be there for her if she needed them.

As the days passed, there was no more talk of Angie and Jayden living alone. Instead, Marcus would be staying at the house with them. Angie rushed straight home from her last college class for the day. Anxious to confront her mother, she carefully considered what she might say. At first, her lips moved, and no words came out. By the time she parked the car at the curb, Angie was talking out loud. "This living situation will not work with me, Jayden, and some strange man in the house with us. How do I know he's not a pervert or rapist?"

Angie hustled through the kitchen door, letting the heavy wooden door slam behind her and announce her arrival. "Mom, where are you?" she yelled.

"I'm in the living room," Pam called out.

Angie slung her leather tote bag filled with books onto the kitchen table and marched into the living room.

"Oh, I meant to tell you; Marcus finally gave me a firm yes. He agreed to stay here with you and Jayden for me. He's going to rent out his house and take care of you guys for me until I get back," Pam said, sitting on the sofa reviewing her travel checklist.

"You have got to be kidding me, Mom! You can't do this. You reel me in and sell me this crap about I can take care of my brother, and just when I start to accept it, you pull the rug from under me. I don't know Marcus, and neither do you. You've only been dating him for a few months, and you already trust him with your kids? I didn't like it when you first mentioned it to me. I like it even less now." Angie yelled, "Who does that?"

"Girl, what are you talking about? You do know Marcus. And I told you that him staying here was possible if he could work it out."

"No, Mom, I've met Marcus; there's a big difference between meeting someone and knowing them. The only other times Jayden and I have even seen him is when he's sneaking out of your bedroom in the morning. Just because you sleep with a guy does not mean you know him." Angie stood in front of her mother with her nostrils flaring in and out and beads of sweat popping out onto the tip of her nose.

"Angie, this is..."

"Mom, I need you to hear me out. This is dangerous, and it's selfish. What if he's a killer or a rapist? What do you know about his background? You don't know what this person is capable of. Do you even care?" Angie's vision began to blur as the heavy tears leaped over her eyelashes and slid down her face.

Pam pushed herself up from the sofa and folded Angie into a tight embrace. "You know I would never put you and your brother in harm's way. Marcus is a good man. Just give him a chance. Talk to him. Get to know him. I guarantee you'll fall in love with him."

Angie abruptly broke free from the hold Pam had on her. Looking directly into her mother's eyes, she demanded, "Are you in love with him? I didn't know you were that serious about him?"

"Well, honey, it's not, and no. I'm not in love with him. We have become very good friends. We respect each other, and I guess we do feel something for each other, but I wouldn't exactly call it love." Pam snatched her eyes away from Angie's pleading glance and then offered her a smile.

"Look, sweetie, I wanted to take the pressure of caring for your brother off you. You were worried about the responsibility I was putting on you. I gave it some more thought and decided you were right. It was too much to expect of you."

"Mom," Angie blurted out.

"Angie, please, don't give me a hard time about this. I've made up my mind, and that's it. Marcus has been on his own for a long time. He knows what to do in an emergency, and he knows the needs of a household. Everything will be fine. I promise, and besides, I will always call you. No matter what happens, remember that you are the one person I will always contact. I just need to know that you're with me on this. I've made the right decision. Trust me," Pam coaxed.

Angie's bottom lip trembled with emotion. She rubbed the side of her pant leg hard with her hand. Tears slid down her face and dripped off her chin onto the front of her blouse.

"Say something, Angie."

"Why? Nothing I say is going to make a difference. Like you said, you've made up your mind." Angie whirled her body around quickly and stomped out of the living room, sending the glass vase on the table by the doorway crashing to the floor. Shattered pieces of glass sang out loudly as they hit the floor. Angie never broke her stride out of the living room, through the kitchen, and out the back door. She slammed it hard enough to shake the frame.

"What in the hell do you think you are doing, little girl, breaking up my stuff?" Pam charged, trailing behind Angie.

Angie yanked shut her car door and backed out of the driveway, leaving skid marks on the pavement as her last statement.

Pam stood in the doorway, glancing back and forth from the broken glass on the floor to Angie's fleeing car that was now out of the driveway and headed down the block.

CHAPTER FOUR

Jayden tugged on his mother's sleeve to get her attention. She hadn't heard him hustle down the stairs, taking the steps two at a time.

Pam jerked her head abruptly to face Jayden after his second strong tug at her. "You startled me. I thought you were taking a nap."

"I heard a bunch of noise. It woke me up." Jayden glanced back at the shattered vase on the floor with his arm outstretched and finger-pointing at it. "I didn't break that, Mom. I promise; it wasn't me."

"I know, baby. I know." Pam stroked the side of Jayden's face with the palm of her hand.

His caramel-colored skin and big eyes seemed to light up with relief that he wasn't about to be blamed for the mess on the floor. "I'll help you get the glass up." Jayden offered with a bright smile that claimed his face and showed off the straight, white teeth his braces had awarded him. "What happened anyway? Isn't that your favorite crystal vase? It had to be Angie because it wasn't me. She's in trouble, right?" Jayden snickered, covering his mouth with his hand.

"Don't worry about who's in trouble. You make sure you stay out of trouble while I'm gone."

"I know you said you were okay with Marcus staying here while I'm gone. Have you changed your mind?"

Jayden dumped the broken glass from the dustpan into the trash can near the sink. "He seems cool. At least I'll have someone to watch the game with." Jayden shook his index finger in his mother's direction. "You know Angie will try to spend all her time with that boyfriend of hers."

Pam inspected the floor to ensure that the last speck of glass had been swept up. "Your sister will take good care of you in my absence. Don't worry. I promise." Pam planted a kiss on Jayden's cheek and wrapped him up into a strong embrace.

"Mom, I am not a little kid anymore."

"Okay, I guess you're too big for ice cream at Baskin-Robins, too."

Jayden laughed and responded with wide eyes and a smile, "Nope, Mommy. I'm not too big at all. Let's go."

Pam and Jayden hadn't been home with ice cream in hand for more than ten minutes when Pam's cell phone rang out with the familiar tune that announced her mother was calling. Good Jesus, she can only want one thing. Why do I feel like Angie called my mother to spill her guts? Pam drew in a deep breath and said lazily, "Hi Mom."

Pam's mother, Mrs. Carter, cut right into Pam without any greeting. "What is this foolishness my granddaughter tells me about you having some man stay with them while you run off to Japan on some scavenger hunt?"

"Madea, don't start. I already told you I am going to Japan and why. You couldn't talk me out of it then, and you can't talk me out of it now." Pam kicked off her shoes and plopped down onto the sofa in the living room. Her fingers clung to the edge of the sofa, and she squeezed hard.

"Girl, you are still just as stubborn as you were as a child. Couldn't tell you anything then, and I can't tell you anything now. You could have just brought the kids to Amarillo and left them with me and your dad. But you are too stubborn for that."

Her mother scolded her like a child for almost ten minutes before Pam cut into her with ice-cold precision. "Madea, stop, just stop. These are my kids, and it's my decision. I am doing what I feel is the best financial move for my family. The kids will be fine. Marcus is a good guy. You are just going to have to trust my decision."

"Pam, I don't know why..."

"I'm leaving tomorrow, and I still have a lot to do. I've got to go. I'll call you before I get on the plane. Talk to you tomorrow." Pam gazed up at the ceiling, mouthing, "Please let me get off this phone, please."

It worked. Her mother said a couple more things and released Pam from the tongue-lashing she'd had more than enough of. Pam grabbed one of the big sofa pillows, covered her face with it, and screamed as loudly as she could. She removed the pillow, took a deep breath, and screamed again into the pillow. A few minutes later, she schlepped up the stairs, finished packing, and crossed the last few things off her to-do list.

CHAPTER FIVE

On the dreaded day of departure, Marcus and Jayden took Pam to the airport. Angie chose not to watch her mother leave for a trip she was against. The time she'd spent with her mother the night before had been memorable and meaningful. They snacked on popcorn and cuddled on the sofa like they used to do when Angie was a little girl. They talked and laughed about old times and cried before calling it a night.

Angie stood in the front doorway, watching them back out of the driveway. Her line of vision was fixed on her mother. I'm glad I apologized for storming out of the house and breaking her vase. She's going to be oceans away from us. I had to let it go. Angie allowed a quiet breath to escape her lungs and out past her lips. She yelled out, "Love you, Mom." Then the car was gone, and so was her mother.

She turned, closed the door, and headed up the stairs, taking them two at a time until she was in her bedroom. Fifteen minutes later, she'd shoved some clothes into two duffle bags and headed down the stairs, out the door, and into her car. Her boyfriend, Jacoby's, house would be her safe haven. She was not staying in a house with a strange man she knew nothing about while her mother was gone.

Jacoby's mother, Mrs. Myers, agreed to allow Angie to stay in her home. It took less persuasion than Angie expected. Jacoby's oldest sister had recently left for college, and their family welcomed Angie to stay in her room until the girl returned for the summer. His mom thought it was unwise and unsafe for Angie to live in the house with a grown man who was a stranger.

Where are your mother's brains in her panties? Mrs. Myers' words sang out in Angie's head as she put her key into the ignition of her car. When Mrs. Myers said it, the words made Angie angry. However, the more Mrs. Myers talked about the situation, the more Angie realized the woman was giving voice to Angie's own thoughts.

Angie pressed her foot down on the gas pedal. Distance from the address Marcus would soon be calling home was needed. "Mom better get back home in six months and not a day later," Angie said aloud, slamming the heel of her fist into the steering wheel.

She thought about the rules Jacoby's mother had made clear to her on the way to the house. Angie knew she meant business when she said, "Break one of my rules, and I will put you out of my house." Her words were stern, and the look on her face said to Angie, "Don't try me." She hated leaving her little brother and would check on him every day. But staying in the house with Marcus wasn't going to happen. Jayden was a minor and had no choice. She did. Besides, she would be back home by the time Pam returned from Japan. Jayden promised not to tell their mother Angie wasn't staying at home. Perhaps she could persuade Marcus to do the same. Angie felt confident her mother didn't struggle flying across the world, leaving her children behind. That thought nagged at her soul but wasn't quite on target.

CHAPTER SIX

Marcus tapped his fingers on the car's dashboard with his eyes glued to the gym door. Twenty minutes late coming out of basketball practice, again. *This kid must think he's something special, and I am on his clock, not the other way around.* He'd driven Jayden back and forth to practice twice, to the arcade, a friend's house, and the mall in just one week. "Dang, I've only been at Pam's a couple of weeks, and now I'm a chauffeur. This crap is about to come to an abrupt halt," Marcus committed to himself aloud as he glanced down at his watch.

Marcus fished out a stick of gum from the armrest of his car and popped it into his mouth. *Maybe I just need to sit Jayden down, talk with him, and help him prioritize the things he wants to do. I'll explain that I can't always be his personal driver.*

He chomped down on the gum for five minutes like it was a tough piece of steak. Finally, the gym door opened, and out marched Jayden. Marcus started up his car, and the engine roared. He pressed a button, and the driver's side window slid down. The frustrated chauffeur spat out the gum and clutched the gear shift between the leather bucket seats so hard he could feel his pulse in his hand. The fifteen-minute ride to Pam's house was quiet. Marcus labored diligently to hold his tongue.

Jayden popped in his earbuds and listened to music on his phone the entire ride. Glad to put an end to the silent torture, Marcus shoved the gear shift into park. Jayden hopped out of the car and pushed the door shut with a heavy hand.

Ten minutes later, Marcus exited the car and entered the house through the back door that led directly into the kitchen. Jayden was in the kitchen eating a sandwich and chips. The needed conversation couldn't be put off any longer.

"Jayden, can I talk with you for a minute?" Marcus tossed his car keys on top of the counter and leaned against it with his ankles crossed and arms folded across his chest.

Jayden said nothing. He stood, grabbed his book bag from the back of the chair, walked over, and placed his glass in the sink. Into the living room, he headed and turned on the flat-screen TV.

Marcus followed him and stopped in the middle of the floor a couple of feet from Jayden. "So, you hop into my car, never speak to me, or say thank you for the ride like I've done nothing at all for you." Marcus waited for a response. Jayden never looked at him or opened his mouth. "Look, I was hoping you would agree to either cut down on some of your weekly activities or see if you can catch a ride with some of your friends."

Jayden's eyes darted away from the TV and landed his visual assault on the target standing in front of him. "Why do you think my mom left you here? She knows what I have to do, and she never has a problem with it. If you don't want to take me where I need to go, you can leave, and my sister will come back home. We don't need you here, and Angie doesn't want you here." Jayden kicked his book bag, which was lying on the floor in front of him. "I'll call my mom so she can explain your job to you. Obviously, you forgot what you are supposed to do." Jayden stood up to leave the room with his cell phone in his hand.

Marcus folded in his bottom lip and felt the pinch of his teeth digging deep into his skin. Is this kid really talking to me crazy? Does he think there will be no consequences for his disrespect and smart mouth?

Jayden walked past his adversary and allowed his gaze to move over him from head to toe, then tossed his pointed words over his shoulder, "You ain't my daddy."

Marcus grabbed Jayden's shoulder and swung him around to face him. Quickly, he clutched the collar of the boy's shirt and pulled his face within inches of his own. "Listen here, you little punk. I know I ain't your daddy. You need to thank God for that. But I'm not your slave or your personal chauffeur either. I'm not here to run your little ass around. I'm here so you can eat. Now, let's get one thing straight, little boy; you'll never talk to me like that again. Understand?"

Jayden's eyelids blinked open and closed several times quickly before two tear drops rolled down his cheeks. He sniffed hard and barked back at Marcus. "Get your hands off me, man."

Marcus ignored his demand. "I tried to help you, but since you're so grown, you work it out. Get around the best way you can. If you can't figure it out, then I guess you just won't get there. I don't care what you do. I'm here because your mother asked me to help her out. Let's be clear. I'm not doing this for you or your sister." Marcus tightened his grip on Jayden's collar and pulled him even closer. "If Angie chooses to be somewhere else other than at home, that's her business. I will still do what I promised your mom I would do. As for you, you will not disrespect me again. You got that?"

Jayden's shaky voice threatened the man who had a chokehold grip on him. "You better get your hands off me. Let me go. Let me go, now." He struggled, attempting to push himself free from Marcus' hold.

Marcus held on tightly, pointing his finger at the struggling kid, almost touching his nose. "You're running your mouth like you can do something to help yourself. You need me. I don't need you. I'll be paying the bills here for the next few months, whether you like it or not. Now get out of my sight." Marcus shoved Jayden onto the floor, and another one of Pam's crystal vases crashed to the floor.

Jayden sat there with beads of sweat dripping from his forehead and his fists balled up tightly. He pounded the floor as he sat with wide eyes, slowly filling with tears that he did not want Marcus to see.

Marcus rolled his eyes at Jayden and snickered, "Not so tough after all, huh?" He walked by him, through the kitchen, and out the back door, which he slammed shut, and he did not look back.

CHAPTER SEVEN

Jayden pushed himself up from the floor, collected his things, and stomped up the stairs to his bedroom, where he wept. He missed his mother. She'd only called him twice since she'd left. With watery eyes and a dripping nose from all his sobbing, he surveyed his bedroom. His new laptop, game system, shelves full of games, even the new basketball team jacket he'd gotten a couple of weeks ago, none of it was what he wanted. Jayden wanted his mother.

He grabbed a Kleenex from his desk, blew his nose hard, wiped away his tears with the back of his hand, and snatched up his cell phone from his bed. His fingers pressed hard and quickly down onto the keypad of his phone. "I'm sure you had no idea that Marcus is a mean jerk. I hate being here with him. This was a mistake, Mom. Call me, please," Jayden pleaded into the phone, clutching it tightly. He sat on his bed bent over with both elbows planted on his knees. He held the phone with both hands while tapping his feet, and his eyes were glued to the screen of his phone. "Come on, Mom. Call me," he yelled at the phone.

The phone didn't ring. Five minutes later, he called his mother again and paced the floor, waiting for her to answer. No luck. Her voicemail spoke to him. He pressed the end button and quickly called another number. His voice quivered with emotion as soon as he heard her voice.

"He pushed me down into the floor."

"What? Who pushed you?" Angie demanded with a loud voice.

Jayden gave her all the details of his argument and scuffle with Marcus. "I don't want him here." His voice trailed off into sniffles and a cough.

"Sit tight. I am on my way," Angie assured him.

Marcus had driven around for a few minutes and found himself back in the driveway scolding himself. "I had no right to put my hands on that kid, no matter how he acted or what he said to me." He pounded his fist into the palm of his left hand. "Now I've got a real mess." Out of the car and through the back door, he pushed himself. He had to apologize to Jayden. He was wrong.

The house phone rang just as he was about to head upstairs. He stopped at the cordless phone sitting on the granite countertop of the island in the middle of the kitchen. He didn't even get the word hello completely out of his mouth before Angie's voice jumped through the phone and attacked him.

"Jayden told me you put your hands on him. You better get your things and get out of my mother's house. Don't be there when I get there, or else," she warned.

Marcus got no chance to respond. The dial tone sang out in his ear. She has some nerve thinking that she'll run me out, Marcus thought. Besides, he had nowhere to go. He had sublet his apartment, and although the new tenants hadn't moved in yet, he had already spent their deposit and first month's rent. He had to honor the contract between them. Maybe he had put himself in a bad situation, agreeing to sublet his apartment, stay at Pam's house, and pay bills there while she was in Japan. He liked Pam, and the five thousand dollars she promised him for helping her out had sealed the deal. But her kids and their disrespectful mouths definitely weren't part of that deal.

His conscience led him step by step to Jayden's bedroom door. Marcus stood quietly for a few moments, then knocked softly on the door. No response, then another soft knock. On the other side of the door, the sound of someone walking across the floor could be heard. Moments later, a quiet fell over Jayden's room.

"Come on, Jayden. I know you're in there. I need to talk to you."

Marcus folded his arms and waited. Still, not a word came through the door.

"I handled the situation all wrong. I wish I hadn't used force to get my point across. I apologize for grabbing you and shoving you down. There was nothing right about that. I'm sorry. I really am, Jayden." He patted the side of his leg with his hand. The kid had to say something or eventually come out of that room if for nothing but to use the toilet.

A few minutes crawled by. Marcus decided it was probably best to leave it alone for now. No need to make things any worse. He retreated from the door and started down the steps. Halfway down, a loud, angry voice called out to him.

"Marcus, where the hell are you?"

A weak grin crawled across his face as he slowed his pace. He decided to let her come to him, curious to see just what Angie thought she was big and bad enough to do.

She met Marcus halfway up the steps, hurling curses as fast as her tongue could fire them. "Have you lost your mind putting your hands on my brother? Only a punk a--, piss poor excuse for a man would shove a kid around."

"Wow, girl, you got a foul mouth on you. Does your mother know you talk like that? You are too pretty to let such ugly words come out of your mouth."

Jayden rushed out of his room and stood at the top of the stairs.

"Are you hurt, Jayden?"

He shook his head no in response to his sister.

Angie stepped within inches of Marcus, pointing her finger in his face, almost touching his nose. "I told you to be out of here by the time I got here. Get your sh-- and get out of my mother's house, NOW!"

Angie was so close to Marcus that he could feel her breath on his face. He stepped back two feet and doubled over in laughter. When he finally stood up straight, a forceful blow crashed into his face. His ears rang like a bell sounding off, and his nose throbbed with pain. Marcus shook his head to clear his thoughts. This girl just punched me like a man. Marcus drew back his right hand and landed a slap across Angie's face that sounded like a crash.

Jayden ran halfway down the stairs, stopped, and leaped onto Marcus' back. All three of them tumbled down the stairs. Hand-to-hand combat had broken out, and the living room was the battlefield. Glass ashtrays, lamps, and even a glass end table were thrown at Marcus.

Angie punched, kicked, scratched, and threw everything she could reach at her enemy. This was a battlefield, and she had the home advantage.

Marcus tried to shield himself mostly and get out of his attacker's reach and the objects dinging him from every side.

Unexpectedly, Angie stopped, sucked in a couple of hard breaths, and dropped to the floor, and cried out, "I miss my mother. How could she leave us like this?" She wailed uncontrollably with her shoulders shaking and sucking in deep breaths as she wept and tried to talk at the same time.

CHAPTER EIGHT

Jayden knelt on the floor beside his sister, wrapped both arms around her, and rocked back and forth with a slow, solemn rhythm that shook Marcus to his core. He brushed away the blood that trickled down the side of his face from the open cut over his right eye. He stood over them, looking down. It had become clear to him. They needed their mother, and she wasn't there for them. That's what all the tension between them was about. Jayden's selfish, unappreciative, bad attitude and Angie's unwillingness to give him a chance was simply driven by the hurt they felt when their mother left. They needed her.

The pain he witnessed pulled him to the floor as well. He moaned as he bent his right knee, rubbing the swollen knot the glass ashtray had caused. He couldn't help it. Marcus pulled both Angie and Jayden into a tight embrace. To his surprise, he felt them reach for him as well. The loud crash of the lamp that fell from the edge of the coffee table and slammed into the floor broke up their embrace. They looked around at the broken glass, furniture, lamps, and all the mess their rumble had caused and burst into roaring laughter.

"Man, you would think a tornado swept through here. Mom would kill us if she saw this mess." Jayden stood, turning around, taking it all in.

"Mom would go ballistic if she saw her house in this condition. I'm sure you know by now, Marcus, that she is a clean fanatic."

"Yes, we better get to work cleaning this disaster up." Marcus stood and leaned over to help Angie up.

Jacoby peered into the house through the side panel of glass at the front door. He swung open the door, and it made a noisy clunk when it hit the door stop on the wall. "Get your hands off of her," Jacoby warned as he lunged forward, caught Marcus by the collar of his shirt, and nearly hurled him across the room and onto the floor.

Marcus' head slammed into the end of the thick glass table, and another battle scar opened its vein and gushed out blood from the side of his face. Dazed for only a few seconds, he regained his focus, ran across the room, and tackled Jacoby. The battle of the Titans had begun. They rolled over and over on the floor, scuffling, breathing hard, and struggling to get a firm hold on each other. Jayden watched with wide eyes while Angie screamed and pleaded for them to stop.

Just as Marcus had pinned Jacoby down and drew back a clenched fist targeted for the center of his face, Angie latched onto Marcus' arm and begged with a piercing scream, "No, don't hit him. Please don't hit him."

The victor looked over his shoulder at the young girl who was trying to rescue her boyfriend, then back at the young man beneath him and realized he was just a kid. Marcus unclenched his fist and stood.

Angie helped Jacoby from the floor and outside to his car. "Jayden, I'll call you later unless you want to come with me?"

Jayden shook his head no. "I'm cool," he offered, glancing back at Marcus.

"Okay, I better drive Jacoby home." She tossed a weak head nod toward Marcus and slid into the driver's seat of Jacoby's sleek black Charger with tinted windows.

They rode to Jacoby's in silence. His throbbing headache forced him to recline his seat and cover his eyes with both hands. Sunlight only agitated the pain, which wrinkled his forehead and made him nauseous.

Angie steered the car into the driveway and hopped out to allow her boyfriend to lean on her. "Let's just get you through the living room and up the stairs without your mother seeing you. At least until you are feeling better."

"Not so loud. My head is about to explode." The words escaped his mouth and landed in his mother's ears.

Mrs. Myer's mouth fell open at the sight of her son scratched up, dried blood underneath his nose, and appearing to be unable to walk without assistance. "Oh, my Lord. What happened to you?" She gently ran her finger over the bruise on his right cheek. It stood out boldly against his light caramel complexion. Her attention swung over to Angie as she whipped her head to the right and challenged the young girl she had invited into her home. "What happened to him? Are you the reason why he's all banged up?"

Pushing past his headache, Jacoby tried to speak above a whisper. "No, Mom. It's not her fault. It was me. I jumped to the wrong conclusion," he admitted.

"Wrong conclusion, what do you mean, wrong conclusion? What is he talking about, Angie? Start talking, and I mean right now."

Angie chewed at her bottom lip, swallowed slowly, and gazed at the woman in front of her who was making her nervous.

"Girl, you better say something," Mrs. Myers yelled with her hand on her hip and tiny, red blood vessels popping out on the cheeks of her pale-skinned face.

"Mrs. Myers, Jacoby came over after my brother and I had gotten into an altercation with my mom's boyfriend, but...,"

"Oh, but nothing; I knew this was going to happen," Cynthia Myers challenged.

Jacoby stood up straight, holding onto his side, cleared his throat, and tried to push out a strong voice.

"Angie, just go to your room and let me talk to my mom, please."

Angie did a quick about-face, determined not to make eye contact with Mrs. Myers. When she'd safely escaped the contempt-filled atmosphere downstairs, she collapsed onto the bed, shielded herself by pulling the comforter over her head, and burying her face into the pillow. It was a hollow escape. The volume of Mrs. Myers' anger-filled voice floated up the stairs to pursue her.

CHAPTER NINE

Marcus shut the door behind him and walked straight to the refrigerator for cold water. He popped the cap on the bottle of prescription painkillers he'd picked up from the pharmacy. Down his throat slid two big pills chased by four big gulps of water. With both hands planted against the refrigerator, he leaned his weight into the door.

"Hey, you made it back. What took you so long?" Jayden questioned as he entered the kitchen and perched himself onto one of the bar stools.

"The emergency room was packed. My eight stitches had to wait in line behind the guy who was rushed in with a gunshot wound." Marcus lightly touched the skin under his chin, which was laced together with stitches. "Thanks for cleaning up all the mess we made in the living room. Sorry, I had to leave that on you."

"The blood and mess everywhere needed cleaning up." Jayden pointed to the blood-laced shirt Marcus was still wearing.

"Hey, look, little man. I really am sorry for shoving you and getting all this chaos started. I feel bad about it," he offered up with weak, pleading eyes.

Jayden cracked a slight smile. "I'm sorry too, Marcus. I was mad at my mom for leaving us and took it out on you. The stuff she usually does for me, for some reason, I wanted to see you run around for me as much as she does." The guilty boy confessed, dropped his head, and fidgeted with the plastic watch band on his wrist.

A hush crowded the room for a few moments. Neither spoke, not knowing what was next.

The loud silence was broken by Jayden popping up from his seat and announcing, "I'll work on my schedule and get rides when I can. Oh, and I can come right out when basketball practice ends."

"So, you purposely..." The adult in the room stopped and swallowed the words about to leap out of his mouth. "Don't worry about it. I will help get you where you need to be as much as possible. We'll just have to work together. Okay?"

Marcus offered his knuckles up first. They pounded fists, and the peace treaty had been signed.

"Can we order a pizza?" Jayden asked with his bubbly, big eyes, expressing his eagerness.

"Yes, my stomach is empty. But I choose the place," Marcus advised, removing his cell phone from his shirt pocket. A twinge of pain shot through his chin. He'd almost forgotten about the stitches and the headache that had pursued him on the way home from the emergency room.

Later that night, crawling into Pam's king-size bed, Marcus wondered if he had made the right decision. Why did I agree to move away from my house to pay bills in someone else's house and be a caretaker to a teenage boy whose father lives nearby? His thoughts became a whisper in the dark. "Why isn't this boy with his father? What am I doing here?" He hadn't known Pam very long, and although he had become very fond of her, maybe he had agreed to the live-in situation with her kids too quickly. Perhaps she wasn't even the right woman for him.

Marcus rolled over onto his back, crossed his ankles, and placed his palms behind his head. Through the open blinds and sheer curtains, he stared out the window while his thoughts tumbled around in his head. Was she the right one? She was at least ten years older than him. She definitely seemed to be money-hungry, which was why she was halfway around the world, away from her family to begin with.

Jayden wasn't the only brat in the family. His mother had been spoiled by someone, as well, and was used to having her way, Marcus decided. He'd noticed that when things didn't go how Pam wanted them to, she'd either throw a tantrum or shut down and not talk until she got what she wanted. He didn't think she was someone he wanted to be with for the rest of his life. "Why in the hell did I move in here?" he asked himself out loud. Sleep continued to escape him for almost an hour. Finally, he drifted off after taking a pain pill to dull the throbbing discomfort stabbing at his chin.

CHAPTER TEN

Pam sat on the edge of the bed in her hotel room. The dim lighting, the stale air, and the frustration that bore into her soul wouldn't let her rest. She'd only called home a few times since arriving in Japan. Her communication with her kids had primarily been text messages, and they had been few and far between. She didn't want to hear the words, "How's everything going? Will you be home soon?"

She didn't want to lie. The truth was things were going horribly. She planted her elbows into her wide-spread knees and dropped her head. Pam couldn't escape the scene that played repeatedly in her head. The day after she'd arrived, her nightmare began.

She had her instructions. Ask for Chu and tell him that she was sent by Kiko, which was Dudley's Japanese name. The two short men behind the counter of the tea shop she'd entered seemed nervous. Their gaze bounced back and forth between her and the door. They pointed at her, spoke to each other in Japanese, and continued pointing using their hands to describe her. She figured they had to be talking about her. Were they measuring her size and height? She wasn't sure. But she was ready to get the heck out of there.

Pam held tightly to the box that she had taken the body toning device out of. She watched the men inspect it as their voices got louder and louder. The short man with glasses approached her and essentially backed her out of the store, speaking loudly. "Tomorrow, tomorrow, you come back tomorrow," were the only words spoken in English.

Pam remembered trying to grab the device from the man. Before she knew what was happening, he'd backed her right up to the exit door, opened it, shoved her out, and locked the door. The man burst into laughter and lifted the device up over his head with both hands in victory.

Pam rubbed the side of her hand, which was still sore. She had banged it on the shop's glass door so hard that she broke the glass and cut her hand. The short man wearing glasses ran into a back room with the other man right on his heels. All Pam could do was look through the broken glass door and yell. A flash from the camera of a woman beside her taking multiple snapshots of Pam and waving people over to see the window that she had broken was the only reason Pam turned and walked away.

Pam shot up from the side of the bed and kicked the trash can near her. It sailed across the room and slammed into the hotel room door. The shrill of her cell phone pulled her over to investigate who was calling. "Darn it, Dudley, again. I don't want to hear your mouth again today." She snatched up the phone from the pillow and, without answering it, yelled at the phone in her hand, "I know, Dudley, I better get that device back, or I'm not getting a dime. Instead, I will owe you a fortune, and you'll take it out of my a-- if you have to. I know, jerk. I know."

According to Dudley, Chu would be out of town for another four days. Somehow, he'd contacted Chu as soon as Pam informed him that she'd given the device to the wrong person, and they kept it. "What does he keep calling me for? There's nothing I can do until Chu returns and contacts me. Jesus, stop calling me," Pam said to the still-ringing phone and tossed it onto the bed. Nothing had happened the way Dudley told her it would. Maybe he hadn't told her everything. Things weren't adding up. What was Dudley not telling her?

Pam stomped into the bathroom, turned on the faucet, and leaned over the rusty sink. She buried her face into her hands, repeatedly splashing cold water onto her face. She stood to face her reflection in the mirror. The tears that slid down her face were camouflaged by the water dripping from her cheeks.

The woman staring back at her wasn't the attractive, jazzy, confident woman Pam knew. This woman had bloodshot eyes, an uncombed head of hair, wore no makeup, and had bags under her eyes that said she and sleep hadn't spent much time together. Defeat and desperation poked at her to go home and admit she'd made a mistake like everybody kept telling her. Her mother's voice rang out in her ear. "Half a million dollars to take a device to Japan; if it sounds too good to be true, it probably is." But Dudley only purchased her a one-way ticket. She was stuck, and retreating was not an option.

Morning came quickly and seeped into her hotel room through the narrow slits in the blinds. Pam rubbed her eyeballs with the heels of both hands. She glanced over at the clock on the bedside table. It was eight o'clock in the morning, and she had actually gotten five hours of sleep. Her achy body and the headache that pricked at her temples told her the five hours felt like one hour.

Forty-five minutes after Pam showered, dressed, and sucked down a cup of black coffee, she was in a taxi headed back to the tea shop where the device had been stolen from her. She slipped a compact mirror from her purse and assessed the red wig, red lipstick, oversized hoop earrings, and dark shades that were meant to disguise her. No way would those guys in the shop recognize her. She checked her purse for her translation book. It didn't help her much the day before, but she just might need it.

Pam climbed out of the taxi a short distance from the shop. She walked slowly until she stood in front of the window and could peer into the shop, hoping not to be noticed. This time, three men were standing behind the counter. The same two men from the day before and another guy, who looked younger, were all in the shop. The younger guy seemed angry with the two men who had stolen the device from her. She watched them for a few minutes and saw the young guy pull the stolen device out of a black bag.

Pam pressed her face against the glass. Yep, it was Dudley's device. She opened the door and headed into the shop, pretending to be a tourist needing directions. The three men scrambled like roaches do when you turn the lights on in a dark room. But not fast enough. She could see the young guy stuff the device under the counter while the other two hurried off to the back and out of sight.

Pam pointed to the translation book and said repeatedly, "Need to buy a tea set."

The guy squinted his eyelids and shook his head, chanting, "No, go. You go." Pam pulled out some cash and waved it at him while pointing at a tea set on a shelf.

The guy shook his head as if he understood what she wanted and pulled out a short ladder with four steps. As soon as the man was on the top step reaching for the pot, Pam shot behind the counter, grabbed the device, and made a dash for the door.

The shop owner turned toward Pam in time to see her snag up the device and stuff it into her big purse. It sounded like he was fussing as he yelled loudly and fast while he moved quickly down the ladder. Pam hustled from behind the counter, reached for the doorknob, and flung the door open wide.

His accent was thick, and his words were strung together. Still, Pam was sure the man said, "Hey, you. Lady, stop." His arms flailed in the air as he stumbled face forward, hit the ground, and continued to yell at Pam.

Oh, now he can speak English, Pam thought. She ran out of the door and down the sidewalk with big red curls bouncing in the air. Her chest pounded, and she ran right out of her left shoe as she bumped into the man in front of her when she rushed by him.

Dang, Dudley was right. This thing must really be worth some money. These people are willing to steal and who knows what else to get this device. Pam jerked her head over her right shoulder to see all three men from the shop chasing her. The short, husky man was leading the pack, shoving people out of his way and pointing at her. Pam ran faster. "Lord, give me strength."

CHAPTER ELEVEN

Several weeks had passed since Angie landed at Jacoby's house. The still of the night finally claimed the five-bedroom brick home. Leaves on the tree outside Jacoby's bedroom window whispered their song as the cool wind serenaded them. The leaves weren't the only noise that kept the night alive. Weren't his parents ever going to stop talking? If they didn't go to bed soon, he'd miss his opportunity to sneak down the hall into Angie's room. That hadn't been a problem since his parents were usually in bed by 10:30 p.m. His stepfather would be asleep if his mother could just stop talking.

It was midnight, and voices still crawled from underneath his parents' bedroom door. They were now just loud enough for him to make out what they were saying.

"I think we made a mistake letting that girl stay here. She's been here too long, and there's too much drama with her family." Cynthia pulled her robe on and tightened the belt with a hard yank. "My son got hurt defending her a couple of weeks ago. That girl is playing games. She's trouble. Not to mention, she's lazy and doesn't do a thing around here to help." Cynthia protested, plopping down onto the bench at the foot of the bed.

"Leave that girl alone, Cynthia. Angie is a fine young lady, and you know your son is crazy about her. She cooked a fabulous dinner tonight, and all you did was complain. I didn't want to tell you this, but her roast beef was the best I've ever eaten."

His wife looked at him through squinted eyelids as thin as a penny.

"Oh, don't look at me like that, Cynthia. Your roast is always dry. It's so dry, it feels like splinters of wood going down my throat." Her husband massaged his throat with his fingers. "Just kidding, babe," he said, sitting up in bed.

"Okay, Charles, don't talk too much. You're about to bite off the hand that feeds you. Her roast wasn't all that to me. It was okay."

He looked at her sucking his teeth, and said, "Whatever, you look green with envy to me. Just leave that girl alone. Jacoby's not a kid anymore. It would help if you tried to be more considerate for his sake. She hasn't done anything, at least no more than our own kids. None of them clean up enough if you ask me, but other than that, she's a good kid going through something. In a few months, she will be gone, and we'll both be glad we helped her out," Charles Myers said, hoping to convince his wife to be kinder to Angie. A deep yawn forced his mouth open wide. "Come back to bed."

"Maybe you're right, for once, old man." She got up, climbed back into bed, and hugged him. "I'll just be glad when it's time for her to leave my house. I don't like her much anymore, especially not for my boy."

"Come on here, woman, let's go to sleep and stay out of that boy's business. You can't tell him who to like."

"That's what you think," Cynthia shot back, punching her pillow several times.

After more than an hour of waiting for his parents to doze off, Jacoby impatiently tiptoed down the hallway, slipped into Angie's room, and pulled back the covers.

Angie pretended to be asleep. A weak grin crawled across her face as she lay still. Jacoby undressed and slid into the bed and scooted up close to her. Once he got comfortable, he slid the straps of her gown off her shoulder. He tugged at her bikini panties until he'd freed them from her hips and tossed them onto the floor. Softly, he kissed her neck and rubbed her plump breasts.

Angie had not moved a muscle. She continued to pretend to be asleep. If he wanted sex from her, he would have to come up with something better than he did to interest her. A few minutes went by, and she could feel her body begin to tingle and excitement trickle through the lower half of her. Then, as usual, the excitement came to an abrupt stop.

The horny boyfriend attempted to mount Angie for his sexual pleasure. She refused to accept the same old boring sex from Jacoby this time. He was a pretty selfish lover who wasn't working with the biggest instrument in the toolbox, which didn't help the cause at all.

"Not tonight, Jacoby." Angie whispered. "Your three-minute, get mine and leave routine won't cut it. Tonight, I want more," she demanded, poking him in the chest with her index finger. "Let's do things a little bit different this time." She flipped him onto his back in her full-size bed and straddled him. She rode Jacoby like a Clydesdale.

Shock claimed his voice, and only a wide-open mouth and bulging eyeballs spoke to his surprise. Suddenly a cry of pleasure escaped his mouth and then a long noisy moan. His body moved in unison with her curvy hips that penned him down like her captured prey. Angie had dated Jacoby for a year, and she had never been fully satisfied by him sexually. She pretended to be asleep each time he'd sneak into her bedroom. She'd hoped that would dissuade him from his midnight creeping. Sometimes, she'd pretend to be asleep throughout the entire sexual encounter. That definitely wasn't hard to do for three minutes. Even that never stopped him from coming to her bedroom late at night. He'd enter the room quietly and exit just as quietly after quickly handling his business. The boy she loved was inept and as clumsy as a child when it came to lovemaking.

Angie could hardly believe his response to her sexy moves. He showed no self-control. She silenced him constantly, but he cried out continuously.

“Oh, Angie,” he moaned, “I love this, baby. Don’t stop,” he called out as if they were in a house all alone. The more she moved, the louder he moaned.

The door to the bedroom suddenly opened wide, and the room flooded with light as Jacoby’s mother flipped on the light switch.

CHAPTER TWELVE

"What in the hell is going on in here? Oh, my God! CHARLES, CHARLES," yelled Cynthia Myers, standing in the doorway with both hands on her hips. She'd gotten out of bed because of the loud sounds coming from Angie's bedroom. "Get off of my son, Angela, and pack your things. I want you out of here, NOW! I have a twelve-year-old daughter here. Doesn't that mean anything to you? What do you think I'm running here, a whore house?"

Angie's knees instantly shot up to her chin to shield her naked body. "My name is Angie, not Angela," she said to Cynthia.

"Girl, I don't give a crap what your name is. Is that all you have to say for yourself? All you can do at this very moment is correct me about the way I say your name. It should've been Angela. Angie is always short for Angela; in case your mom didn't know that. Now, you get the hell out of my house. I told you my rules before you moved your little trifling, slutty tail in here. You just violated my main rule. You disrespected my house, you little hussy." With her fists clenched, Cynthia bridged the distance between her and Angie with three wide steps and yelled, "Did you hear me?"

"But Ma, I came into her room. This is my fault," explained Jacoby with a sheet wrapped around him, shielding his nakedness.

"Yeah, Jacoby, that's obvious." His mother slapped him hard on the back of his head. "But you didn't rape her? You were just being stupid and disrespectful by screwing some little hussy right down the hallway from my bedroom in my house."

Cynthia's eyes and hot words bore into Jacoby like a spear. "Hasn't she ever heard of just say no? Her mama should've taught her that, and that's what she should've done in my house. She should've said no. She's the one who needs a place to stay, not you, and certainly not me. How dare you defend her?" Cynthia's face was red, and blood vessels sprouted through her cheeks like the roots of a plant. Her light complexion gave way to her anger, which continued to mount with her nostrils flaring in and out.

Cynthia pointed her skinny, manicured finger at Angie sitting in bed, hiding her body beneath the comforter she'd snatched up from the floor. "First, my son gets his face beaten and bruised because of you, and now this. That's it." Cynthia took a step closer to Angie. "Get moving, girl. You only have a few minutes to get your things together and get out of my house before I start throwing you and your crap out on the front lawn."

Without a word, Angie scrambled to locate the robe that had been kicked off the bed during her and Jacoby's steamy romp—just as Mr. Myers stumbled in, half asleep and confused.

"What is going on in here? Honey, why are you up? And you're yelling loud enough to wake the dead." His eyes floated over to Angie, who pulled the comforter up tighter against her chest. He looked over at Jacoby with his bare chest and boxers on backward. The scene became clear to him. Mr. Myers' eyelids opened wide, and his chin dropped as he stepped further into the bedroom for a closer look. "I know you all not doing the nasty up in this house," his gaze aimed right at Angie.

"Come out of here, Charles, before I knock your damn head off," yelled Mrs. Myers, snatching him by the arm. "You want to know why I'm up? If you can sleep through what I heard coming from this room, you wouldn't wake up if a freight train came through the bedroom. These two silly kids thought they could get away with having sex in my house. Not hardly. Nobody gets their groove on up in here, but me and my husband."

"Since when? It's been a minute." Charles Myers confessed, clearing his throat.

"Charles, I'm going to pretend I didn't hear that." She rolled her eyes at him and focused on Angie. "Girl, your time is running out. Get your things. I'll be waiting for you downstairs." Cynthia stomped out of the room and down the hallway, with her husband following close behind.

"I'm still trying to figure out the last time we did the nasty thing you're talking about," her husband inquired, shaking his head.

"CHARLES, this is not the time," Mrs. Myers tossed back and hustled quickly down the stairs.

As Angie shed a waterfall of tears, Jacoby helped her pack most of her things and promised to bring the rest to her house the next day. Angie apologized to his parents. Mrs. Myers folded arms, wrinkled brow, and her foot tapping rapidly on the floor, let Angie know she wasn't moving fast enough even as she walked out of the front door.

Jacoby walked Angie to her car and placed her bag in the back seat.

"Maybe we should chill for a while. Let things cool off. Your mom is right. I should've never let you in my bedroom. I could've locked the door. She was clear about what she expected when she agreed to let me move in. I can't blame her for being angry."

"No, baby, it was my fault. I take all the blame. I don't want to cool it, Angie. I love you. Everything will be okay."

Angie closed the car door and let down the window. "We'll talk later." Tears welled up in her eyes as she pulled away from the curb, leaving Jacoby standing in the middle of the street with his head hanging down. She glanced into the rear-view mirror at him. What a mess. Everything is such a mess.

CHAPTER THIRTEEN

When Angie pulled into the driveway of her mother's house, she sucked in a deep breath and pushed it out slowly. What was next? She wasn't sure, but her body was tired. Slowly, heavy steps took her to the back door. Angie tipped inside as quietly as possible. But no need for that since Marcus stood in the kitchen wearing only pajama bottoms with a bottle of water turned up. His hairy chest could not hide the rippled muscles that claimed his chest and left her speechless.

"Uh, I uh, sorry, I know it's late." Her eyes darted to the clock above the window and back to Marcus. "I had a situation at Jacoby's house, and I wanted to stay in my room tonight. I hope that's alright."

"Oh, of course, it is. I would never try to keep you away from your home, Angie. You didn't have to leave to begin with. I'm going back to bed. I just got a little thirsty."

"Wow, good taste, Mom," Angie said, louder than she thought while watching Marcus walk away.

"Did you say something?" He turned to inquire.

"I just said I miss my mom."

Marcus walked out of the kitchen, up the stairs, and out of sight. But the faint traces of his cologne lingered behind. Angie took in a big whiff of the cologne-laced air surrounding her, then sat down at the kitchen table. I better call Mom. She punched the number one on her speed dial and counted the rings. One, two, three, four... still no answer. A text message would have to do.

I miss you, Mom. I know you'll be gone for another four months. Just checking on you. By the way, Marcus isn't so bad after all. LOL! Call when you can. Luv you!

On Angie's way to her bed, she walked by her mom's bedroom door.

Marcus was near the door, zipping up his jacket. "Going out for a jog?"

"Yeah, it's what I do when I can't sleep."

"Okay, be safe. I'm going to bed. I'm tired, and I've had enough drama for one day. Goodnight." As Angie peeled off her clothes and climbed into bed, her cell phone rang with a familiar tune. The caller ID read "MY FUTURE." She answered with a smile in her voice.

"Hey, Sweetie."

"Did you make it home yet?"

"Yes, Jacoby, I made it home. Sorry, I didn't call." Angie propped her head up on two pillows and gazed out her bedroom window.

"Baby, again, I'm so sorry about tonight. I feel terrible. It's all my fault.

I wish I hadn't come into your room. I miss you already."

"It'll all work out. It feels good to be in my own bed anyway," she admitted, snuggling down under the covers.

"You got me over here daydreaming about that tight butt of yours. You had me screaming like a little girl. Where'd you learn that stuff you did to me? When we got together, I thought you were a virgin, and you've always followed my lead. That definitely was not the case tonight. You were like a different person."

"I just wanted to try something different, and I never told you that I was a virgin."

"Well, virgin or not, I need to know when you can put some of those sexy hot moves on me again?"

"We'll have to discuss that another time. I'm exhausted; I'm going to sleep. I'll call you tomorrow." She stretched her arm over her head and yawned silently. "Goodnight."

"So, you're not a virgin, huh? Ain't that a..." The silence announced that Angie had ended the call. He pulled the phone away from his ear and stared at it.

After a week back at home, Angie wondered why she'd ever left. Marcus worked at the hospital during the day and worked a part-time job at least three nights a week. She had all the freedom she needed with little to no distractions from Marcus or her kid brother. Her classes kept her busy, and she hadn't seen Jacoby in a few days, except from a distance on campus. She was anxious to get together with him, but time had not presented itself.

"What are you two doing?" Angie asked Jayden and Marcus as she entered the house.

"What does it look like, Sis? We're playing chess. Marcus taught me how to play, and I've been kicking his butt ever since," Jayden announced confidently.

"Yeah, right, in your dreams, little man. If you won, it's because I let you win," said Marcus, laughing.

"Whatever. Well, take this, since you let me win," Jayden boasted, making a move that ended the game.

"Okay, you got me again, but don't let it go to your head."

"You should try, Angie. It's cool, and you'll probably beat Marcus, too. He's actually a better teacher than player."

They all laughed at Jayden poking fun at Marcus. Jayden got up and left the room. Marcus gestured to Angie to take a seat and try her luck. After Angie caught on, she did beat Marcus.

After a couple more games, Marcus announced he had some errands to take care of. "I'll see you later. I better get going."

"Have you talked to my mom, Marcus?" Angie inquired.

"No, I haven't in about a week. We text each other here and there. She wanted to know that everything's all good with you guys."

Jayden appeared in the doorway. "Hey Marcus, can you drop me off at my friend Joey's house? I'll ask Joey's mom to bring me home in a few hours. I'm sure she won't mind."

"Sure, Jayden. And Angie, I have to work my part-time job tonight. It will be after midnight by the time I get back to the house. So, hold down the fort."

"That's cool; just lock the door behind you. I'm going to take a nap. My next class isn't until six this evening," Angie said, stretching and yawning. She called Jacoby for a lunch date and told him she'd leave the door unlocked, just in case she was in the shower when he arrived.

"All right now. That is what I'm talking about. I'll be right over," Jacoby committed. His voice sang out through the phone line.

Angie prepared a special lunch for them, expecting him to arrive twenty to thirty minutes after their phone call. She prepared two salads with marinated strip steaks; seasoned to perfection, her signature golden peach pie and iced tea. When he didn't make the lunch date, Angie put away his food and went upstairs, turned on Chris Brown, from her play list, and got into the shower. Minutes later, she pulled back the shower curtain to step out, and Jacoby's nude sculpted body stood there.

He reached in and turned the water back on, gently pushed her back inside the shower, and joined her. He kissed her lips, and her eyelids, then he licked her cheek like it was cool, tasty ice cream. His mouth slid down her neck, over her shoulders, and found her plump nipples standing at attention as his touch had commanded. With no concern about drying off, they got out of the shower, kissing the whole way from the bathroom to Angie's bedroom.

In only seconds, Jacoby pulled Angie on top of him. "Take control, baby, you know, the way you did at my house the night we got busted. Let me see you work it." He licked his lips, latched onto both of her breasts with his palms, and closed his eyelids.

Angie gave him what he asked for. Just like before, he squealed and moaned, yelling out her name. It wasn't long before Angie joined the chorus with her own sensual sounds while they both got lost in ecstasy.

Marcus opened the front door, shaking his head. It was a wasted drive out to the job since he'd mixed up the date he'd agreed to work for his friend. I could have been home watching the game. A man's voice, moaning and groaning, grabbed his attention the moment he shut the door. What the hell? I know Angie is not in here having sex with her boyfriend in her mother's house. With each step Marcus took up the stairs, he considered what he would say to Angie. This type of disrespect could not go without reprimand.

When he reached the top of the stairs, the voices that escaped Angie's bedroom calmed his rage and captured his interest. The sound of Angie's voice laced with pleasure crept through his veins like a slow venom. He stood there, legs heavy, unable to move, and his manhood throbbing. What was he doing to her that gave her so much pleasure? Her sultry whimpers pulled him into the adjoining bathroom shared by Angie and Jayden's bedrooms.

Angie's bedroom door was slightly open. Anxious lovers hadn't taken the time to secure their privacy. Slow steps closed the distance between Marcus and Angie's whimpers. The sliver of light that crept through the partly open door allowed him to see Angie straddled Jacoby, rocking to the beat of Chris Brown's jam, "Residuals." Marcus watched Angie and Jacoby move with rhythmic timing as one person, close and nearing their destination.

Marcus' thoughts placed him in bed with Angie. It was his body she was entangled with. He could feel her heartbeat against his chest. He moved up and down inside of her and waited for each quiver of her body to touch him.

Angie's head hung back; her eyelids closed as she bit down on her bottom lip. Her large breast bounced to the motion. Marcus could feel the touch of her skin against his. Jacoby gripped Angie's bottom, helping her make every down stroke. As the two reached their climax, Marcus realized his hand had found his hardness, and he stroked it, wishing his thoughts were a reality.

The fantasy was over, and he'd better make his escape. He tried to quietly back out of the bathroom, but lost his balance on the slick, wet floor and fell. The loud thud surely had to announce that their privacy had been breached. The couple stirred, certain they had heard a sound—but too lost in the moment to care.

Marcus feared that the bathroom door would be forced wide open in seconds. Was he about to be found out? Would his lust and sinful desire for a young girl he couldn't have be uncovered? Exposure wasn't an option. He forced himself up from the wet floor and scurried to his room.

CHAPTER FOURTEEN

Hidden away in Pam's room behind a locked door, Marcus hoped he was safe. He sat on the bed, hoping Angie and Jacoby wouldn't come looking for the peeping Tom they'd heard in the bathroom. He squeezed his forehead hard with the heels of both hands. I wish I hadn't seen Angie like that. Marcus couldn't shake the picture of Angie's naked bottom from his mind. Could he ever look at her the same again? Somehow, he knew he wouldn't. She was beautiful and sexy but so much younger than him. Yet, he found himself wanting her just the same.

Marcus told himself more than once that the young lady was someone he could never have. She belonged to Jacoby; besides that, he was dating her mother. That reality shook the thought out of his mind. He shot up from the bed and fished his cell from his jacket pocket. Cassie wasn't who he wanted, but she would do what he needed. He hated dealing with Cassie because she was so possessive of him. She'd made a scene once when she saw him out in public with another woman. She'd even threatened several women's lives, keyed their cars, and flattened tires. Usually, Marcus warned women about her so they wouldn't be caught off guard.

Pam's encounter with Cassie came to mind as he reconsidered calling her. He could almost hear Pam's shaking voice in his ear as she described the crazed encounter she'd had with Cassie. Marcus had run into a neighborhood Walmart and left Pam in his car. Cassie recognized the vehicle and tapped on the window, pretending to need directions. When Pam let down the window, the cold steel barrel of a gun was pressed into her cheek. Cassie cocked the handgun. "I don't know you, but I'm sure you know me. I'm Cassie, Marcus' woman. You've heard of me before, haven't you? Oh, it's okay this time. I don't hurt females who try to take my man the first time I catch them. But know this, if I ever see you with my man again, I will hurt you so bad that you may not recover." He and Pam had argued that night about Cassie. They'd almost broken up over it.

However, that night, he told Pam about assault charges that a few women had against the obsessed Cassie. She had sliced one woman's face to shreds with a straight razor after following her home from a date with Marcus. Because Cassie's father was an attorney, she was out of jail the following morning. She paid a healthy fine, at least her wealthy father did, and she walked.

Cassie had ruined many prospective relationships for Marcus over the years. He tried to keep his distance because he knew Cassie was dangerous. But periodically, his desperate desires for sex would overpower him and cause him to seek out Cassie when no one else was available. Each time, Marcus left with an empty and regretful heart. But Cassie took his interest in sex as the possibility that his heart would one day be hers.

After seeing Angie with Jacoby, Marcus had to quench his thirst for a woman's touch. He knew Cassie was the woman to do just that since she had mad love for him. She had no shame in performing whatever sexual act it took to prove that to Marcus. He rubbed his finger over the small scar on his shoulder that Cassie had tattooed him with by planting her nails there. Then he pulled up her number on his cell and pressed the call button. As usual, when she received the call from Marcus, she welcomed him with open legs and met his sexual needs.

Two hours later, Marcus returned home and entered a dark, quiet house. He heated up the meal Angie had prepared for Jacoby, devoured it, and then went off to bed. Cassie had worn him out. With just barely enough energy to walk upstairs, he climbed into bed and fell into a deep, coma-like sleep.

On another side of the world, in Japan, Pam was far from enjoying a peaceful sleep. The police knocked on her hotel room door with questions about the stolen merchandise. Chu beat the police there. He and Pam remained quiet until the police left. Chu warned Pam that there was a warrant for her arrest. He was instructed to hide her out for the remainder of her stay in Japan. He'd promised to keep her safe until he could purchase her ticket back to the States. Chu's daughter would deliver the ticket two days before she was to leave. Pam was afraid to move a muscle.

Just before Chu left, he gave Pam her final instructions. "There's a price on your head. Those people feel you dishonored them by stealing their property," said Chu.

"What do you mean their property? They took it from me first. The massager belongs to Dudley, I mean Kiko. He invented it. They must be crazy," Pam protested as she shot up from the small wobbling table in the corner of the room.

"Lady, I no make you understand. It goes much deeper than you can comprehend. Just get some rest, and I'll make sure your last few days here are safe ones. And for both of our sakes, you better hope I can find a buyer for this device before too long."

"Wait a minute, Chu. What do you mean by my last few days here? Do you mean here in Japan or here on earth?"

Chu laughed and shook his head on his way to the door. "I don't see what's so damn funny, JAP. My neck is on the line, not yours," she yelled after him.

Chu laughed even harder, with his plump belly jiggling as he closed the door.

Pam surveyed the room, taking in a panoramic view. The dirty walls, stained carpet, broken sofa, and the rickety fold-up bed made her want to stand up all night. No way was she about to sleep on that bed. She gave in and reluctantly sat down on the sofa. She was at the mercy of Chu, who she wasn't altogether sure she could trust.

Oh Lord, she thought. What have I done? I know my kids think I'm crazy. My daughter's birthday is next month, and I'm going to miss it. I know they're just lost without me. And Marcus probably hates that he's there. I should've let those kids go and stay with my parents.

Pam picked up the Styrofoam cup of soda next to her foot and hurled it into the wall. She spoke aloud in frustration to the empty room. "I was so busy trying to get this stupid money that I didn't give Marcus much consideration either. Wow, I think I messed up again. That fine man is not going to wait for me to get back stateside to have sex. If he ends up being with someone else, then I guess I will have to accept that. I just better not find out about it if he wants to be with me when I get back home."

CHAPTER FIFTEEN

Angie walked out of her college business class and pulled out her iPad to check her midterm grades. A broad, toothy grin claimed her face, two B's and two A's. "That deserves a celebration," she boasted to herself as she walked to the parking lot. She dug deep into her purse until she felt her phone. There was only one person she wanted to celebrate with. The phone rang twice and went to voicemail. She called the landline phone. Jacoby's mother's voice sent a chill through Angie's veins as she bit down on her bottom lip.

"Yes," Cynthia said with a stern tone.

"Hello, Mrs. Myers. May I speak to Jacoby, please?"

"Well, Angela—sorry, I mean Angie. I'm not sure if he can come to the phone right now, but hold on, I'll check."

Angie heard Jacoby's hearty laughter on his way to the phone.

"Hello."

"Hey, Jacoby, I was calling to tell you..."

"Hey Angie, I need to call you back. I'm doing something for my dad."

Mrs. Myers chimed in on the line, "Coby, honey, don't keep Brianna waiting. You two have a class soon. You need to be leaving."

Angie gasped. She slapped her hand into her chest, slammed her car door shut, and stabbed the end button on her cell with her thumb. What the heck was going on? Jacoby has been acting a little differently for the last few weeks. But another girl? Adrenaline and anger claimed her body. She twisted her shoulder-length hair around her finger. Maybe his love for her was fading, and she had simply refused to accept the signs that dared her to notice. There were fewer calls from him; he rarely returned her calls, and they had no recent late-night phone dates. How did she miss it? She had been busy with classes and studying for her midterms.

Jacoby always preached about the two being honest with each other, no matter what. He was the only person in her life who had been truthful about everything until now. He'd made her feel safe and secure. When her mother disappointed her, he was there to console her. He was always able to give her a different perspective. She loved him, and he loved her. Why would he stop now? This could not be happening. She needed him. She didn't have anyone else right now. Her mother was gone. Who would be her confidant, and who would love her?

Angie thought back to the girl Jacoby mentioned having a class with. She remembered how awkward it felt to hear him talk about her. Yes, she was cute. But she wasn't all that, at least not enough to make Angie worry. Jacoby wasn't a shallow guy. The girl would have to have more than looks going for herself. Everybody liked Jacoby. He was intelligent, fine as hell, and he cared about people. Angie knew girls had their eyes on him, but that didn't worry her because what she had with Jacoby was real. She thought it was, but that foundational belief was starting to crack.

They had been through some things with their families that made them close. There had been no reason for insecurity until that phone call. Now Brianna goes to his house to pick him up for class. He has a car. Reality hit Angie. She bumped the heel of her hand against her forehead. Jacoby's mother picked up the phone purposefully to cause a conflict between me and Jacoby. She was angry at herself for not realizing sooner that their relationship was changing. Should she confront him and the girl? Did she think she was just going to take her man? And nothing was going to be said or done about it. Brianna didn't know her, but she was about to meet her soon.

Angie whipped her car into the driveway and shoved the gear shift into park. She sat silent and motionless for a couple of minutes. Tears stung at her eyes while her bottom lip quivered. Her head slowly inched down until it rested on the steering wheel. It was then that her stream of tears flowed.

CHAPTER SIXTEEN

Jayden came home hurriedly to prepare for his basketball game after soccer practice. He was used to his mother supporting him at his games, but everyone was too busy with their own lives. Angie usually had a hard time refusing him anything. Maybe she would come out and watch his game. He walked down the hallway and knocked on her bedroom door.

"Yeah, who is it?"

"It's me. Can I come in?" Jayden asked. He heard her unlock the door, and then it parted slightly. He waited a minute, then went inside and stood at the foot of the bed. "Girl, you look a mess. Have you been sleeping all afternoon? And this room is messier than mine." His head moved from side to side as he surveyed the clothes on the floor and fast-food wrappers on the bed.

Angie tossed an empty plastic water bottle at him. "Boy, what do you want?"

"Will you come to my game tonight?"

"Why? Do you need a ride?" Angie questioned as she sat up on the side of her bed.

"No, I don't need a ride. I'll be riding the bus with the team. I just want you to come. You never come to my games anymore. Bring Jacoby, too."

"Don't mention that jerk to me." Angie shot up from the side of the bed and kicked the dirty clothes in front of her. "I'll think about coming to your game. Leave the information on the kitchen counter. Now get out of here. I'm trying to take a nap."

Angie climbed out of bed an hour later and slipped into the jeans and T-shirt she'd worn earlier. Although her heart ached, and she preferred staying in bed, she didn't want to disappoint her brother. Somebody needed to be at his game, and Pam sure couldn't. She brushed her teeth, threw on a hat, and searched for her hot pink Nikes. Finally, she checked the note on the counter for the location of the game and headed out.

Marcus returned to a quiet house and decided to take advantage of it. He turned on the TV, found a basketball game, and planted himself on the sofa. He scarfed down a couple of ham and cheese sandwiches and dozed off in front of the TV. His ringing cell phone snatched him from the dream that had claimed him. Pam's frantic voice reached right through the phone, forcing him wide awake and attentive quickly.

"Slow down, Pam, slow down! What's going on?"

"Marcus, I'm in trouble."

"What? Why? How are you in trouble?" Marcus sat straight up and scooted forward to the edge of the sofa.

"I can't talk long. Some Japanese people took the gadget from me when I first got here. I saw where they put it; I stole it back from them. Now, the police department has a warrant for my arrest. I had to check out of the hotel because the police kept hanging around waiting for me. Chu, the guy Dudley told me would be my contact, put me up in one of his houses to hide out and told me not to leave for any reason. It's a real dump." Pam looked around the dusty room, noticing the stains on the carpet while brushing off her pant leg. "I've been here ever since; I don't know when I'll get home." Pam stood looking out of the window into the yard across the street and down both ends of the block, noticing each car that went by. She didn't plan on anyone sneaking up on her.

"Wow, do you think you'll be back by the date we agreed upon? I need to be able to move back home as we planned. You know I only have tenants for six months."

"I don't know. Didn't I just tell you I didn't know when I would get back there? Are you hard of hearing or just an insensitive jerk? I'm a million miles away from home, and your selfish a-- is worried about when you can get back to your raggedy a-- house. Damn!" Pam shot back as she slammed the window shut.

"What the..." Marcus yelled in surprise. "Woman, who in the hell do you think you're talking to? I'm doing you a favor. It's not my fault that you're on another continent. Your greedy, money-hungry, get-rich-quick, scheming a-- got you in the mess you're in now."

"You are an inconsiderate bastard. This conversation is over, and so are we. You can go to hell."

"You're right about one thing; it's definitely over," Marcus agreed loudly and pressed his back onto the sofa. He surveyed the room. He was sitting in someone else's house with someone else's things, and that someone else was selfish and ungrateful. He got up from the sofa, marched upstairs, and climbed into someone else's bed.

Twenty minutes into a deep snoring session, Marcus was summoned from his sleep by a loud noise at the front door and Angie's frantic voice yelling. He got out of bed and trotted down the stairs. Before he reached the bottom, Angie crashed into him as she ran up the steps, almost knocking him down.

"What is it? Angie, what happened? Are you okay?"

Crying, breathing hard, and sniffling at the same time, she managed to say, "No, I'm not okay. I went to see Jayden play tonight. The game just happened to be at Jacoby's sister's middle school. He was there with some girl. I was so humiliated. I thought I would throw up right in front of them."

"Where is Jayden? Is the game over?"

"No, I just left. He'll ride back with the team."

"Calm down. Sit here. I'll be right back."

Marcus returned with some tissues and a cold towel. He handed them to her. "Blow your nose and wipe your face. It'll make you feel better. Tell me what happened," he advised, sitting down on the step next to her.

Angie did as she was instructed, then took a deep breath and pushed out her anger and humiliation onto Marcus with words that flowed like a pot boiling over. "I didn't see them until halftime because we sat on opposite sides. I got up to go to the concession stand and saw him walk up with his arm around this girl. They were hugging and kissing each other like they were in a bedroom somewhere. I couldn't believe it. He was too busy to talk to me earlier today when I called him. But he had time to take some girl to a game. He was so busy hanging all over her that he didn't even see me." Angie muffled a scream with her hand and stomped her feet fast several times onto the step beneath her.

Marcus burst into laughter. "What are you doing having a temper tantrum?"

Angie glanced over at him, giggled, and said, "Don't make fun of me."

"Did you see this coming? Is this guy a player, or what?"

"No, he's not a player. Yes, I guess I did see some signs, but I don't understand," cried Angie, burying her face into Marcus' chest.

"Everybody plays a fool, sometimes, Angie."

"Huh?" she said, looking up at Marcus while being ushered to the sofa.

"That boyfriend of yours or ex-boyfriend is young, more than that, he's stupid. No real man would ever cheat on a sistah as fine as you. Those hazel eyes of yours can hypnotize a man."

"You're just saying that to make me feel better—and it's working. Continue." They laughed. Marcus and Angie talked and laughed for almost an hour about some of his relationships and how he'd boohooed from a broken heart a couple of times in his younger days.

Jayden walked into the house, and before Angie or Marcus could say anything, he confessed Jacoby's sin. "I saw your boyfriend at the game with that girl. Acting like she was his girlfriend and not you, Angie. I didn't get a chance to talk to him. If I had, I would have told him that he was no longer welcome in our house. He's bigger than me, and I know he'd beat the brakes off me if I tried to go at him. Just wait; in a couple of years, when he decides he wants you back, I'm going to beat the crap out of him for you, okay?" Jayden headed up to his bedroom. When he reached the top of the stairs, he yelled down, "I mean it, Angie."

"Well, it's late, Marcus. I think I'll go to bed, too. Thanks for listening. I do feel better."

"No problem." Marcus stood. "Listen, people will come and go in your life. Everyone that comes into your life is not meant to stay. Can you imagine how confusing and chaotic life would become if everyone stayed? We have to let the people who want to leave, leave—even when it hurts. But time heals all wounds."

"I know, but I don't want to let him go. I love Jacoby, and I know he loves me, too. He's only acting like this because of his mother. She hates me because of something that happened while I was staying at her house."

"Seriously, Angie, you think his mom has that kind of control over him and who he dates?"

"Well, yeah. And then again, I don't know, maybe not. Anyway, I'll figure it out. Maybe Jacoby's already figured it out for me. My brain is overloaded. I'm going to bed." She stepped in close to him and kissed his cheek. "Wow, you smell good. What is that cologne you're wearing?" A weak smile turned up the corners of her mouth.

"It's called Patrick by the K. Company."

Angie sniffed again and backed away quickly, smiling. "My mother loves a perfume they created called Bella, but I think I like their male line of cologne better."

Marcus moved through the downstairs, checking for locked doors, turned out the lights, and then climbed the stairs to Pam's bedroom. He stretched out his long legs, grateful for the king-size bed. Nearly thirty minutes passed, but sleep still refused to come. Pam's sharp words continued to stab at him. He was there with her kids, and she had the nerve to be slick at the mouth with him. Should he leave and make his exit the profound statement that he didn't give a darn? Maybe he would stay since it seemed like Angie was going to need him, and to his surprise, he wanted to be there for her. It was no longer about Pam.

CHAPTER SEVENTEEN

There he is that lying cheat. Just walking around with no remorse for his actions. We've made eye contact. So, he can't turn, go the other way, and act like he didn't see me. Angie sucked in a deep breath, opened and closed her right fist tightly a few times, and prepared to be within a couple of feet of Jacoby.

"Hey, Angie. How are you?"

"Well, I guess I could be okay, but I'm a little confused. My boyfriend broke up with me without telling me. He's running around with some chick who has a baby and a baby daddy. And I hear she's still involved with the guy. I'm sure you know him. He's a Kappa. His name is Mac."

"Angie, I know all about that, and it's over between them."

"I didn't even know it was over between us. When were you going to tell me—when you got engaged? On the day you got married? When?" Angie's head bobbled from right to left as she assaulted him with her words. With her index finger, she stabbed Jacoby in the center of his forehead hard, which caused him to take a step backward.

"Hey, don't push me," he advised, with a wrinkled brow and deep voice.

"Are you kidding me? After all the dirt you've done. You're lucky that precious car of yours isn't sitting on four flat tires and there isn't sugar in the gas tank." Angie threatened through gritted teeth with her face just inches from his.

"Yeah, right. I can't talk right now, Angie. I've got to go." He shifted the weight of his book bag onto his other shoulder. "I'm in a hurry."

"Jacoby, just tell me what I did? Why did you suddenly stop caring for me? You started seeing someone else without saying a word to me. How could you be so cold? Is it because of the way your mom feels about me?" Her voice squeaked with emotion as she forced the tears not to fall that pricked at her eyes.

"I can't talk to you about this right now. I'm meeting Brianna, and I don't want her upset if she sees us together. Call me tonight, and maybe we can talk." He started to walk away.

"Are you serious? You don't want Brianna to see you talking to me? What is this? I'm your girlfriend. You never cared before who saw us together. How could you do this to me?" Her left cheek trembled.

Brianna moved toward them, closing the distance between her, Jacoby, and a possible explosion. Her visual assault went from Jacoby to Angie and back to Jacoby. She waited for one of them to say something.

"It's not what you think, baby," Jacoby offered Brianna, with wide eyes. "She's just trying to find a way to accept us."

Tears taunted Angie's eyes, burning and itching, daring her to lose control of them. She refused, willing her tears to stay put. No way was she going to let this chick that took her man have any satisfaction in seeing not even one tear fall. She opened her mouth to tell the girl off, determined to be in control of the situation. To her surprise, Brianna didn't bring any level of confrontation to the face-off.

"It's okay, Jacoby. Can I talk to you for a minute, please?" she questioned with a soft voice.

He led her a few feet away from Angie. "Sure, what's up? You look like you've been crying. What's wrong, sweetheart?"

"No, I'm okay, really. My son isn't feeling well today, and I need to pick him up from daycare. Is it okay if I use your car?"

"No problem. Whatever you need, baby," He slipped the keys from his pocket and handed them to her.

Hmm, he's handing over the keys to the car that he cherishes so much. He never did that for me. "You know what?" Angie said, stepping to them. With red eyes, a quivering lip, and clenched fists, she faced Brianna. "This is some crap. Did you really think you were just going to take my man, and I wasn't going to check you? You don't know me. I will..."

Jacoby tossed Angie a hard look and ushered Brianna to his car.

"Yep, that's the best thing for you, to get to stepping, trick," Angie yelled after Brianna, waving her hands in the air, challenging her to come back.

Brianna ignored Angie and pleaded her case with Jacoby. "You're such a sweet guy. I hope that I am not asking too much. My dad can't pick me up after class today. I need to get some things done, and I may have to take my baby to the doctor. I should be done with your car around eight. I can come to your house, and maybe we can do something special tonight. Is that okay with you?"

"That's fine. Go ahead and take the car. I'll get a ride." He leaned in for a quick peck on the lips.

Angie grabbed her stomach, made a gagging noise, and bent over as if she would throw up at the sight of them kissing.

"I'll see you at my place at eight. I look forward to that something special." He tried to kiss Brianna's mouth again, but she quickly turned her head, and his kiss landed on her cheek. "Hold on to that until later," she offered, walking away with a wide smile.

Seconds later, she trotted off down the sidewalk, twirling Jacoby's keys around her index finger.

When Brianna was out of sight, Jacoby walked up to Angie. Her tears were flowing now. Sadly, the tears did not move him. "If you want to talk, you can give me a ride home after class, and we can talk then."

Maybe if we talk, he'll think about how things were with us. Yes, that mind-blowing sex I threw on him at his mama's house. The friendship that we both shared, and the way we cared about each other. The thing between us that I thought was love.

Jacoby snapped his fingers in front of Angie's face. "Are you giving me a ride home or not?"

"Yes, and we can talk, right?"

"Yep, I'll meet you in the parking lot by the auditorium at 3:00 o'clock."

The day could not go by fast enough for Angie. She was anxious to talk with Jacoby and work things out. The conversation didn't go the way she'd hoped. The ride to Jacoby's house after class did not provide Angie with the conversation her heart needed to hear. She was disappointed when Jacoby insisted on going straight home. They drove along with Jacoby only offering up one-word answers. He was just using her for a ride. Her heart wouldn't allow that to matter. She was in his presence, and that gave her hope. She would take any time she could get with him, even if it was possibly their last time together.

Jacoby didn't care much about what Angie thought. He needed a ride home, and she wanted to be with him. He would give her the time it took to drive to his house from the college campus. After that, time was up. He'd made plans to romance Brianna later that night. That was his only concern.

Brianna claimed with any new relationship; she lived by her necessary three-month rule: no sex. They had only been dating for a few weeks. Although they were usually together, Jacoby thought she seemed distracted; he still found her irresistible. There was no way he was waiting for two more months. He was sure that by being a gentleman, buying her things, pampering her, and now letting her use his car, she would want to have some hot sex. He planned to encourage her to toss that crazy three month rule out of the window tonight.

The second Angie pulled her car up in front of his house, before she could turn the ignition off, Jacoby's mouth opened, and words poured out. "I'm sorry, Angie. I promise I didn't mean to hurt you. You'll find someone else. I'm not even worthy of your feelings. I didn't mean to fall for someone else, but sometimes, stuff just happens. I still care about you, and I want the best for you, but right now, it's not me. I'm sorry." He shook his head and lifted both palms in the air as he gave up on their relationship.

"Jacoby, you're making a mistake. That girl has a baby, and most of the time, that means baby daddy drama. Are you sure that's what you want for your life?" She gripped the steering wheel so hard that she could feel her pulse in her fingers. "I love you, Jacoby, and I know there is no way she could feel that way about you. She wouldn't even let you kiss her. Didn't you notice that? What is wrong with you? This time last year, you loved me. Hell, this time last month, you loved me. I will never understand what could've happened that quickly to change your feelings for me. It had to be your mother. I know she hates me."

"I don't understand it, either. I don't know what it is. It's just something about her. I love the girl, Angie. I wish for your sake that I'd never met her, but I can't go backward. I don't know what you want from me. My decision is final. I'm not doing this with you, anymore. It's time for you to let go and move on."

She reached for his hand as he opened the car door. He snatched his hand away before she could touch him, exited the car, and slammed the door.

It was an emotional drive home for Angie. The tears which pooled in the corners of her eyes before streaming down her cheeks blurred her vision. She ignored cars that blew their horns at her when she swerved into their lane, driving recklessly. Before she made it home, she pulled onto the side of the road and gave into the emotional storm raging in her heart and mind. She screamed, cried, and pounded the steering wheel with both fists. "Help me, Lord. It hurt so much."

While Angie sat on the side of the road in tears, Brianna drove into a beautiful, gated community. The homes were adorned with Queen Anne architecture, manicured lawns, in-ground swimming pools, picture windows, showcasing white baby grand pianos, and custom-made furniture. There was no doubt that this part of town hosted homes of people with wealth.

She checked the rearview mirror and followed a car into the wrought iron gates that closed slowly behind her. She parked on the street, walked a half mile up an inclined sidewalk to a house, and rang the doorbell. An older Mexican woman opened the door. Brianna saw her son shuffling behind the woman and hurried right past her to hug her boy.

"Hello, my little man. I've missed you."

The woman did not speak. She walked out of the room, leaving Brianna alone, smiling at her son, who babbled, "Mommy," repeatedly. Brianna took her son, Miles, into the huge living room and played with him for the next two hours.

Isabella Gonzales walked into the living room carrying papers in her hand. "I need you to sign these papers before you go. They came today," she stated, waving the papers back and forth before she handed them over. "You make me very happy, senorita, Brianna. Gracias, gracias."

"No thanks necessary, Isabella. I could never repay you for the joy that you've brought to my son and me." She placed Miles into Isabella's arms and signed the papers one by one.

"How did you get here?"

"I borrowed a car from a guy on campus."

"Is he someone special?"

"No, he's nice, but I dare not make that mistake again. He's just a friend. I don't know when or if I'll ever be ready for another relationship. I'm not sure it's worth it, and besides, one month from now, we will both have what we want. That definitely does not include a third wheel."

The two ladies embraced while Miles stood between the two of them. "Well, sweetie, Mommy has to go. I'll see you later. I love you." She kissed both his cheeks and snuggled his face up against hers. Reluctantly, she slowly walked away leaving him whimpering and reaching for her.

CHAPTER EIGHTEEN

"Thanks for allowing him to sleep over. I will pick him up tomorrow by 10:00 a.m." Marcus ended the call with the mother of Jayden's friend, Jeremy. Perfect, Jayden would be spending the night with his friend. He would have the house to himself, and he did not have to work. His plan was to relax a bit and maybe call Cassie later for some sexual healing. He called up his friend and tried to explain his on-again, off-again non-relationship with Cassie.

"Cassie knows why this thing is what it is. Whether she likes it or not, she created this crazy scenario between us. I hit it when I want to and disappear when I want to. We don't have a relationship, and the stars will never line up for that one." Marcus switched the cell phone to his other ear and propped it up with his shoulder as he washed his hands.

"Man, you are a cold brotha. Sounds like if she's dealing with all of that, she must really like you," his friend D. offered.

"She likes me, and she likes drama. Anyway, she's not the one for me. She's too easy. She let me hit it the first night I met her. We met at the club, partied, had some drinks, and headed to her place. I never saw her again until four months later. She called me claiming she was pregnant with my baby."

"Man, she hit you with the baby daddy knockout punch."

"She cried and swore the baby was mine. You know me; I've wanted to be a father for a long time. I just never met the right woman. But I decided to give it a try, and I would take a DNA test if needed. We had the baby, and the baby had my heart right from the beginning. Hell, I even moved in with Cassie before she gave birth. So, we played house, mommy, and daddy. Now, here's the kicker." Marcus shook his head, remembering the painful event.

"The guy she dated before she and I hooked up swore the baby was probably his. He kept insisting that Cassie allow him to do a DNA test. She wouldn't. So, I decided to do one to shut the guy up."

"Oh, wow. I think I see the writing on the wall," D. chimed in with a deep tone in his voice.

"I was at the house by myself when the DNA results came in the mail. When I read the results, all I could hear in my head was, 'You are not the father.' I may as well have been on the Maury Povich show. I packed up my stuff, put the DNA results on the kitchen table, and left."

"So, a year and a half later, I ran into her at the same nightclub where we originally met. She and the guy didn't make it, and she kept trying to get me to take her back. Not in this lifetime. But if she wants to dish it out, and I'm hungry, I'll take it. And that's the end of the story." They both laughed.

"I got to get out of here and get to work. I'll check you later," D. told his buddy.

"Cool, the game is about to come on anyway. Check you later." Marcus shoved the cell phone into his pant pocket and thought back to a conversation between him and Cassie.

It was an honest mistake, Marcus. I really thought my baby girl was your daughter. She should have been your child. You're still angry with me. But I'm never going to let you walk out of my life. We are always going to be connected.

Maybe she meant that we would always have a sexual connection. Anytime I call, she answers the phone and is always willing and able to serve up the loving. I hope that's what she meant. She is a little crazy. Marcus' brow wrinkled, and a frown claimed his face.

She's not that crazy, Marcus told himself. He thought back to what Cassie had said to him a few months ago during their last hotel rendezvous. "You and I, here in this hotel, it's just about sex. There are no emotions involved on your part, right?"

He remembered himself nodding his head and Cassie pulling the sheet over her naked body and covering her breasts. She knows. She knows there is nothing between us but sex. Marcus plopped down onto the leather chaise lounge, snagged the remote, and flipped through the channels until he landed on the Houston Rockets game.

The kitchen door slammed hard, sending a ripple of noise through the kitchen and into the living room. So much for watching the game in peace, Marcus decided as he got up to see what was going on.

Angie slung four bags of groceries onto the countertop, leaned against it, closed her eyelids, and took a deep breath.

Marcus cleared his throat, calling attention to himself. "Do you need some help?"

"No, I'm just pissed right now. I cook when I'm upset." She pulled the items out of the bags and placed them all on the countertop.

Marcus threw up both hands to surrender as he started backing out of the kitchen. "Well, I will get out of your way."

Quickly removing her eyes from his chiseled and hairy chest, she managed to speak. "I don't want to talk about it, Marcus. I just want to cook. Have you eaten?" she asked, pulling down an apron from the hook near the refrigerator.

"No, not yet, and I am a little hungry."

"I can use a hand if you've got time. You can be my prep chef." With both hands, she waved him back into the kitchen.

"Okay, I don't know what that is, but I know how to take directions. What are we having?" Marcus inquired, peeking over Angie's shoulder and rubbing his palms together.

"Hmm, let me surprise you," said Angie, smiling for the first time that day. "That's usually what I say when I'm not exactly sure, but I'm sure you will enjoy it. Do you like Mexican food?"

"Yes, love it. What do you have in mind?"

"Maybe we can start with some appetizers, mini-quesadillas, taco chicken nachos, and some tortilla pizzettes. Then, a nice light Gazpacho soup or salad, your choice, and lime-poached swordfish with corn and chili salsa as the main course. The showstopper is the dessert, lemon cheese quesadillas with mango sauce. So, you ready?"

"Oh, yeah, I'm ready—ready to eat. That sounds delicious and pricey. You really roll like that?"

With a hearty laugh that erupted from her throat, Angie responded,

"No, I have a hook-up with the butcher at Chandler's Deli. It's my girl Vanessa's brother-in-law. He owns the place. He gives me great deals because he knows I love to cook. I could never afford all this."

Marcus and Angie cooked, laughed, and ate until they couldn't shovel down another bite. Marcus glanced up at the clock. A couple of hours passed. "You know, Angie, I can't remember ever having Mexican food that good. That may have been the best Mexican meal I've ever eaten. I'm stuffed."

Angie stood and took a bow as she stretched out her apron to both sides. "Glad you enjoyed it."

"Seriously though, I thoroughly enjoyed it all, and the company, as well. Thanks, Angie, for a great meal."

"I was pretty upset when I got here. I'm feeling much better now. Thank you, Mr. Blue, for your company. Blue, that is an odd last name."

"Okay, don't be making fun of my name." Marcus tossed a half smile to Angie.

The shrill of Angie's cell phone interrupted them. "Excuse me a second." She slipped her phone from her purse and walked into the next room. The volume of her voice faded into a whisper.

"Have you been drinking? Why would you want to see me? You made it clear that I needed to move on. So, what's up with the change of heart suddenly?"

Marcus could hear bits of Angie's conversation and wanted to hear more. He inched closer to the door.

Angie's voice climbed above a whisper, "Okay, okay, of course, I want to work things out. I'll be there shortly."

Marcus stepped to Angie in the middle of the doorway. "Please, tell me you didn't buy that. That was your guy telling you that he needs you, right? Don't you recognize a booty call when you hear one? That's exactly what just happened."

"You don't know what you're talking about. There was more between us than sex."

Marcus snapped his fingers twice in front of Angie's face. "Come on, Angie. I'll bet anything that he was dumped earlier by his new girl, and now he wants to get busy with you."

"That's not true. He sounded like he'd been drinking, and he realized he'd made a mistake choosing someone else over me. I told you I prayed earlier, and it looks like God has answered my prayers."

"You believe that? You just said yourself that he'd been drinking. You think God would put you in the hands of a drunken man? You're talking crazy, but then again, you are only twenty-one."

"What in the hell is that supposed to mean?" Angie took a step backward. "I'm leaving. I don't have time for this. What do you know about God and what He would or wouldn't do?" Angie challenged, grabbing her purse and keys from the bar stool in the kitchen.

Marcus grabbed her arm. "Hold on a second, Angie. I didn't mean that. Just hear me out, please. I'm no saint, but I believe in God, and I know a little bit about Him. My parents had me in church all my life. My mom is a prayer warrior. All I'm saying is that God doesn't bless mess, and in my opinion, that's what this is, Angie."

"Your opinion, Marcus. You know what they say about opinions, don't you? They are just like butt holes, and everybody has one."

"Listen to me for just a few minutes. Let me tell you how the night will go with this guy."

"Okay, Marcus, but make it fast because I have to go."

Standing in the middle of the kitchen floor, Marcus talked to Angie for another five minutes—nothing he said altered Angie's determination to answer Jacoby's booty call. The wind chimes on the front porch were still spinning after Angie swept by it, got in her car, and was already two blocks down the street.

CHAPTER NINETEEN

Jacoby turned up a beer bottle and gulped down the last foamy swallow. He dropped down on the couch and pulled out his cell phone. "Brianna, this is Jacoby. Call me when you get this message. I had plans for us tonight. I wanted to take you to my favorite restaurant, and I had tickets to see Kevin Hart at the Funny Bone. I understand that your son is sick. Just give me a call tomorrow. Goodnight, beautiful."

Jacoby leaned his head back on the sofa and squeezed his eyelids tightly. He could see Brianna's face and hear her parting words in the message she'd left him earlier that evening. "I'm sorry about tonight, Jacoby. I wanted to get together, but my son is still not feeling well. I will call you tomorrow. I'm sure he'll be better then."

Angie pulled into Jacoby's parents' driveway. No cars. Thank goodness. Jacoby said they would be out late.

Jacoby had opened another beer which he'd downed five minutes before the doorbell rang. He opened the door wide for Angie to come inside, then walked back into the living room.

The scent of his cologne lingered in the air. "Polo cologne, Polo outfit, and a fresh haircut, hmm," Angie whispered.

With a slight slur in his speech, he tossed an invite at Angie. "Let's go upstairs."

"What do you mean go upstairs? I thought we were going to talk about us getting back together."

"Hey, I told you I made a mistake. We can talk about that tomorrow. I need you right now, baby. Please, don't turn me down, Bri..." He cleared his throat. "I mean Angie. Sorry about that. I—I—I've been drinking." I want you, baby. Can't you see that?" His outstretched hand pleaded for her to come closer.

Angie moved toward him as he stepped to her, pressing his body against her, pinning her against a wall. He kissed her neck and stroked her breast.

Her body and soul wanted this man. He was her man. Sleeping with him would be the payback Brianna deserved for trying to steal her boyfriend. Marcus' warning continued to play in her head like a song on repeat. It's just a Booty Call.

Jacoby pressed his manhood harder against Angie, unbuttoned her blouse, and slid his tongue up and down between her breasts. He slipped the bra strap over her shoulder and tasted her nipples, which were now free for him to enjoy. He planted his hand deep down into her jeans. There, he found her moistened treasure, which caused him to become even more aggressive.

Angie inhaled a slow deep breath as she fought her desire to allow him to slide his finger inside of her. Seconds went by, and she could feel herself quickly giving in to her hunger for his touch. His hands felt good, and his tongue against her skin excited her. His lips left her hard nipples and claimed her lips, then her neck. Could he possibly get any harder? His rod was throbbing against her, and it beckoned her. She reached down to touch him and felt her moist nectar ooze out into her panties. "Oh, my God."

Jacoby placed his hand over hers and guided her hand to massage his manhood, which ached to be released from his pants.

The moist spot between her legs wouldn't let Angie deny the pleasure she felt. Her body yearned desperately for him. She needed him to make love to her as he had done before.

Time wasn't on his side. Angie couldn't be there when his parents got home. He peeled off his shirt, stepped out of his pants, and seconds later, stood naked in the living room. As he lay on the carpet, he pulled her down on top of him. He wanted sex, and he wanted it right then and there; on the floor would do. Foreplay was over.

Jacoby squeezed her breast with both hands and sucked viciously at her nipples.

"Ouch, that hurt. You're being too rough," Angie protested, grabbing at her breasts.

"Sorry, take these tight jeans off," Jacoby replied, yanking on her belt loops.

His harsh demand snapped Angie right out of the seductive spell he'd cast upon her. This wasn't lovemaking. It was an animal attack. She was afraid that if she didn't stop it quickly, she wouldn't be able to, and he would win, leaving her a humiliated mess.

Marcus was right. Angie pushed Jacoby's hands from her body as he struggled to get her pants down.

"Stop it! I'm not doing this. If you meant what you said and want to be with me, call me when you sober up. I'm out of here." Angie stood up, grabbed her sweater from the floor, and put it on. She snatched up her purse and keys from the floor, as well. She left Jacoby on the floor with wide eyes and a wrinkled brow. Before she could get into her car, he'd made it to the front door.

"So, it's like that, Angie? How are you going to do this to me? You said you wanted to work on this thing between us." His hand moved back and forth in the air between them.

Angie looked over her shoulder, "The only thing you want to work on is the thing between your legs."

"Okay, so you were lying to me again. You know, like you lied about being a virgin. You don't turn me down. I broke up with you. You said you wanted to work it out. The only way to work this out is for you to come back in here right now. Get back here, right now, you whore."

Angie didn't respond. She kept a steady pace to her car. Wow, I can't believe he would call me a whore. And I was stupid enough to think he loved me. Marcus was right. Everything he said was exactly right. "I hate you, Jacoby. You're a stupid jerk," she spat, glaring at him as he stood naked in the open doorway. Her words were loud, clear, and laced with emotion and tears.

Angie closed the car door and pressed her foot hard down on the gas pedal. She needed distance between her and the man who'd broken her heart twice. She hoped Marcus was still up. She wanted to tell him that he was right. Everything he'd said was true. When she pulled into the garage, his car wasn't there. She called his cell phone. It went to voicemail. She didn't leave a message.

Disappointed, Angie entered the house, threw her keys on the counter, and plopped onto the couch. What had just happened at Jacoby's house wouldn't let her go. She couldn't turn off the instant replay in her mind. She could see herself being pawed at and used. The word "whore" sounded off in her ear like a crystal-clear surround sound system. Where was Marcus? She needed him.

It was almost two in the morning, and Marcus hadn't come home or returned Angie's call. "Marcus could be out on a booty call, himself. What would my mother think? On second thought, what do I think? Men have some nerve. Jacoby would've used me tonight if it hadn't been for Marcus. It's funny how he described it so well, play-by-play. Now I know why. He knows the game because he plays it, too. I guess they all do.

The sound of her own voice made her look around the room. The house was quiet, and suddenly, the room was way too big. She shook her head, pushed herself up from the sofa, turned off the lights, and schlepped upstairs to her bedroom. She undressed, pulled back the cover, climbed into her bed, and pulled the covers over her head.

Meanwhile, Marcus lay in Cassie's bed, being awakened for round two. He had no plans of going home before sunrise, and Cassie knew all the right moves to make her man stay put.

CHAPTER TWENTY

The phone rang for the sixth time and rolled over to Angie's voicemail.

"Sorry, I missed you, baby. I hate I won't be there for your birthday party. When I get back, I will make it up to you and take you shopping. Love you." Pam ended the call but squeezed the cell phone tightly. The timing of her trip sucked.

She'd already left a message for her mom and dad, lying that everything was great and going according to plan. The lie tasted bitter as it spewed out of her mouth since she still couldn't get out of Japan, and there was no buyer for the device. She had to lie. She couldn't stand to hear her mother say, "I told you so."

She looked around the dingy room dressed in cobwebs, dirty carpet, and a stench that smelled like spoiled food. It was worse than the first rat den Chu had tucked her away in for her so-called safety. He needed to get her exit plan worked out and find the correct person to whom she needed to hand the device.

Pam's concern for Jayden pushed thoughts of her current dilemma aside. He never seemed to be home when she called, and she could rarely get him on his cell phone. The last time she spoke with

Marcus, he'd told her that Jayden had spent the night with his buddy, Jeremy. Jayden had two friends named Jeremy. One was a good kid from a decent family that Jayden had known since elementary school. The other kid was bad news.

Pam got up and pushed the takeout food to the center of the table.

Jayden knew which Jeremy he was allowed to hang out with. She wasn't going to give it any further worry. She would check with Marcus or Angie the next time she called home, just to make sure he wasn't hanging out with the wrong Jeremy. Pam didn't think she'd be talking to Marcus much. She'd tried apologizing to him about the unpleasant conversation that caused them to put the brakes on their so-called relationship. Yet, Marcus didn't seem too receptive to her apology. Now, with every call, he only answered questions about Jayden and Angie and engaged in no other conversation with her. Pam walked over to the counter and scrolled through her text messages.

Whatever, Pam said to herself. Hopefully, he'll forgive me soon, and we can see where this thing goes with us. One thing is for sure; he knows how to please a woman in bed. I am not about to give that up, especially if I don't have to. Pam tried to quiet the thoughts in her head as she sat down in the recliner chair, tossing a frown over at the bed in the corner, which she refused to sleep in.

Pam finally fell asleep with thoughts of Jayden nagging at her. She hoped he was doing well in sports and keeping his grades up. But Pam was too far away to know Jayden was spending his time with the wrong Jeremy. He was the bad seed that his older sister was raising because their mother was in prison for killing their father.

While Pam slumbered on the other side of the world, Jayden's life was taking on a major makeover. The bad seed had latched onto Jayden the moment Pam left town. Jayden spent most of his free time with Jeremy now that his mother was gone. He knew Jeremy's home life and the kids he hung around with were not what he was used to. But Jayden liked Jeremy and wanted to be his friend. He would soon discover that friendship didn't mean the same thing to Jeremy. He and his friends were all members of a gang called the Bloods. After hanging out for a few weeks with Jeremy, Jayden had graduated from being a nerd playing basketball to failing grades and smoking marijuana. He knew he was headed down the wrong path. But he didn't know how to stop the locomotive barreling down the track to destruction.

Marcus and Angie had been too busy to notice that Jayden spent less and less time at home. They had no idea that Jayden had quit the basketball and soccer team. He couldn't tell them what was going on because he'd told lie after lie, and they were all getting along pretty well now. He couldn't ruin that. His dad worked a lot, and Pam had instructed him not to let his dad know she was out of the country. What was the answer? How could he get away from Jeremy and not be labeled a punk?

Jayden walked home from Jeremy's house. He kicked a rock along the sidewalk as he went along. He wished he could kick Jeremy out of his life as easily as he'd kicked the rock. Man, this has gotten way too crazy. Jayden was weary of the constant talk about plans to hurt people, breaking into houses, and experiment with drugs.

He shoved his hand down into his pocket and pulled out the marijuana Jeremy had given him to maintain his high. He walked over and tossed it down the street drain at the curb. This thing with Jeremy had gone too far. Jayden kicked the rock again, accepting that he needed to pull back from Jeremy and avoid him. Jayden finally realized Jeremy was not the kind of friend he wanted. His life was too close to the edge of danger, a danger that Jayden had decided he wanted to flee from. What made me think that getting high, skipping school, vandalizing buildings, and scaring old folks was cool?

One final hard kick and the rock took flight, sailed across the street, and hit a car. The car alarm sounded off with a piercing screech to

Jayden's ears. His head swung left and right, searching both sides of the street. There was no one in sight. He took off down the sidewalk with his shirt tail waving in the wind behind him. His baseball cap took flight and flew off his head. He glanced behind him. He'd gotten that autographed ball cap for his birthday. He wanted it. But the sound of the man down the street cursing and screaming, "Who in the hell busted my window? I'm calling the cops," made him abandon the cap and pick up his speed. He couldn't let the car owner see him. When he was blocks away, he continued to run, sucking in air, and while sweat dripped down his face. He would soon realize he couldn't outrun all his problems.

CHAPTER TWENTY-ONE

Angie was tired after a long day of classes, errands, and shopping. The night had claimed the sky, and finally home, she went to her bedroom and changed into some shorts and a tank top. She trotted back downstairs to clean the kitchen of the mess she'd made before she'd left. She noticed Jayden's book bag hanging on the coat rack in the hallway. He's been awfully quiet lately. And he hasn't bugged me to come to a game lately, either. Maybe he got out of practice early. He's always tired after basketball practice.

She pulled the note off the refrigerator. I have to work late. Lock up and hold down the fort. Marcus used the same note every time. It was worn and wrinkled now, and it was hard to see the words anymore, but Angie knew what it said.

She sat in the kitchen on a barstool and listed all the things she would need for her birthday party. Her grandparents wanted to pay for everything, and she planned to take them up on it. She looked forward to her big day. She expected at least twenty-five people to show up. She called her friend Vanessa to see if she still planned on helping her decorate for the party.

Standing at the front door, Angie watched the young couple across the street holding hands and kissing. Vanessa's voice shut down thoughts of her and Jacoby.

"What's up, girl?" Vanessa answered, with a smile in her voice.

"What are you so happy about?" Angie questioned, still gazing at the couple.

"You still wearing that stank attitude of yours? I told you to stop sulking over that trifling Jacoby."

"Girl, please. I'm not thinking about that fool. I'm done with him." Maybe walking away from the door and the seemingly happy couple across the street would make her statement a little less of a lie. She sat down at the foot of the stairs, not wanting to wake Jayden.

"Where is that fine specimen of a man, Marcus? You guys home alone?" Vanessa's laughter drifted through the phone and landed on Angie's nerves.

"Get real. Nothing is happening with me and Marcus. I don't think much is happening with him and my mom either. Not the way he stays out late creeping and coming up in here at 5:00 a.m. sometimes." Angie brushed off the leg of her short shorts and turned up her nose at the thought of Marcus. "He doesn't have to worry about me sharing my business with him again. I thought we'd made a connection that night as friends, of course. But I guess I was wrong. All men are just dogs."

"Dang, girl, it sounds like you two made more than a friend connection. Sounds more like a love connection. On the real, if I didn't know better, I'd think you were jealous. You sure you're not trying to push up on your mama's man?" Vanessa's stifled snicker didn't go unnoticed.

"You are not funny. I would never cross the line with my mother's boyfriend. That would be foul. Who does that?"

"I don't know, but he is FINE. You let me know if you don't want him because your mama should've known better than to leave a good-looking chocolate brotha like that all by his lonesome. He can rob this cradle any day, boo."

"Vanessa, you are so crazy. Leave my mama's man alone. He's off limits, no matter how FINE he is." Angie stabbed the air with her index finger as she scolded her friend. "Anyway, I called to make sure you are going to help me decorate for my party?"

"Absolutely, the party is going to be jumping. The decorations have to be on point."

"Okay, sounds good. I'll call you later."

Angie moved over to the front door. The couple were still on the porch. The young man was down on one knee, holding something in his hand, and the red-headed girl with bouncing curls jumped up and down, screaming. Angie shook her head from side to side. "Happy today and cursing each other out tomorrow. It won't last. Few marriages do."

While loading the dishwasher, Angie considered Vanessa's comment about her jealousy of Marcus spending the night away from the house. She had to shake any thoughts of Marcus or him spending the night with some woman. She started the dishwasher and then completed her guest list with a checkmark next to the last item that needed to be purchased. The deadbolt on the front door sounded off. The heavy wooden door parted. The jealous girl's eyes darted to the wall clock. "It's almost midnight. I should've been in bed. Ouch," she yelled after bumping her knee on the table, hurrying to gather her party planning notes.

"Hey, Angie. Are you okay?" Marcus asked, tossing the mail onto the counter.

"Yes, I hit my knee getting up," Angie said, still rubbing her knee.

"You're up pretty late. Somebody is going to be tired in class tomorrow."

"I was working on some last-minute things for my party and lost track of time."

"Oh, yeah. Your birthday is soon. How are your plans coming along?"

"Pretty good. You're on the guest list. I hope you're planning on being here."

"Well, you know I work most nights. I was sure you wouldn't want an old guy like me at your party anyway."

"Yeah, right, not at all. Why wouldn't I want you here? Actually, I'm counting on you being here. I've told everyone about my mom's handsome, really cool boyfriend. My friends want to meet you."

"Angie, I'm sorry to disappoint you, but your mom and I sort of called things off weeks ago. She didn't tell you?" Marcus rubbed his chin.

"No, she didn't," Angie tilted her head to the left. "What happened? And why are you still here with us?"

"Well, when I tell someone I'm going to do something, I keep my word. But if you think you can handle these bills and want me to leave, then I will. I might have to put a woman and her two kids out of my house, but I have to do what I have to do."

"No, that's not what I meant at all. I don't want you to leave, and I know Jayden doesn't, either. It's cool having you here. What happened with you and my mom? You know what, on second thought, never mind. Don't explain. It's none of my business. You're a good man, Marcus. Anyone can see that." She muffled a wide yawn with her hand. "I'm going to bed."

"Good night, Angie. I think I'll turn in, too," Marcus replied, watching her walk away. Those short shorts hugging her hips and the spandex top that offered up her breasts said she was not too young for anything. Marcus pulled at the trimmed beard at the tip of his chin.

He shut off the lights when he reached the top of the stairs and walked into the master bathroom. Marcus peeled off his clothes and allowed a much-needed cold shower to cool the raging fire racing through the lower half of his body. He fought the thoughts of Angie as the cold water beat down on his waning body and hard manhood. He couldn't be attracted to Pam's daughter. It wasn't right, and it wouldn't work anyway.

Out of the shower and his half-wet body lying across the bed, he punched the pillow several times. He looked up at the ceiling fan as it spun around in the dark. His thoughts tumbled around in his head at the same speed until sleep finally cast its' spell.

Down the hall, Angie squeezed her eyelids together tightly and attempted to push the image of Marcus out of her head. She needed desperately to quiet the thoughts of Marcus that plagued her. She whispered into the dark, "I can't like him. I can't be attracted to him, and I definitely can't be thinking about sexing him down." Twenty silent minutes passed before her mind shut down, and sleep rescued her.

CHAPTER TWENTY-TWO

It was party time, and the house was decorated with blue and white balloons. A DJ was hired to keep the music rocking, and the kitchen counters and the island overflowed with all kinds of food, from pizza to barbeque ribs. Angie was busy checking things out before her guests started to arrive.

"Happy Birthday, Angie."

"Thanks, Jayden. I need your help today. Don't go too far, okay?"

"I won't. I'll be right here working like a Hebrew slave for you. I'm going over to Jeremy's later. Just let me know what you need me to do." He continued pressing buttons on his hand-held game.

"Well, the first thing you can do is see if you can spend the night at a friend's house. You do not need to be at this party. I do not want little tots running around," Angie told him, twirling across the floor.

"Tots? Whatever. You wouldn't Turn Up if Ma was here."

"But she's not here," Angie delivered with a wide grin. They both laughed.

Marcus entered the kitchen from the basement. "You've got it looking like a club down there. Don't party too hard tonight."

"Thanks, I'm almost done with everything. Just have to make the punch, take the homemade cookies out of the oven, and get dressed." She stepped over to the oven and pulled the door open to peek in at the cookies. "I wish you could stay for the party."

"Yeah, me too. But I got to get to work. Well, happy birthday! I hope you have a good time tonight. Your party may still be going strong when I get off at midnight."

Two hours later, Angie's Hawaiian themed birthday party was loud and live. As more guests arrived, they plucked out beaded necklaces and their color choice of lei from a basket near the door. Angie and some of her friends wore grass skirts over jeans and coconut bras over bikini tops.

With a cupcake and a smile, Angie had personally paid her neighbors a visit to warn them about the noise level she expected. They liked Angie, and each thanked her and gave her a loud-noise party pass for the night.

The blue Hawaiian punch that started out pure and innocent had been corrupted as the night went along, and Angie was feeling the effects. She stumbled over an ottoman while walking across the floor to meet Vanessa, who was yelling over the music. Angie sucked down her fourth cup of spiked punch and shoved the empty cup at her friend.

"Hey, you better slow down. You know that punch has alcohol in it, right?" Vanessa sniffed the empty cup.

"I thought it tasted different. It is so good." Angie licked her lips. "I wish Marcus was here. He is just the nicest guy ever and so sweet. He smells so good, and he was so helpful to me today."

"Sounds like you are feeling him a little too much," Vanessa offered up.

They both laughed and poured another cup of punch.

"No, he's..." and they said in unison, "My mama's boyfriend," shouting to be heard over the music.

"Yeah, I know exactly who he is," Vanessa teased, watching the moves being made on the dance floor.

"Well, technically, he's fair game because they broke up weeks ago," explained Angie. "I mean not for me, but... anyway, he's a good friend," she offered up in laughter.

People were shouting "Happy Birthday," and challenging Angie to step out on the dance floor.

The tall, slim girl with glasses who had been appointed to be the doorkeeper rushed up to Angie. "Did you invite Jacoby? He's at your door and looking too good. If you don't want him, please give him my digits. I'll gladly take him right off your hands." The girl planted both hands on her hips.

Angie stomped to the door, holding her stomach and clearing her throat. Jacoby stood in the doorway as she approached him. "What are you doing here? You definitely weren't invited."

A few of her guests looked toward the door where they were, but most of her guests just kept partying.

"Sorry, Angie. I know I shouldn't have come, but I didn't want to miss giving you something for your birthday. This time last year, you were out with me. Now we're not together. What's up with that?"

"You know what's up with that. So, let's not go there." Angie's eyes roamed his tall stature from head to toe.

"Don't you miss me? I messed up, Angie. I realize that now. I forgot just how much you mean to me. If you could just give me another chance, I promise that I'll make it up to you. I really do love you. This is for you." He lifted the red gift bag in his hand and eased it toward her.

Angie shoved the gift bag back at Jacoby. "No, thank you. If you had said that the night you called me a whore, I would've taken you back in a heartbeat, but now it's too late. I won't be bitten by the same snake twice. I'm sorry, Jacoby, but I finally did what you told me to do. I have moved on. Now, I don't mean to be rude, but obviously, I'm busy. Can you please leave?" She waved her hand toward his car parked in the driveway.

A cloud of laughs and muffled comments came from the small crowd standing near the door close enough to hear Angie give Jacoby the unexpected big blow-off.

"Now, you can be through with the man, but you do not have to be stupid. Take that gift, girl. It's your birthday." Vanessa grabbed the bag from Jacoby's hand.

In a split-second, Angie snatched it right out of her clutches and thrust it back at the long-faced Jacoby, who was still standing in the doorway. "Tell your mom I said I'm done with the both of you. That should make her happy." She closed the door slowly, forcing Jacoby to back out of the doorway and onto the porch.

"I'm getting a headache," Angie announced, rubbing her stomach.

Vanessa met her with a bottle of cold water in one hand and a mini croissant sandwich in the other. "Eat a little something and drink some water. Maybe you will feel better."

"Party over here," Angie yelled, after sucking down another cup of the spiked blue nectar instead of the water and raising the empty cup into the air.

Marcus glanced down at his watch as he reached for the doorknob. It was 1:00 a.m., and the music was still blasting through the walls and door to greet him as he entered the house.

Vanessa ran into Marcus on her way up the stairs to get another cold towel. "I am so glad you're here. Angie is in the bathroom, and she can't stop throwing up. Man, this is crazy." Vanessa circled her hand in the air, "The party is over, people. You got to go," she yelled out at the crowd.

The slim doorkeeper peered over the rim of her glasses at Vanessa. "I got it. I'll get everyone out. Just take care of Angie."

Marcus rushed to find Angie. The floor was a mess, and she was sitting on the edge of the bathtub, gagging over the toilet. Vanessa came back with a cold towel and swabbed down Angie's face. Ten minutes later, Vanessa and Marcus helped the sick birthday girl upstairs to her bedroom.

"Is Marcus here, Vanessa?" Angie asked, as her head hit the pillow.

"Yes, he's here. He helped me get your heavy behind upstairs."

"Don't tell him I love him, okay?"

"Okay, I won't, I promise," she committed, looking over at Marcus with wide eyes and shrugging her shoulders. She mouthed to Marcus, "She's drunk and doesn't know what she's saying."

"She is definitely drunk to say something like that. Yeah, it's just the alcohol talking," he tried to convince himself. "Okay, Vanessa, I'll go downstairs and make sure everyone is gone and lock up."

"I think he loves me, too. He just doesn't know it yet. I'm never going to drink again." Angie moaned and wiped the sweat from her forehead.

Marcus stopped in the doorway to listen.

"Go to sleep, Angie. You are talking way too much." Vanessa took her shoes off and pulled the cover over her friend.

"No, I want to sleep with my man tonight. You know he and my mom broke up. So, that makes him anybody's man, right?"

"Angie, be quiet. Marcus is right over there." She nodded her head toward him and wrinkled her brow.

"Marcus, baby, I love you. I told you that already, didn't I?" She slurred her confession and stretched out her open hand to him.

"Vanessa, you need to get your friend something to eat. She needs to sober up." Marcus fled the bedroom. He needed to escape the confessing tongue that had to be teasing him. No way were her words true. Minutes later, Vanessa trotted downstairs and stopped in the kitchen.

"Thanks for taking care of Angie. Her mother would have a fit if she had known what went on here tonight," Marcus offered softly. He surveyed the countertops with half-eaten plates of food, the trash can was overflowing, empty soda cans on the floor, and there were four empty bottles of gin that peeked out of the corner of the trash can.

"Hey, no problem; Angie is my girl. If I were you, Marcus, I'd go to bed. Leave all this stuff until tomorrow. You just got off work."

"Yeah, maybe I will do just that. I'm definitely leaving that bathroom that Miss Angie messed up." They laughed out loud.

"Amen. Cleaning that mess up should make her stay sober."

"Exactly," Marcus said, walking Vanessa to the door. He locked up and went to bed.

Moments after he'd slid into bed, a sliver of light crept into his bedroom when the door opened. Angie sauntered to his bedside, climbed in, and snuggled up close to him. Her skin touched his and set his body on fire. "I want to sleep with you tonight, Big Daddy."

CHAPTER TWENTY-THREE

When Angie told Jayden that he could hang out at Jeremy's house for the night, he knew she meant Jeremy Pearson, his teammate and friend. Jayden had become a manipulator. Instead, he went straight to Jeremy Rungman's apartment in the projects. Anything and everything went on there. The only things constant at Rungman's were roaches, his sister, Candy, and her friends smoking weed, drinking, and walking around nearly naked.

No one around there that Jayden knew worked, since most of the girls had at least three kids and received Public Assistance. They got high, had sex, and used profanity like it was their native language. Men hung out in front of the apartment, roaming the grounds like lions seeking out their next prey. As usual, by nightfall, everyone was coupled off for the night. Two things were sure to happen: girls would fight over guys and girls would come up pregnant with a new baby daddy. That meant a few extra dollars from Public Assistance and WIC.

When Jayden walked into Jeremy's apartment that night, he knew that was not where he needed to be. There he was smack dab in the middle of another lie. He had gone home for the last few nights and pretended to be tired. He went to bed early, knowing his sister would think he'd been to basketball practice. Yet, he couldn't remember the last basketball practice he'd attended. But one thing was true, he was exhausted mentally. He wondered how he could've gotten himself into such a mess and how he could get out of it. He wanted to tell someone. Marcus or his father, either one would do. Jayden decided he couldn't do that since he was afraid that he'd put them in danger with the same gang that was pursuing him. He'd waited too late. He was in too deep, and now he had a tough decision to make, and he'd been given one week to make it. His time was up. If he hadn't gone to Jeremy's that night, there may have been some unwanted guests at Angie's birthday party.

Jayden's grade school friend, Jeremy, along with some of his other friends, told him that he could say "no" to joining the gang. He could just walk away. He considered that, but he would not have the protection of a brotherhood if someone from the streets tried to hurt him. That was what the gang of boys told him was one of the benefits of joining their gang. Jayden knew that meant they would be the ones from the streets trying to hurt him the moment he said "no." What could he do? If he agreed to join the gang, he was also agreeing to the initiation process, which meant he had to take a beating. And he might have to hurt someone. A stranger, someone he didn't know and had never done a thing to him. That made no sense. How could he possibly do that?

"So, what's up, Jayden?"

Jayden walked by a dirty diaper on the floor, two snotty, nosed toddlers playing on the dirty floor, and several beer cans on the table in the living room.

"What's up, Casper? I see you have your boys with you. Why does he have eight other guys with him? They all came to hear my answer, I guess. Probably ready to beat me down if I don't join tonight. Jayden let his eyes roam each face. Each one of them tossed him a stern look that was as hard as their muscle-ripped bodies. Jayden stuck both hands down into his pockets and balled up both fists tight but out of sight of all the stern onlookers.

"Well, we all want to know what you decided," Casper proclaimed, with a thick, husky voice and his eyes glued to Jayden. "We hope you make the right decision." Casper pulled back his thick arm and delivered a heavy blow to Jayden's shoulder.

Jayden clenched his teeth and snatched his hands from his pocket to rub his shoulder. "Hey, what was that for?"

"Just a little medicine to make you think," Casper assured him, taking a couple of steps closer to Jayden.

"What's the deal? Where's your head? You're in, or you're out. What's it going to be? It's simple. You don't need to take all day," Jeremy advised with both arms folded across his chest.

Jayden thought about his mom. He wished she would bust through the door and tell those thugs to leave her son alone. But she couldn't help him since she needed someone to help her thousands of miles away. There was no way for that to happen since his mother was on the other side of the world.

Pam was cooped up in a house that felt like a prison. No word yet from Chu on a buyer for Dudley's device, and Pam was ready to go home without a dollar if she had to swim the ocean to get there. She'd tried calling Angie to wish her a happy birthday, but no answer. "Happy birthday. I hope your day was special. These international calls are way too expensive. So, text me tomorrow and tell me all about your birthday. Love you."

Pam's head moved side to side, surveying the big nasty room with only the roaches and the mice to keep her company. Just as she tossed the phone onto the sofa, a mouse ran over the top of her foot and made a squeaking noise. Pam jerked her feet up onto the sofa and flung the unopened bottle of water next to her in the direction of the mouse. "I hate this place. Chu needs to sell that so-called valuable device so I can get the hell out of here."

She had not seen Chu in over a week. She had no one to interact with and nowhere to go. She hadn't spoken to anyone other than Chu, except the petite Japanese woman next door, who looked to be about her age. She didn't speak great English, but Pam could usually make out what she said. Pam snapped her fingers and popped up from the sofa, cautiously glancing over into the corner where the mouse had run off to.

Pam was determined to get out of that house and away from the stench, at least for the night. That just had to happen. She hurried across the floor, out the front door, up the steps, and knocked hard on the back door of the small house next door.

As soon as the petite Japanese woman opened the door, Pam started talking. "I want to go out dancing. Where do the navy men hang out?"

"American men? They go to the Blue Rider," she smiled and nodded her head up and down.

Hanai, "Can you please take me? I really need to get out of that house," begged Pam. Before she could get an answer from the woman, Chu showed up in the alley between the houses. He waived his hands hard and fast, beckoning for Pam to come to him.

"I'll be back. Think about it. I really need you to go with me."

Pam was still four feet away from Chu, and his tongue was already chewing her out. "Why you out of house? You out in the open. Price still on your head. Get in house. Get in right now." He led the way, scurrying up the stairs with his short legs.

Up the steps behind Chu, Pam followed, pleading her case. "I am tired of being cooped up like a prisoner. I haven't seen anyone hanging around, and the police have no idea where I am."

Chu grabbed the two bags of groceries he'd left at the front door when he'd first gotten there. "Here food for you. Stay in house. Dudley paying me to keep you safe. No make trouble for me."

The next few things he said were all in Japanese. He shook his head violently as he delivered what Pam thought was a tongue-lashing for her.

"Okay, Chu. I'll stay inside." Until you leave, she thought to herself. No way would she dare mention going out with Hanai.

"You not leave this house. You stupid woman. You want to die?"

Pam quickly closed the distance between her and Chu. Standing over his four-foot, nine-inch frame, she looked down and scolded him. "I'm not one of the docile Japanese women you can talk to any kind of way and boss around like a child. You got the wrong one. And if you..."

Chu shook his head, walked around her, and headed for the door. "Stay in house. You listen. Stay in house." He babbled something loudly in Japanese and walked out of the door, closing it behind him with a loud noise.

Pam flung the door open, and the doorknob slammed into the wall. "Chu, I am tired of this. Sell the thing already. I'm ready to get out of this hell hole." She slammed her fist into her thigh.

Chu didn't turn around, and he didn't respond. He kept walking until his silhouette faded into the bright sunlight.

Seconds later, Pam was back at Hanai's and convinced her that she needed to go out. "These people don't know me. I will only be here for another few weeks. I am desperate to have some fun," she assured her.

“I show you where to find the men. I take you there tonight, but I can’t stay. Have sick mother,” said the woman.

“That’s fine. I understand. I can take care of myself. Just get me there,” she told Hanai as she left her house.

CHAPTER TWENTY-FOUR

Pam was excited for the first time since she'd arrived in Japan. She washed, dried, and curled her hair. Then, she painted on make-up and slid on a tight, short, purple and black dress she'd taken from Angie's closet. Black Michael Kors pumps and fishnet stockings were a necessity. "Look out Sailor Boys," she told the reflection of herself in the mirror.

As soon as she entered the club, the cloud of smoke choked her and sent her into a coughing frenzy. Jesus, you can still smoke in public places here. That is crazy. Her eyes burned from the smoke and the swarm of people inside made moving around challenging. "There are a lot of American men. This is what I need," Pam whispered into the smoke-filled room. Looks like I have choices. She went to the bar and chatted with men over the loud music. She worked the dance floor with a partner and sometimes without. Finally, winding down, Pam sat at the bar alone and ordered a third Singapore Sling. She sipped on the smooth, sweet combination of gin, cherry-flavored brandy, pineapple, lime juice and grenadine. Pam licked her red lips and placed the glass on the bar.

"Can I have a taste?" the dark chocolate man beside her asked.

"Of my drink?" Pam questioned, pointing at her glass.

"No, of those delicious-looking lips of yours."

"I don't kiss strangers."

"Then allow me to introduce myself. My name is Randall," he offered with a toothy smile.

Pam introduced herself. He wasn't dressed like a sailor, but he was handsome. As her lips moved, the man's gaze was fixed on them glancing from her eyes back to her lips. Just as Pam stood, Randall covered her lips with his and thrust his tongue down her throat. She shoved him away from her and brushed the taste of him off her lips with the back of her hand. "You jerk. Get the hell away from me." Pam turned and walked across the room and blended into the crowd until she couldn't see him any longer.

She stood at the dance floor's edge and allowed the music's beat to soothe her. She closed her eyelids and moved to the beat unaware that midway through the song, she had attracted an uninvited partner until he pinched her butt.

"Hey baby," he said and winked at her.

His breath and the smell of fish and alcohol slapped her. Her eyelids popped open and so did her mouth. "Get the hell away from me. I don't want to dance with you. You had no right to touch me; you pig."

He walked away from her briefly and came back with a buddy who was even more aggressive than him. They managed to get Pam in between the two of them, and they touched her breast and butt with both hands.

"Stop it, you freaks. Keep your damn hands off me," she yelled and took wide steps to get away from them.

The men laughed and jabbered loudly about her as they walked behind her. She cursed the men all the way to the bar. They laughed and pointed at her as they turned and headed toward the exit, still talking about her to each other.

Pam sat at the bar and threw back at least three tequila shots before returning to the dance floor. More than one man watched her as she swayed to the beat of a slow groove. The alcohol seduced her, and she liked the feeling. A tall sailor with a clean-shaven face and a dimple in his chin stared at her from his seat in the corner. He sucked down the last swallow of Hennessy from his glass and swirled the ice around and around. He pitched his glance from Pam to the two men at the table next to him, who were pointing at her. The tall sailor strained to hear what they were saying as they smiled and continued to point at her. He could only hear bits and pieces of their conversation. Yet, he heard enough to know their thoughts were evil.

One of the men at the table with a bulging muscle that sported a tattoo of a skull dancing on his right bicep wiggled his tongue in Pam's direction, stood, grabbed his manhood, and took two steps toward Pam.

The tall sailor stood, took four wide steps, and stood in front of the man with the tattoo on his arm. He narrowed his eyelids to deliver a piercing, determined expression that conveyed his message before his words declared it. "She's not that kind of girl," he proclaimed. "She's just drunk. Now, back off. I'll see to it that she gets home. No need for you to make any further plans concerning the woman in the purple and black dress dancing alone."

The man glanced past his aggressor and took in Pam's slow, seductive moves for a few seconds, then held up both hands as he surrendered to the firm warning that had been issued. He backed away and returned to his seat without uttering a word.

When the song ended, the sailor who'd just rescued her, without her knowledge, walked slowly up to Pam. He touched her arm gently.

"Miss, my name is Andre. You look like you could use a ride home. Are you okay?"

Pam's eyes roamed his body from head to toe, twice. Her words were slurred, "No way. I'll call a cab. I'm fine; don't touch me. I came by myself, and I'll leave by myself." He waited while she fumbled through her purse to locate her phone. When she finally fished it out, it was dead. "Crap," she shook the phone and threw it back into her purse.

"Last offer," the man said. "I'd be glad to make sure you get home safely."

Pam curled her lips and drew in a short breath. "I guess so. I don't really want to, and don't you think for one minute that I'm giving you any of this good stuff just for a ride home." Pam patted the spot between her legs.

"You're a tourist. You are definitely not from around here. Everything about you says that. I just don't want to see anything happen to you. That's it; that's all."

The ride to Pam's was quiet. She leaned her head back on the headrest, and two minutes later, she was asleep. She'd given him the address. So, he let her sleep. When they got to Pam's, he squeezed her hand. She woke up, looked to the left and right of her, realized where she was, and slid out of the car. "Thanks, I'm good."

He walked her to the door and waited for her to get the door unlocked.

Once she pushed the door open, she swatted his hand and giggled. "Get your hungry ass away from here. I told you that I am not giving up anything."

"Ma'am, I was just trying to be sure you got home safely. That's all. I didn't want anything from you," he assured her.

"Sure, that's what they all say. Now, take your weird ass on. What do you want, a freaking medal?" she yelled, closing the door. She started undressing before she made it to the bedroom. She heard his car pull away.

A loud sound swept through the house and rattled the windows in the bedroom. Two men kicked in the front door and stormed toward Pam with wide eyes. One threw his empty beer bottle into the floor and yelled, "There that whore is. Get her."

"Get out of here before I call the police. Get out, get out."

The short plump guy reached her first and dragged her from the bedroom and onto the front room floor. They snatched off her clothes as she kicked, scratched, and screamed.

Her strength seemed to drain from her body. Her hands felt heavy, and tears blurred her vision as she continued to struggle. The tall, muscular guy with glasses spread her legs open and kept them open with his knees while he unfastened his pants. "I got something for you." He pulled his manhood out, held it in his hand, and shook it at her. With one thrust, he was deep inside of her.

Her piercing scream, which sounded like a wounded animal, was muffled by the other man who held her wrists over her head with one hand and put his other hand over her mouth.

The man snorted and grunted like an animal while he pounded and stabbed her insides with every inch of him. "Good, right? You want some more of this hard stick, don't you?"

Tears rolled down the sides of her face and seeped into the dirty, stained carpet. Her strength had left her body. The struggle was gone from her, and her muffled screams were now weak whimpers. She counted the last few thrusts. One, two, three... and the man heaved his last couple of painful stabs into her body, jerked hard, and rolled off her.

The other man wasted no time flipping her over, mounting her, and thrusting himself inside of her from behind. His forceful thrusts tore at her insides. She screamed as loud as she could from the core of her soul. She got one last scream out before the first animal who'd savagely raped her stuffed a dirty rag into her mouth.

Pam could feel what she thought had to be blood pouring from her bottom. Her stomach was plagued with cramps, and seconds later, the dinner she'd eaten earlier erupted and climbed up from her gut.

They left her on the floor like a discarded piece of trash once they'd ravished her body. The last assailant zipped up his pants and repeatedly mocked and insulted her. His voice was hoarse and thick as he wiped the sweat from his face with both hands.

"All we wanted was a dance. Now, look at what you made us do. I hope it was good for you because it was damn good for me." He cleared his throat and harked up a wad of thick yellow spit and spat it down into her face. "Now, who's the freak? Isn't that what she called us?" He looked over at the guy wearing glasses for confirmation.

"Yeah, among other things. I remember her calling us a couple of faggots. Wasn't that it, sweetheart? Didn't feel much like faggots just now, though, did it?"

After they'd had their fill of mocking her, they discussed going back to the bar for another drink.

"Hell, a drink sounds great, but I could use a cigarette after that, and I don't even smoke," the short, plump guy responded, who'd taken the second round of ravishing Pam.

"I know what you mean," the other man said, licking his lips. "She was a good piece. Maybe we'll come back for some more another time."

"Hmm, not a bad idea," the other sailor agreed.

Pam willed herself up from the floor, pushing past the pain that snaked through her body. The filthy fluids that drained from her vagina slid down both legs. She managed to stand and hobble to the kitchen. No way in hell will they... Move your feet Pam. Fury energized her. She snatched a large butcher knife from the countertop.

Before the two laughing assailants stepped off the porch, Pam stumbled forward and plunged a knife into the back of the first man who had violated her. He took two steps and fell into the short, chubby man, who turned, saw the blood dripping from his friend's back, and his eyes darted to Pam. He drew back his fist and punched her in the face.

She fell with a loud thud. Her hands flew to her eyes. One was already swelling and changing colors. Blood dripped from her nose onto the porch. She tried to lift her head and then drifted out of consciousness.

"Why did you do that? You stupid bitch." He bent down and tried to help his friend up.

The wounded man coughed up blood. His friend wrapped his arms around him tighter as his body weakened, and he struggled to stand up. Blood oozed from the man's back, staining the clothing of his accomplice.

"Come on, man, you're going to be alright. We have to get you out of here. Stay with me, now."

Down the steps and into the yard was as far as they got. The bleeding man dropped to his knees, drew in a gurgling loud breath, and slumped to the ground, dead.

CHAPTER TWENTY-FIVE

Hanai headed out of her front door to get the newspaper. As she stood on the front step, she glanced over in the direction of Pam's house. There was a man struggling to get up from the ground. "Help, you need help? He sick?" Hanai yelled out to the man while waving the newspaper in his direction.

The man's head twirled from side to side to see where the voice came from. His eyes landed on Hanai. He immediately rose and sprinted off, leaving the body of his dead friend behind, and he did not look back.

Hanai's short legs carried her across the yard. She stopped and glared down at the man on the ground. She poked his shoulder with her fingertip and hopped back. No movement. She poked him harder and noticed the blood still oozing from the wound in his back. "Oh, him look dead." She took two quick steps backward, turned, and headed up the steps.

"Hello, hello. You in there?" She called out, pounding on the door with the heels of both hands. When there was no answer, she turned the knob and pushed open the door. Her hand flew to her chest as she sucked in a hard breath at the sight of Pam on the floor, clothes torn, blood on her face, body, and the floor. Fear spoke to Hanai, She dead! The sight in front of her gripped her as she stood still and surveyed the room. Was there anyone else in the house? There was no noise. Only silence spoke in the room.

Cautiously, Hanai tiptoed closer to the body on the floor trying not to step in the blood. The faint rise and fall of Pam's chest told her she wasn't dead. She found a linen closet and yanked out sheets and towels. After covering Pam's body with a cool wet towel, she gently swabbed Pam's swollen face until she regained consciousness.

"So, so sorry. What happened?" Hanai questioned with watery eyes.

Pam's head was spinning. She could hear Hanai's voice but struggled to make out her face since one eye was swollen shut and her vision in the other was blurry. The storm of a headache that raged in her head made it difficult for her to collect her thoughts.

"Help, I get help for you." Hanai spoke fast, glancing from Pam and back to the door.

Thoughts of the attack flooded her memory, and the horrible thing that happened to her began to be clear in her mind. Pam's eyes grew large, and her hands trembled. I stabbed one of them. Is he dead? Is some of the blood on me his blood? She lifted her hand to try and wipe away the blood that covered both hands and her chest. Pam needed to be clean. She wanted to be free of the filthy blood and semen that made her a victim. She brushed at her body with weak strokes attempting to get the foul stench of the violation of her body off her.

Pain swept through Pam's body and demanded medical attention. She was afraid to leave the house or call for medical care. There was still a dead body in the yard. How could she do that? Chu had warned her that leaving the house was dangerous, and she hadn't listened. However, what happened to her had nothing to do with her business with Chu and Dudley. Chu had no idea what trouble she'd found on her own. It would be daylight soon and the man lying in the yard would be discovered.

"I call police. You need doctor." Hanai squeezed Pam's hand. "I get help for you."

Pam swallowed hard and frowned at the taste of blood in her mouth. "No doctor. I can't."

Hanai nodded her head and stepped away from Pam to call the police. Then she struggled and stumbled across the floor, through the yard, and passed the dead body, almost dragging Pam into her house. Thirty minutes later, there was a hard knock at the door. Pam was hidden away in the back bedroom. Hanai placed her index finger on her slips. "No sounds. Be back. Police at door."

Pam hovered somewhere between asleep, awake, and half dead it felt like. A single tear slid down the side of her face and lingered in her ear lobe. She mouthed, "Thank you," because no sound could climb up from her dry throat.

Hanai told the police all she knew of the dead man in the yard was that he was there when she got her newspaper. When they asked if she knew who was living in the house next to her, Hanai lied. The police told her it appeared that a woman was staying there and something bloody and horrible had taken place next door. Hanai stuck to her story, "Saw nothing heard nothing. I was sleeping."

Finally, the police left and assured her they would return. The following day Hanai told Pam about the police, their questions, and that they were sure to be back.

Pam felt that she owed Hanai at least the most important facts about the night that would change her life forever. She started with the two men harassing her on the dance floor at the club. All the details of her rape spilled out of her soul into words that were painful for her to say and hear.

Hanai swabbed at her eyes as she listened to the heart-wrenching description of what happened next door, and she hadn't heard a thing. Maybe if she had not told Pam about the nightclub, this terrible thing would not have happened to her. "I sorry," she told Pam, sniffling hard.

Pam's weak voice tried to offer Hanai absolution, "It's my fault. I should have listened and not gone out." She patted Hanai's hand and said, "You have been very kind to me." Pam's brow wrinkled, and her one open eyelid narrowed. For a couple of moments, she tried to remember where Dudley's device was. Had the men taken it? Did she have it out lying around when they broke into the house? The wrinkles across her forehead disappeared. She remembered moving it and placing it under a loose floorboard in the closet. It's safe. She assured herself. As soon as she had enough strength in her body, she would go next door to make certain.

Pam was unaware that Chu was pounding on the door of the house where the horrible deed had taken place. No response. He pounded harder. Still, no response. With his ear pressed to the door, he listened. There was no noise, no movement. He unlocked the door and was greeted by the blood that covered the floor. Chu shook his head and slammed his right fist into the palm of his hand. He scurried from room to room, with his heart beating faster with each room he entered. Where was the gadget? He'd better try to find it. He pulled out drawers and dumped them onto the floor, turned over furniture, and even checked the refrigerator and freezer. The place was now in complete shambles, and he was still empty-handed. No gadget.

Pam must have been killed or abducted along with Dudley's multi-million-dollar gadget. "She stupid American woman. Damn it!" He kicked the drawer lying on the floor. It took flight and flew across the room and crashed into the wall. "I told her not to leave house. Now we both in danger." Chu stood in the middle of the floor and pounded his head with both fists. What was next? Danger would pursue him.

CHAPTER TWENTY-SIX

The phone rang at least five times before Marcus reached over and snatched the cordless phone from the table next to the bed. "Hello," he croaked out, looking at the digital clock on the nightstand that told him it was 4:20 a.m.

"This is Officer Foster of the Dallas Police Department. We have a victim here at the Dallas Regional Hospital named Jayden Carr. Am I speaking to his father?"

Marcus sat straight up in bed, swung his feet over the side, and stood up. "Yes, I mean, I'm his guardian, Marcus Blue. Why? What's the problem, officer?"

"Sir, Jayden was found lying on a sidewalk unconscious and bleeding. His school ID was in his back pocket. I have to warn you; he's been beaten pretty badly."

"Are you sure it's him?" Marcus asked, grabbing his pants from the end of the bed and stepping into them.

"It's him, alright. This is the number he gave us to call when he regained consciousness. We were told that his injuries are the result of a gang initiation."

"What? Jayden's only twelve years old." Marcus shook his head and took a step forward. "He went to spend the night at a friend's house. What do you mean, gang initiation?" He asked while sticking both feet into a pair of Jordans.

"Sir, I suggest you get here as soon as possible," the officer advised and hung up the phone.

"Damn it, Jayden! What the hell?"

Marcus flung open the bedroom door and sprinted down the hall to Angie's room, yelling on his way, "Angie, I need you to get up. Get up now."

Still hung over from her birthday party, Angie mumbled, rolled over, and pulled the covers over her head. Marcus snatched the covers off her and searched her closet for clothes and shoes for her to put on.

"Hey, what are you doing? Oh, so now you want to get with me? You turned me down and put me in my own bed last night, remember? You suddenly had a change of heart? Well, it's too late, Marcus. Now get out of my room."

"Get dressed right now," he demanded, throwing clothes onto her bed.

"Put these on, quickly. We have to get to the hospital. Jayden's been hurt."

"Jayden... what are you saying, Marcus? How? He spent the night at Jeremy's." Marcus' words sobered her up quickly. She jumped up and pulled on her clothes. Her attention darted to the clock at her bedside. "Are you sure?"

"Yes, I'm sure. The police just called. They said that it was gang related."

Angie gasped loudly and swung her body around to face Marcus. "Gang related? That's impossible. My little brother doesn't belong to any gang. He doesn't even know anybody in a gang. Are you sure they said Jayden? It must be a mistake." Angie tried to convince herself and Marcus.

Seconds later, they were downstairs, slamming shut the doors of Marcus' car. His tires screeched as he sped down the block. The tread marks left behind confirmed his concern for the boy he had come to genuinely care about.

After parking the car, Marcus and Angie pushed through the glass double doors of the hospital and hustled to the information desk. "We're here for Jayden Carr. I'm his sister." The woman behind the desk typed the name into the computer and gave them directions to the Intensive Care Unit. When they arrived, a doctor was in the room with Jayden. The nurse at the ICU desk gently cautioned them to wait outside the room until the doctor came out.

The moment the tall man with a stethoscope stepped outside the room, Angie attacked him with questions. "Doctor, what happened to my brother? Is he going to be alright?"

"Well, your brother was severely beaten. His injuries are very serious. He's in critical condition but should have recovery fully. However, it will take some time. There are multiple contusions to his body, a closed head injury, a detached retina of the left eye, two cracked ribs, a broken nose, and..."

"Oh my, God." Angie interrupted, as tears slid down both cheeks.

"You can see him now. He needs to rest. Please keep your visit short."

Angie and Marcus stepped into Jayden's room with the doctor following close behind. "Jayden, what in the world happened to you? Who did this?"

Jayden opened the only eye he could long enough to see his sister turn and bury her head in Marcus' chest. His other eye was bandaged along with his head. He was groggy from pain medication, and his vision was blurry.

"Doctor, how long do you think he will need to be here?" Angie questioned, rubbing her brother's arm softly.

"Unfortunately, we can't be sure. He does need to be monitored to ensure there's no swelling of the brain and no seizures. At the same time, he's a lucky kid. Some kids don't make it when they get initiated into street gangs. Many times, they're found dead. Keep your visit short, please," the doctor advised as he left the room.

"Street gang, not my son. What the hell is he talking about, Angie?" Jayden's father, Doug, questioned, walking through the door of the hospital room. "What happened to my son?" His head swung from one side to the other. "Where is your mother?"

He walked to the side of the bed, looked down at Jayden, and fury stood up inside him. His eyes were wide and wet. He walked across the room to the window and stomped back to the bedside. His gaze bore into his son's bandaged and badly bruised face. Then, his attention shifted quickly to Angie.

"Angie, tell me what happened to my boy. I've been trying to call Jayden and your mom for weeks, but neither of them has returned my calls. I've even been to the house. No one is ever home. Where is your mom, Angie?" He watched as Angie dropped her head into her hands and began to sob. "What's going on here?" Doug demanded. "Say something, girl!"

"I don't know, Doug. I don't know," Angie blurted out, crying harder and louder.

"Their mom is out of town," Marcus offered, stepping in front of Angie.

"Who are you?" Doug asked, moving towards Marcus. "What do you have to do with any of this?"

"I'm Marcus Blue. I'm staying with Pam's kids until she gets back into town."

"What? Where is she, and how long have you been staying with my son? Somebody better tell me something." His focus jumped from Marcus to Angie and back to Marcus.

"My mom is in Japan, Doug," Angie offered.

"Japan? What the..."

"Sir, please," interrupted a nurse, who heard the noise and stepped into the room.

"I need you all to take this outside of this room. I don't want the patient to get upset. As you can see, he has suffered some serious injuries," she stated, opening the door for them to exit the room.

Standing in the hallway, Angie explained to Doug why Pam went to Japan.

"This is just another one of her wild-ass ideas. You tell her for me that this one nearly cost my son his life. She doesn't get another chance to put my boy in danger. When he gets out of here, he's coming home with me for good." He slammed his fist into the palm of his hand. This whole thing is crazy and should never have happened."

"No, Doug, please don't take my brother." Angie stepped closer to Doug and clutched the sleeve of his jacket.

"Get the hell away from me, Angie," Doug said, throwing his hand up in the air, breaking her hold on him.

"All of you kept Pam being out of the country a secret. What if my son had been killed? You'd better pray he makes a full recovery, or you will have to answer to me," he declared, pointing to Marcus.

"You let my son run around until he got involved with a gang. That's because you don't care about him. He's not your son." Doug stabbed the air with his index finger as he directed his angry tone at Marcus.

He turned to Angie with his eyes bulging with anger. It was her turn.

"I'm surprised at you, Angie. I thought you gave a damn."

"That's not fair, Doug. I love my brother, and you know it." Angie's bottom lip quivered.

"I care about him, too. He said he was spending the night at Jeremy's house. I talked to Jeremy's mother," Marcus offered up with a strong voice.

"Man, this is not the result of one night at Jeremy's house. You don't know where he was and who he was with. Did you ever meet Jeremy's mother face to face? No, you just took his word that was where he was because you didn't give a damn. Now, get the hell out of my way before you find yourself in the bed next to my son. I need to call my attorney." He pushed past Marcus, shoving him aside. "Angie, tell your mother what I said. Jayden goes with me," Doug declared and walked back into his son's hospital room.

Angie whimpered and tried unsuccessfully to stop the waterfall of tears as she peered through the cracked door of Jayden's hospital room. "It kills me to see him like this. I am so sorry he didn't trust us. He never said a word about the mess he got himself into. He must have felt so alone. Marcus, how could he have gotten mixed up with people like that right under our noses? He wouldn't have done this if my mother was home. This is all her fault."

Marcus reached for Angie's hand and pulled her away from Jayden's door. "Don't blame your mother, Angie. I take full responsibility. She left me to watch over him and now look at him. I let her down. I let Jayden down."

"No, Marcus, this is her fault. It was selfish of her to leave us here anyway. She was being selfish as always. Grandma and I both warned her that something tragic could happen."

Angie understood Doug's anger about what happened to Jayden. He had a right to be angry. But Angie was angry, too. Her mom would know that and feel her anger soon.

CHAPTER TWENTY-SEVEN

Angie sobbed, swatted away tears, and blew her nose half the way home. When they entered the house, Marcus dropped down onto the couch and threw his head back.

Angie tried to reach her mother. The phone went straight to voicemail. She sat down on the opposite end of the couch from Marcus. She tried her mother repeatedly. No answer.

"Should I leave her a message?" Angie inquired.

"No, your mother shouldn't have to find out about her son like that. Let's just keep trying until she answers,"

"I can't get the image of Jayden out of my head. I just keep seeing his handsome face banged up with a broken nose and a mangled eye. What about my brother's eye? Oh my, God. What if he loses it?" She blew her nose, and tears clouded her vision. "It could affect the rest of his life. How can I explain this to my mother and grandmother? They will both hate me, and I don't blame them." Angie covered her face with both hands and sobbed loudly. "I should've paid more attention. He's my brother. This is my fault." She shifted in her seat and rubbed her palms up and down both thighs.

Marcus reached over, pulled Angie into his arms, and held her close as she wailed. "This is not your fault," he whispered, guiding her head to his chest. He stroked her hair gently to calm her. They fell asleep and slept for two hours. Marcus would've slept longer except he felt soft strokes across his chest that aroused him. He was surprised at how quickly he had become aroused.

Does this girl know what she's doing? He thought. She must still be asleep. Maybe she's dreaming or has forgotten who I am, her mother's ex. She was drunk when she got into bed with me, but today she's completely sober. His thoughts began to fade as his body relaxed under her touch. Marcus wasn't sure how to react. He'd lusted after Angie since he'd seen her in bed with Jacoby. He knew people would agree that it was morally wrong for him to be with Angie. People would probably say he was a disgusting pervert. They'd wonder how he could make a move on Pam's daughter. People wouldn't care how it happened. It wouldn't matter. He just knew they'd blame him and him alone.

While Marcus was thinking about the nature of what was on the rise, he heard Angie say softly, "You can relax. In case you're wondering, I know exactly what I'm doing. Don't act like you don't want me, Marcus. I see how you look at me. I see you, and you're always watching me. It started the day you saw me in bed with Jacoby, remember? I guess you came home early or something."

Marcus sat in silence, but his thoughts spoke loudly. Oh wow, is she reading my mind, or what? I had no idea Angie saw me watching them. She never said a word.

"You wanted me way back then. It was all over your face. You didn't see me looking at you because your eyes were closed. You were caught up in the moment just like Jacoby was as our bodies touched. I performed for you that day. I wanted to teach you a lesson for being so nosy. Neither of us had any idea it would lead to this. You tried to slip out of the bathroom, but you stumbled. You want to go back in time and pretend it never happened, but let's face it, we have not looked at each other the same way since. The funny thing is, looking back, I realize Jacoby didn't deserve the way I made love to him."

She sat up and whispered in his ear. "I never did to him what I want to do to you."

"What?" Marcus managed to say, feeling the dryness of his throat. His eyes met hers.

"Yes, Marcus Blue, it's true. I said it." She pulled the drawstring on his jogging pants to loosen the waistband and reached inside. Her desires had prompted a mutual response from a particular part of his body, which was what she'd hoped for. She stroked him gently with her hand and felt his arousal harden and throb.

Marcus wanted to snatch every thread of clothing off Angie and make love to her as if his life depended on it. But he struggled with whether or not to join her in this forbidden quest. Beads of sweat painted his forehead.

Angie grinned at his obvious nervousness.

"Angie, I'm just not sure this is right. Everyone will go against us on this. I'm your mother's ex-boyfriend, remember? Besides, I'm a lot older than you. I don't want to hurt you. This is serious. Once we go there, there's no turning back, and then what? If you've ever heard of Pandora's Box, this is it. You are beautiful, and yes, I admit it, I did see you that day. I've wanted you for myself ever since. But you were off-limits then and still need to be off-limits for me now. I've tried to put you out of my mind." Marcus brushed his hand against his manhood to tame it and gain control.

Angie leaned forward and looked into his eyes. "But you couldn't get me off your mind, could you, Marcus? I know you want to do what you think is right. I don't want to hurt my mother. I love her. This has nothing to do with her," Angie said, planting soft kisses on his chest.

Marcus inhaled slowly and held his breath, attempting to resist the impact of her touch.

"There can't be anything wrong with two people who genuinely care about each other being together. You can try to deny it, Marcus, but you and I both know it's true. You see, I'm not worried about you hurting me because you would never do that. You love me. I can feel it. You can't wait to come home from work and find me waiting for you."

Marcus fought back a smile and cleared his throat instead. He adjusted the bulge in his pants to provide himself with some relief from the ache between his legs that inched through the rest of his body. This cannot be happening. I can't allow this to happen. His mind protested, but his body surrendered to Angie's touch.

"I know you want me. I know because I love you. When we're here together, nobody else exists. As much as I hate to admit it, my little brother deceived us. He was able to do that because we were distracted by each other." Angie was silent for a few minutes as she watched Marcus try to hide the excitement and desire that crawled through his body.

"What we feel for each other will hurt other people. I'm not sure that it's right to allow that to happen." God, I want this woman. But it's just not right. He stood and took two steps away from her, hoping to quench his desire. It was wrong, and he needed distance between them.

Angie refused to allow him to put distance between them. She got up and walked over to him, kissed his lips and then his neck. Her tongue moved up his neck to his chin and then to his bottom lip. She nibbled on it, tasting its softness. Then she parted his lips with her tongue, took his tongue captive by hers, and the seductive dance began.

Marcus met her in that moment. They kissed long, deeply, and passionately. Eagerly, they continued to taste each other. Suddenly,

Angie broke away from him and walked upstairs. He never took his eyes off of her. "I want you right now," she confessed.

Marcus followed Angie silently, his eyes fixed on her as if under a spell. When they reached the top of the stairs, she pulled her shirt over her head and unfastened her bra, baring her breasts for his pleasure. Her perky, plump nipples stood at attention and faced Marcus, daring him to take her succulent berries into his mouth.

He latched onto her right nipple, tasted its sweetness, and moaned with the pleasure it delivered to him. With his hand, he rubbed the throbbing manhood between his legs that ached and spilled his wet sexual release into his underwear.

Angie gently removed her nipple from his mouth and ran from him, laughing and shedding items of clothing on the way to the bedroom. He did the same, starting with his shoes and then his shirt. He chased her—and when he caught her, they plunged onto the king-size bed in the Master bedroom—Pam's bed.

Marcus kissed her and held her tightly. His desire was an ache that he needed a remedy for. With her supple breast in his mouth, his finger searched out the core of her hot moist body and slid inside.

Angie gasped loudly and panted with pleasure. Her moist center was warm and pulsating. "Marcus, that feels so good. Don't stop. Please don't stop."

"If you think that feels good. I've got something even better for you, baby." He drew back his finger, licked her juices from it, and gave her two hard licks between her legs, then plunged his tongue inside of her for two minutes of erotic teasing. She twisted and wiggled beneath him with a sexual pleasure that was new to her. Just as she called his name for the third time, Marcus plunged deep inside of her hard and fast with every inch of him that he had to give.

As Angie felt his hard manhood climb in and out of her, she screamed and pledged her love for him. Three minutes later, they reached a very audible and satisfying moment of ecstasy together that was the most pleasure either had experienced. They both were breathing hard, with tremors of ecstasy still shooting through their bodies. Marcus dismounted her wet, sweaty body to lie next to her.

"I love you, Marcus. I really love you," Angie whispered softly.

"Angie, you are a special young lady. It is hard for me to admit, but I love you, too."

They both fell asleep. The morning sunshine was shining through the window when Angie opened her eyelids. Marcus was still sleeping, and that wouldn't do. She blew softly into his ear, then planted a juicy kiss on his lips. "Wake up, old man. My kisses should stimulate you."

His eyelids parted, and a weak smile crawled across his lips.

"Everything about you stimulates me." He rolled over on his side to face her.

"Really? So, you still think this is a bad idea?"

"You know, Angie, all of my relationships have been built on either good sex or just sex, and the ones that lasted any length of time lasted mostly because of sex. I've been in love, but I've never been in a situation where I got a chance to know someone before we had sex. We've been here together in the same house for nearly five months. I've gotten to know you pretty well. And I know that I never want to hurt you."

"Is that a yes? We are going to give us a try?" She touched his bare chest with the palm of her hand.

"My heart tells me yes and not to pay attention to all the reasons we shouldn't. It will be an uphill battle, but yes, we are." Marcus pulled Angie into his arms, and they lay silently in the comfort of their warm embrace and drifted back off to sleep.

CHAPTER TWENTY-EIGHT

Angie woke up, showered, dressed, and headed back to the hospital to see Jayden. She left Marcus a note. He was still sleeping off the great sex and the verbal commitment they'd made to each other to try and make things between them work.

Angie hadn't been gone long when the phone next to the bed summoned Marcus from his sleep-like hibernation. He reached over and snatched up the phone, and with his eyelids still shut tight, he answered the phone, "Yeah."

A stern female voice lashed out at him. "What do you mean, yeah? Who says that? That's no way to answer a phone. You must be Marcus because the kids in my family know better than to answer a phone like that. This is Mrs. Carter, Pam's mother. What in the world happened to my grandson? How in the heck did he get involved with a gang? My daughter left him in your care, and he ended up in the hospital, beaten half to death. Now, she may lose custody of her son because of your sorry behind. If you know what's..."

"Ma'am," Marcus interrupted, his eyelids wide open, and he sat straight up in bed. "I asked Pam if she allowed Jayden to spend the night with friends. She told me the names of the boys he could hang out with. Angie let him spend the night with one of the guys because she didn't want him at her twenty-first birthday party. He wanted to go to his friend's house, and I didn't see anything wrong with that. It wasn't anything out of the ordinary. Jayden occasionally spends the night with friends, even when his mom is home. I left it up to Angie and Jayden because I had to work until midnight."

"Oh, so now it's Angie and Jayden's fault. Passing the buck and negligence are signs of irresponsibility, young man. I knew this was a bad idea from the start. I told Pam this was going to bite her square in her..."

"Listen, ma'am, this is not Pam's fault, and it is not mine. I'm not passing the buck. Angie and I tried to look out for Jayden. He had some friends we didn't know about," Marcus explained, scratching his head.

"Well, you should've known about them. That's why she left you there. I will never believe you agreed to stay there because you were so crazy about my daughter. Obviously, you didn't stay to look out for Jayden, either. I'd be willing to bet my life that you've had your eyes set on my granddaughter's rump roast from the very start. That's been your plan all along, hasn't it? You can admit it. I understand. My daughter is too old for you. This whole thing is blowing up in her face, just like I told her it would."

Is this woman psychic? She couldn't possibly know that Angie and I spent the night together. This is what we can expect from everyone once they learn about us. Marcus' thoughts kept him from responding.

"Well, say something. Don't get quiet on me, now. What's the matter?

Did I hit a nerve? I thought so."

"No, ma'am, you're wrong," Marcus finally said. "I was just making sure you were finished. I didn't want to interrupt you."

"Don't get sassy, young man. I haven't reached my daughter. But I think she would agree that I should take care of the rent, bills, and my grandchildren until she gets home. You need to get out of her house before somebody else gets hurt. I'll be there next week to make sure that happens. I will give you that much time. I will have my grandson, Nelson, with me. It would be in your best interest to start packing now and be gone when we get there. Until then, I will be at the hospital checking on my grandson, and I don't want to see you there."

The dial tone informed him that she was finished talking. Marcus punched the headboard twice and then rubbed his knuckles.

Pam was in excruciating pain and had no idea what was happening on the other side of the world with her son, Angie, or Marcus. Pam woke up and reached for her cell phone. She felt around the bed near her and found nothing. It's next door. I left it. She tried to open her mouth to call out to Hanai, but she could barely part her lips. Tears welled up in her eyes. Her thoughts were flooded immediately with the faces and the grimy touch of the men and the pain they inflicted on her body. Lord, I need to talk to my kids, and I can't even open my mouth. She could not believe that she'd been the victim of such a gruesome rape. She just wanted to go home. She scolded herself. I should've left here months ago, money or not. Marcus was right. I did come here on the notion of getting rich quickly. Nothing should've ever been important enough for me to go this far away from my family and for this length of time. Pam balled up her fists, stretched her fingers out wide, then balled her fists up so tightly she could feel her pulse in her hand.

Pam left the old, worn sofa in Hanai's home for the second time to peep through the blinds to see if anyone was hanging around her hideout next door. Her fear of being arrested or killed drove her painful steps across the room. Hanai's mother walked up behind

Pam with a tray of food. When Pam heard the noise behind her, she stumbled, nearly knocking the tray from the woman's hands. She limped back over to the sofa and slowly sat down.

The small-framed Japanese woman spoke to Pam. "You need eat. Food, I have food for you." She shook her head back and forth, almost making Pam dizzy. "Can you eat? Your mouth and face, they big? You need doctor."

"No, I don't want to eat, and I can't go to the doctor." Pam touched her face gingerly and winced at the pain even a light touch caused.

"Yes, you must go. You need doctor. Face ugly," said the woman, twisting her own face to show Pam how she looked to her. Hanai's mother put down the tray, left the room, rushed back in, and held up a small mirror in front of Pam's face.

"What in the..." Pam managed to eke out through slightly parted lips, shocked at her badly bruised and swollen face. No wonder she was in such pain. There was no avoiding medical attention, which meant that she would most likely have to tell the doctor about being raped. What am I going to say to the police? They are sure to be called. I need somebody. I can't call my kids. They would panic. I've screwed up things with Marcus. I need to try to make it right with him. He's a good guy. Pam pounded both fists against her chest in frustration and allowed the tears to wash down her face over bruises that stared back at her in the mirror.

CHAPTER TWENTY-NINE

Jayden was being released from the hospital and going home with his father. Doug Carr worked quickly to get temporary custody of his son. Angie had packed some of Jayden's clothes, his laptop, and several pairs of his Jordan shoe collection and took them to the hospital. She passed Doug at the nurse's station and went down to her brother's room.

"Hey, I got the stuff you asked for." Angie dropped two duffle bags in the chair and sat down on the side of the bed next to Jayden. "I'm going to miss you." She brushed her index finger over the top of his bandaged eye.

The doctor was hopeful that the surgery on his eye was successful, but that was yet to be determined. They wouldn't know for sure until it was time to remove the bandages in several weeks.

"Under the circumstances, you have no choice but to go with your dad. He's doing what's best for you. Anyway, you need to be far away from those thugs who hurt you." She drew in a slow, quiet breath and rubbed at her eyes, determined not to let the tears poking at them fall.

"I'll be okay. Don't worry about me." He grunted as he reached over to hug his sister. It would be a while before Jayden would be completely healed. His body ached, and his eyes were still sore.

Doug entered the room with papers in his hand. "Okay, we can leave as soon as the wheelchair gets here."

"Wheelchair, I don't need a wheelchair," trying to convince his dad with a pleading stare.

"And just how do you expect to get down the hallway, stand in the elevator down eight floors, then down a long corridor, out the front door, and to the car? I'm not carrying your big butt. You can barely stand up. You're getting in the wheelchair."

"Okay, Dad, okay."

"Now that you are feeling a little better, tell me what happened the night you were attacked."

Jayden leaned back on the bed, closed his eyelids, and spit out the gruesome details about the night he was violently beaten because he refused to join the gang.

"Well, thank God you had the good sense to say no. If you had joined that gang, worse things would have happened to you than the beating they gave you. Trying to get out of the gang could have cost you your life." Doug brushed his hand over the top of his son's head. "We've got a lot of talking to do."

Doug looked over at Angie, "You're welcome to come and see your brother any time."

"Thanks, Doug," Angie flashed a smile at him and shook her head up and down.

"I'll give you guys a few minutes to talk. I better check on that wheelchair."

"I love you, Jayden. I promise to call you every day and visit as often as I can."

"I love you too, Angie." He was silent for a moment. "Tell Marcus I said thanks for everything, and I'm sorry for causing so much trouble." He rubbed his arm, which was in a sling.

"Marcus just wants you to get better. I'll tell him." She pinched his leg and pulled at his ear. "At least you will be safe at Doug's."

Angie told Jayden that Marcus had been forced to leave the house. "I tried to talk him out of leaving, but Nana made it clear that she didn't trust his motives, and she wanted him out. I told Marcus that our mother would be furious with Nana for interfering with the arrangements she made for her household. But you know Nana."

"Yeah, mom will have a fit," Jayden agreed.

"But he won't listen," Angie told him with droopy eyes.

Angie couldn't tell Jayden the truth. Marcus didn't want their grandmother to know that she was completely right about him and Angie. Although they were together, it hadn't happened the way she'd implied.

"I wish I'd had the chance to convince Nana to give Marcus a break. I would've admitted to her that I deceived you and Marcus on more than one occasion. I led you to believe I was with my real friend, Jeremy Pearson. I had no business getting involved with Jeremy Rungman or anyone like him. He has a rap sheet as tall as I am. Everyone knew he was bad news except me." Jayden pressed his hand hard into the bed.

"Teachers warned me about him, and so did Mom. She said although she felt sorry for him, no good mother would want her child with his kind. I should've listened to Mom. The beating was way more evidence than was necessary to prove that point. Now, Nana blames Marcus when it was my fault."

"Don't worry about it," Angie said, rubbing his back. "Everyone makes mistakes. You just have to learn from them," Angie advised.

Jayden clung to his sister and held her tightly. "I promise to stay out of trouble. I promise."

Angie kissed him on the cheek, broke the vice grip hold Jayden had on her, and exited the room before disobedient tears could fall.

Angie drove home from the hospital sad about her brother and because Marcus was leaving. Angie and Marcus were counting down the days before Marcus had to vacate Pam's house by order of Grandma Carter. With only four days left, they tumbled around in Pam's king-size bed—laughing, playing, and teasing each other with light foreplay. Marcus lifted his head from the soft skin of Angie's inner thigh. He was certain he'd heard a door close and voices downstairs. "Shh, listen," he warned Angie.

Silence claimed the bedroom as they both lay still but attentive. He was right. Seconds later, the voices moved closer to them.

"Oh my, God, Marcus, that's my grandmother," Angie whispered in a panic, throwing back the covers in search of her bra.

Mrs. Carter had decided, without warning, to come to her daughter's house less than a week after her phone conversation with Marcus. She lived four hours away, in a town near Angie's oldest brother, Nelson, who had driven her there.

Angie bolted across the bed to lock the door. Marcus hustled to the bathroom, stumbling, attempting to step into his underwear.

"Angie's not in her room. Maybe she's sleeping in her mother's room while she's away," proclaimed Grandma as she approached Pam's bedroom. She turned the doorknob and discovered the door was locked.

One, two, three heavy knocks on the door rattled through Angie's body like shock waves. She slid the second leg of her pants up her thigh and over her hips. Two more buttons and her bountiful bosom would no longer be exposed.

"Angie, honey, are you in there? It's Nana."

Angie belted out a roaring yawn as if she had been asleep. "Yes, ma'am, Nana. Let me get something on. I'll be right there." Angie ran her hands over her head and rustled up her hair to support the lie that she had been asleep.

"Nana, I'll be right back. I need to check on something," Nelson said, heading back down the stairs.

While Mrs. Carter waited for Angie, she searched through every room upstairs, opened the closet doors, and checked underneath the beds. I better not find a hint of anything that tells me that slick young man did not leave this house like I told him to do. Satisfied, she hurried back and stood in front of Pam's door. "Girl, open this door," she commanded with a stern tone.

When the door opened, Angie's grandmother whisked right by her.

"Child, I got to get to the restroom."

"Hold on a second, I don't think there's any toilet tissue in there. You can use the bathroom in the hallway," Angie declared loud enough for Marcus to hear her warning.

Her grandmother never slowed her pace. "Yes, there is. There's a whole roll in here," she yelled back.

Angie sat at the foot of the bed, biting her nails and tapping her foot on the floor. The bomb was about to explode any minute since Marcus was sure to be discovered. She covered her mouth and held her breath when she heard the squeaky closet door open and close without any yelling or one curse word bouncing off the walls. When her grandmother walked back into the bedroom, she rushed up and draped her arms around her neck.

"I am so glad to see you." Angie held on tightly. She needed a few seconds to wipe the guilt off her face, which she was sure her grandmother would be able to see.

"I'm glad to see you too, honey. Are you still dating that nice boy, Jacoby?"

"Yes, ma'am," Angie answered quickly, looking behind her. Why is she asking me about Jacoby?

"Why do you seem so nervous? I know you haven't been sneaking that boy over here all hours of the night because your mother is gone." They stood in the middle of the bedroom floor. Mrs. Carter's head was cocked to the right, and her purse perched in the bend of her arm as she snapped her fingers at Angie. "Answer me, girl."

"No, definitely not. Believe me, his mother makes sure of that. I'm not her favorite person." Her words were half true. Jacoby wasn't spending the night, but Marcus sure was.

"Okay, I was just wondering." Mrs. Carter tugged at Angie's blouse, which stopped just above her navel. "Where is the rest of this top of yours?"

Angie giggled, "Nana, this is the style," she told her and changed the subject. "Come on, let's go downstairs. I'll fix you some coffee."

She placed her arm around her grandmother's shoulders and guided her through the hallway and down the stairs.

Her brother was closing the garage door when they made it to the kitchen. Their eyes met. He mouthed, "I know."

Angie ignored his silent challenge and gave him a warm greeting. "Hey Nelson, how's it going?"

They embraced, and Nelson whispered in her ear, "I guess you think you're grown, huh?"

Angie broke free of his hold on her and looked away to face her grandmother. "Have a seat, Nana. I know you must be tired from the long drive. How's Poppa?"

"Oh, he's fine. He wanted to come, but he has a new puppy, and he doesn't want to leave him right now. He's not housebroken yet. We would have gone home to piles of poop all over the house." She turned up her nose and shook her head like a bobblehead doll. "You know your Poppa is all about dogs."

"Well, tell him to expect my usual Sunday evening call." She poured a cup of coffee for her grandmother, and she could feel her brother's eyes boring into the back of her head. She refused to make eye contact with him. When she turned around to hand over the cup of coffee, Angie sidestepped Nelson, not wanting to make eye-to-eye contact.

After a few minutes of coffee sipping and chit-chatting with Angie, Mrs. Carter said, "I need you to take me to the realtor's office. I need to pay the rent for a couple of months. I've only gotten a few text messages from your mother lately, and she's not sure exactly when she'll be back. She was pretty sure it would take at least a few more weeks."

"I can't wait for my mom to come home. Marcus has definitely done all he could to help me and Jayden." Angie picked up the rubber band on the counter and stretched it out from one side to the other. "Why did you make Marcus leave?"

Nelson sat at the table and listened to the exchange between his sister and grandmother while he bit down into an apple he'd grabbed from the bowl on the countertop.

"What's the point in him staying here if Jayden's not here? He could be a rapist or something. You don't need to be here with some strange grown man. Your mother should be ashamed of herself for leaving him here with you guys in the first place." She pushed the coffee cup away from her. "I know your mom is going to be upset with me. No matter, I'm doing what's best for you children since she won't."

"He's a nice guy. He really is. But he's gone now." The rubber band popped, stung Angie's finger, and flew across the room. "Ouch," she squealed.

Nelson burst into laughter. "That's what you get."

Angie narrowed her eyelids, and with a wrinkled brow, growled at him, saying, "Shut up, Nelson." She didn't want any secret he may have uncovered to come bouncing out of his mouth.

"I understand, Nana, but I don't know where the realty office is. My mother usually handles that." She needed to get her grandmother back on the road to home. Marcus must be about to suffocate in that closet. That was the thought that made her bite the nails on her left hand.

Mrs. Carter clutched her purse and said, "I have the address right here. Your granddaddy and I have paid your mother's rent before." Her grandmother reached over and swatted her hand. "Stop biting your nails. Girl, you sure are acting nervous."

Angie's line of view shot over to Nelson, who met her with a stern visual assault.

He tossed the half-eaten apple core into the trash can across the room, leaned back in the chair, and challenged his sister, "Yeah, Angie. What's wrong with you?"

"Nothing is wrong with me. Let's find that rental office. I don't want you guys to be too late heading home. You know that traffic will be getting heavy soon. Besides, I don't want grandma worn out." She slid off the stool in front of the island and led the way to the front door.

"Yeah, I just bet you don't want us to be too late leaving for home," Nelson's words stabbed at Angie's back.

She led the way out of the kitchen and to the front door while crossing her fingers on both hands. I need to get them out of here as quickly as possible.

CHAPTER THIRTY

Pam had not spoken to any of her children in three weeks. Her children, mother, and Marcus had unsuccessfully attempted to contact her. Maybe it was for the best. Jayden was feeling much better and had been released from the hospital. Yet, there was still a storm brewing since Pam had no idea Jayden's father had temporary custody of him, and Angie had temporary custody of Marcus.

Pam lay in bed at Hanai's house, wanting desperately to call her parents and say, "Please, help me. I messed up. I want to come home," even if it meant admitting to her mother that she had been right about everything. The thunder electrified the sky with sprouts of light that crept across the dark blanket that made the evening look like midnight. The raindrops that slid down the windowpane moved at the same pace as Pam's tears which crawled down her face. I should have called my kids every night. I took Marcus for granted, and I was unappreciative. I should've told Doug I was planning to leave the country, but at the time, I just didn't want another naysayer to tell me that I was making a huge mistake. I will make it right when I get home—if I get home. Pam pressed the power button on the phone. It had finally charged. She was anxious to find out what was happening on the other side of the world.

There were several anger-filled, threatening messages from Chu and Dudley. She would've responded to them, but the pain in her broken jawbone wouldn't allow her to have a heated discussion with anyone. The conversation with either of them was sure to be a hot one. So, contacting them would have to wait since her mouth was wired shut for the next several weeks. Delaying medical attention had only made her broken jaw worse. Now that the surgery was behind her, hopefully, healing would be a hundred percent. Speaking was temporarily not an option while her tears flowed plentifully.

The string of text messages and voicemails from her family, which spilled into her ear, stung at her nerves and sent an ache that pierced her heart. She had been gone too long. I need to get home. Lord, heal my body. Let me make it back to my kids. Lord, please keep them safe for me. She punched out a three-word text to all her kids in a group message. **I love you**. She rubbed the glass screen of the cell phone, wishing that a simple motion would take her home.

The voicemails and text messages from her family urged her to call home. Pam fell asleep, believing each message was sent to guilt her into coming home. She couldn't call home; she couldn't even talk. Besides that, she couldn't tell them she was attacked and raped. While she kept her secret for the time being, her family had a secret, too. Soon, those secrets would collide.

CHAPTER THIRTY-ONE

"Nana, I've got to go. Don't call the Red Cross just yet. I got a text from mom last night. All she said was, **I love you**, but at least we know she's okay. I tried to call her back when I noticed the text. But she didn't answer. We've got to tell her about Jayden." Angie shifted the book bag on her shoulder.

"I better hear from your mother soon. Or I'm going to be on a plane.

Your mother can do some crazy stuff, but she's my only child."

"I know, Nana. I hear you. She's okay. Tell Poppa hello for me. I'll call you tomorrow." Angie ended the call and smiled at the picture of Marcus that immediately popped up as her screen saver. She was also concerned that she hadn't heard from her mother, though she didn't suspect anything was wrong and didn't want her grandmother to worry. As he exited his car, Jacoby spotted Angie walking across the college campus. He called out her name and ran to catch up to her. He didn't expect her to talk to him, though she was surprisingly cordial.

"What's up, Jacoby? I see you got your car back."

"Yeah, finally, after it was found at the Mexican border. I can't believe Brianna would just run off with my car. I thought she loved me." Jacoby yanked the baseball cap on his head down over his eyes.

"What goes around comes around."

"I know that's true. Angie, I've missed you," he confessed as they walked along the concrete path next to the water. "I keep wondering how I could spend a year loving someone, then give her up because I thought I'd found someone better. I told my mom I'd made that mistake—partly because she didn't like you. She finally admitted that she shouldn't have interfered with our relationship. She wants to see you. My sisters, well, you know they adore you. We all miss you. I didn't know what I had until..."

Angie stopped abruptly and faced Jacoby. "Yeah, I know. You realized what you had when Brianna tricked you and used you. Well, I'm sorry, but I'm no longer available. I have a man. A real man, and what I feel for him, I've never felt for anyone else." A grin zipped across her lips, and her eyes lit up.

Jacoby turned his head, looked off into the distance for a moment, and turned back to face the girl that he realized he wanted. "Yeah, well, I hope the rumors aren't true, Angie."

"What rumors?" Her grin faded.

"I heard you were messing around with Marcus, your mom's boyfriend. You remember him, right?" He tugged hard on the straps to his backpack.

"Whoever I am dating is none of your business. If you hadn't cheated on me, I wouldn't have this wonderful man in my life. At first, I was angry with you. Now, I realize you did me a favor."

Two girls walked by them, and both allowed their eyes to sweep down Jacoby's body. "You better hold on tight to him, girlfriend," the girl with the thick auburn mane tossed out.

"You can have him. He's a dog that hasn't been trained yet, if you know what I mean?"

The two girls laughed as they walked further, and Jacoby tugged even tighter on the backpack straps until one popped and the backpack hung halfway off his back.

"Not funny, Angie. But okay, if you say you're in love, I have to accept that, no matter who it is. Just remember that I'm here if you ever need me. I just can't see how you could get over me so quickly and now profess your love for someone else." Jacoby leaned in and kissed her cheek.

"Are you serious? I remember saying those very words to you. If you think really hard, you might remember how you answered me. I do." Her thin finger with a red nail bounced in his face. "Now, I have to go. What you think and feel about me is no longer my concern. Take care of yourself. Bye!" Angie whisked her body around and strutted off in her three-inch heels and tight jeans.

Before Angie made it to her next class, which she was now late for, her cell phone sounded off. The ringtone told her it was Vanessa.

"Quick, girl, I'm late for class. What's up?"

"911, girl, I need the 411. When did you and that fine Marcus start getting busy? I knew it was going to happen."

"What are you talking about?" Angie walked over to the grassy area and sat down on a bench.

"Don't try to play me. I got a text from your brother, Nelson. He asked me if you and Marcus were sleeping together."

Angie's mouth fell open. "What? When? Why would he ask you that?" Angie rubbed her palms together and looked to both sides of her as if others were in on the secret.

"Don't worry. I lied and told him that nothing like that would happen between the two of you. If it did, I would know about it since you and I don't keep secrets. What a joke. You definitely kept the thing between you and Marcus a secret."

Vanessa's giggles jumped through the phone and poked at Angie. "Why do you keep saying that? What makes you think something is going on between us?"

"Girl, stop it. Nelson saw Marcus' car in the garage when he and your grandmother came by unexpectedly last week. Just so you know, he said the upstairs hallway smelled like straight-up sex and that they must have interrupted the two of you."

"We weren't having sex. We were just kissing and fooling around..." Angie's hand flew up to her mouth to keep the words from flying out. But it was too late.

"I knew it. I knew Marcus was hitting that. Okay, spill it, and stop lying."

The silence that claimed the phone line was loud. Angie rubbed her hand down the front of her jeans several times and out came the truth. She told Vanessa all about her and Marcus. They talked right through Angie's class as she professed her love for Marcus. Her conscious mocked her for daring to be excited about her man, who had been her mother's man first.

CHAPTER THIRTY-TWO

Doug and Angie watched intently and stood close as the doctor removed the bandages from Jayden's eye. The side of his face and eye socket were sore, swollen, and badly scarred. The doctor assured them that the soreness and swelling were temporary as he examined Jayden's eye.

"What about the scars, Doc?" Jayden's father probed with a clenched fist.

"Well, sir, plastic surgery may be something you want to consider since..."

Jayden interrupted, "I'll wear these ugly scars to remind me of my bad judgment and disobedience. No surgery."

"Some of the scars will heal, but there are sure to be some permanent scars, as well. Now, for the good news, the surgery was a success. Your retina should heal by at least ninety-five percent, which is great, considering you nearly lost your eye."

After doing a general eye exam, the doctor advised that the strength of the eye would improve and that the vision would continue to get better. "Continued care with an Ophthalmologist for several weeks will be necessary. You were very fortunate, young man," the doctor proclaimed, placing a firm hand on Jayden's shoulder.

"Jayden announced with a smile, "I can see, Dad. Things are a little fuzzy, but I can see."

"The fuzzy vision will clear up completely in a week or two. Stop by the desk on your way out and make a follow-up appointment." The doctor gave them all instructions on how to take care of his eye and left the room.

They left the doctor's office and headed for Pam's house. Doug was determined to pick up the rest of his son's belongings. Jayden had left several messages for Pam to call him as soon as possible. He didn't want to tell her what happened to him on a voicemail. He did want to warn her that his father had found out she was in Japan. He knew his mom would be upset when she learned that his dad had been granted temporary custody until she returned. And he planned to take Pam to court for full custody.

Jayden tried to push the thought of a custody battle between his parents out of his head as he stuffed clothes into his duffle bag. He glanced over at the phone on his nightstand and wished his mom would call before he left. The silence in the room touched him like a cool breeze. He zipped up his jacket, slung his bag over his shoulder, and closed the door to what used to be his room.

Jayden sat quietly in the car as he headed out of town to his father's house. He flipped down the visor and stared into the mirror. He stroked the scars to the right of his eye.

His dad reached over and flipped up the visor. "Son, I know you love your mom and want to live with her because that is what you are used to. I need you to understand that I must do what's best for you. You are my only son, my only child. I can't leave you in a situation that I know is dangerous."

"I know, Dad," Jayden responded, gazing downward. He was well aware of the danger of him living with his mom when she returned. "That gang will not just let me walk away. Living with Mom will make me an easy target, because there will be nowhere I can hide." It was his disobedience and lies that snatched him from the home he'd shared with his mother and sister. He had lived with them all his life. Living anywhere else just felt wrong, even if it was with his dad.

Angie walked in the door of Marcus' apartment after a full day of classes, dropped bags on the counter, kissed him, and walked straight into the bedroom.

"Do you want to go out for dinner tonight?" Marcus asked.

"No, I've already taken care of it. Give me a minute. I'll be right out." She wanted to have dinner with her mom and her brother. She wanted things to be the way they used to be. That wasn't possible. Jayden had been taken away, and who knew what would happen with her and Marcus once her mom did come home? Everything was just so crazy. She bit at the nubs that used to be long fingernails as she entered the bathroom.

She took a shower, pulled her hair into a bun on top of her head, and painted her face with a subtle hint of makeup. Next, Angie put on black and yellow sheer lingerie, three-inch, black leather sandals that laced at the ankles, slipped on a short, black satin robe, and strutted into the kitchen. The scent of her perfume drew Marcus' attention away from the ball game.

"Well, aren't you just the sexiest, most gorgeous thing I've seen all day?"

"Thank you. I've got a great meal planned for us," she replied, as she bent down to pull out cookware from the cabinets and hide the sadness in her eyes that would soon become the truth on her lips.

The lingerie and Angie's perfume pulled Marcus out of his chair. He stepped behind her, wrapped his arms around her waist, and gently kissed her neck. "Can I have dessert first?"

Angie turned to face him, lifted her breast with both hands to tease him, and firmly said, "No, I thought we'd start off with a couple of appetizers, jalapeno pepper, shrimp cocktail, and sausage stuffed mushrooms. Then we'll have marinated beef tenderloin with loaded mashed potatoes and a steamed vegetable medley. For dessert, we'll dip strawberries in a mocha fondue."

He lowered his head to stroke the caramel-colored, circular birthmark on her right breast. "How did I ever get so lucky?"

"Don't speak too soon," Angie advised. "You may not feel that way after dinner."

"Nothing can change the way I feel about you." His lips overtook hers, and his tongue stroked hers until his manhood rose to attention.

She stepped back, glanced down at him, and a grin claimed her face.

"Have a seat, sir. There will be time for that later."

An hour later, Marcus complimented nearly every bite. "Baby, this is fantastic. When do you find the time to prepare meals like this? You already had the tenderloins marinating. I never saw you in the kitchen last night before we went to bed."

"I know. I couldn't sleep. I got up and did most of the prep work last night for our dinner." She moved the food around on her plate with her fork, taking only three bites.

"Why couldn't you sleep? Is everything okay?"

She put her fork down, stretched her hand across the table, and touched his hand lightly. "I love you, Marcus. You know that, but I've had to make a decision that will affect us. You won't like it. I don't like it." A tear streaked down her cheek, and she quickly wiped it away with her hand.

Marcus stood, took three steps and he pulled her into his arms. "What's wrong, sweetheart? Please, tell me." Marcus rubbed her back as he felt her tears drip onto his shoulder.

"Marcus, we're going to have to end this," she told him with a shaky voice.

He stepped back, lifted her chin, and searched her eyes. "What are you talking about?"

"It's over between us." Angie sniffed hard and wiped her nose.

"Why would you say that? We're just starting. I thought things were going well between us."

"Time hasn't stood still just because we fell in love with each other. My mother will be home soon. I just can't hurt her. She's going to be devastated when she finds out about Jayden getting hurt and Doug having custody. I don't want to add to that. Besides, she's going to be all alone. You and I being happy and my mom being miserable just isn't right." She swiped at her wet eyes with the heels of her hands while putting some distance between them.

"Baby, no. Please don't do this. We can work it out. We'll explain to your mom that it just happened. Love just happened. No one can control who they fall in love with." He took a step toward her.

Angie put her hand up, gesturing for him to stop. "I love you. You know I do. This is just as hard on me as it is on you, but after tonight, I'm going home, and I'm not coming back. I've got to end this thing between us. I need you to make love to me one last time."

This time, she didn't stop him. Marcus came close to her; he brushed away the tear that dropped from her eyelash with his thumb. "We love each other. I want to marry you and take you away from here. You can't sacrifice your happiness for your mom. She does exactly what she wants to do all the time. Does she care what you think? No. You didn't want her to go to Japan, but she went anyway, and this is the result."

Angie heard his words and fought not to allow them to sink into her heart.

"Even what happened to Jayden is because of her decision to leave.

You're a smart, caring, beautiful woman. You haven't done anything wrong. It's not wrong for you to love and be loved." He stepped away from her, allowing his gaze to wash over the sadness in her face. Marcus slid both hands back and forth over his bald head. "Maybe you can keep me a secret until you decide the time is right to tell your mom about us. That could work."

"Baby, you know the truth always has a way of being discovered. I don't..."

"Shhh. I'm not letting you go." He silenced her debate with a kiss that overpowered her and persuaded her she couldn't let him go. Marcus led her quietly to the bedroom, tasting her body slowly, pleasuring the sweet, hot core between her legs more than once.

Angie wasn't silent in giving herself to him. With every deep stroke he plunged inside of her, she clung to him, saying, "Don't stop. Please, don't stop." They reached the sensual mountain top together in a moment of ecstasy that sent quivers of pleasure through their bodies. In the darkness of the room, a sad silence crept in and hung there in the air.

Angie inhaled a deep breath of courage, heaved herself up from the bed, and wasted no time preparing for her departure. She showered, dressed, and grabbed some of her belongings, stuffing them into an oversized bag. Marcus sat on the edge of the bed, trying to think of something to say that would make her change her mind. The words never came. She had chosen her mother over him. There was no winning that battle. He followed her as she walked to the door.

"Is it okay if I keep my key for a while? I'll need to come by later to get the rest of my things."

"Of course, it is. Keep it as long as you like. Angie, can't we talk about this some more?" Marcus placed his hand on the door and leaned his weight against it. "Aren't we worth it?"

"You're just making this harder. There's no way that our relationship won't hurt my mom. I can't do this. I just can't." Tears rushed down her face. She grabbed the doorknob. "Let me go, Marcus. I need to go right now." Her pain became audible with whimpers laced with more tears.

Her mind was made up. Preventing her from leaving was only causing her more pain. No words came to him. Slowly, he moved aside and watched her walk out of his apartment and out of his life.

It wasn't long before Angie was back at her mother's house, in her bedroom, sprawled out across the bed, sobbing. Her phone vibrated with a text message from Marcus.

I know you have to do what you think is best. We did open Pandora's Box, and I don't know how to close it. I'll let you go for now. You didn't leave me much choice. But wrong or not, I'll pray every day that you'll come back to me. I finally found the love of my life. Somehow, we have to fix this.

Angie pressed the phone against her chest and released a scream that felt like a roar.

CHAPTER THIRTY-THREE

Pam was on her way into the doctor's office to have the wires removed from her jaw. She was afraid of what her face might look like. But she was anxious to be able to talk without pain and eat solid food. Her phone vibrated in her purse. She ignored it, assuming it was Dudley again. He'd called her three times in the last hour. He'd left her daily messages expressing his anger and promising her bodily harm if she returned to the States without his device. Would he really harm her? No way for her to be sure.

She could take the unsuccessful journey back home with the wires out of her mouth. Thank goodness the police hadn't found her or made the connection between her and Chu. As far as she knew, Chu owned the house. Hopefully, the authorities couldn't track him down and tie him to her. The charge was murder. Chu might give her up quickly to save himself. They called it murder. Pam called it justice.

Pam's reason for being in Japan had seemed simple to accomplish when she arrived. Though now, it seemed virtually impossible to do. She wished it had been simple. It turned out to be the most challenging quest ever. Now, she just wanted to get back to the simple life she'd left at home. I got to get home to my children and try to get my man back. I need something stable in my life because everything else has gone to hell in a handbasket. Pam gripped the handle of the office building door. She squeezed it tightly, sucked in a dose of courage, and pulled at the heavy door to enter. Her jaw had to be okay, with no permanent damage, and she had to find a way to get home.

The removal of the wire from her jaw was successful. But it was two weeks before her jaw was strong enough to talk and sound close to normal. She said goodbye to Hanai and her mother, and headed to the airport, putting her escape plan into action. Pam intended to enter the airport incognito, hoping not to be recognized by Chu, Dudley, or any of their comrades. She wore a mushroom hat with a visor nearly covering her eyes and a matching infinity scarf around her neck. Her eyes were hidden behind dark sunglasses. Her eyeballs shifted from side to side, and she gazed down the walkway as far as she could see. Lord, let me get out of this country and back to the U.S., and I will never do anything as crazy as this trip again, I swear.

Anxious to board the plane, Pam headed through the security gate, scanning the area to ensure that none of her troubles had followed her. Good thing Chu had given her an open-ended ticket a few weeks back. All she had to do was show proper ID to board the plane. Fear raced through her body as she passed through security and walked to her boarding gate. Lord, don't let the police slap handcuffs on me before this plane takes off.

Seconds later, a voice behind her called out, "Miss, excuse me. Miss."

Pam froze. Should she run to the door? No use in that. They would simply drag her off the plane. Maybe if she pretended to faint, they wouldn't handcuff someone who was unconscious.

"Miss," the stern male voice called out again.

Pam spun around, irritation flaring. "What?" she snapped.

The tall man handed her the infinity scarf that had been around her neck. "You dropped this, and it's such a nice scarf. I thought for sure you wouldn't want to lose it." The man panted a couple of times and heaved in a deep breath. "I tried to stop you sooner, but you got through security so quickly that I had to almost run to catch up with you."

"Thank you, sir. That was incredibly nice of you." She plunged her hand down into her deep purse. "Let me give you a little something for your troubles."

He touched Pam's hand gently. "No, there is no need for that. Have a safe trip." He turned and walked away.

Finally, eight feet from the door to board the plane. A tear slid down her face. Maybe she wasn't going to jail and could make it home to her children. Thank you, God!

The voice over the intercom steered Pam to her boarding gate. "Final boarding call for flight 327 to Dallas, Texas."

Pam handed the woman her boarding pass at the gate. United States, here I come. Once she buckled her seatbelt, she pushed out a quiet, cool breath that slipped through her lips. "One step closer to home." Pam closed her eyelids tightly. She focused on every sound that she heard. Nothing sounded alarming. No heavy steps marched toward her, no handcuffs clicking, no voice telling her she was under arrest, or voices mocking her as she was arrested. "Whew," she said quietly and exhaled.

The door of the plane was closed and locked. She heard static through the speaker before the flight attendant spoke. Pam finally felt secure that she was about to be on her way home. She could feel the plane backing away from the boarding gate door as it prepared for take-off. She lay back in her seat and closed her eyelids. Pam planted her hand on her chest and tried to slow her breathing. A voice clutched at her heart and caused fear to inch through her body.

"Ladies and gentlemen, our departure will be slightly delayed. Please remain calm and seated. We will be taking off shortly."

The plane jerked, came to a crawl, and stopped. The door opened, and a Navy officer walked onto the plane. He passed a piece of paper to the flight attendant as he spoke with her briefly. Then his search began, and he took short, slow steps down the aisle toward Pam. His head moved from one side of the plane to the other.

"God, help me," Pam whispered, scooting as far down in her seat as possible and pulling her hat lower to cover her eyes. Please, God, don't let him be looking for me.

CHAPTER THIRTY-FOUR

Two weeks passed, and Marcus struggled to adjust to life without Angie. He thought of her daily and sometimes caught himself smiling about some of the funny things she did. Even though he promised to respect her decision, he texted Angie every night, saying, **I love you. Pray for us. I am!** Angie never responded.

Marcus spent as little time as possible at his apartment. He couldn't stand to be there without Angie. He signed on for overtime at both jobs. He'd begun studying for his RN license. He made pretty good money as an LPN, but once he was licensed as an RN, he would more than double his salary. Then, he could quit his part-time job as a Federal Express security guard.

A solemn moment shook him. Marcus stuffed the last item of clothing into a suitcase. He needed to get away. A weekend trip to his family reunion in San Antonio, Texas, was perfect timing. He looked forward to seeing his mother and the rest of the family. It saddened him that Angie wasn't going with him. She'd planned on accompanying him before their one-sided decision to split up. He knew she would love his family, and they would adore her.

Pam would be home from Japan soon. Angie would have her own reunion. A part of him felt sorry for Pam because of the turmoil her leaving had caused. She would have some hard things to face once she was home. She'll want to know why I didn't pick her up from the airport and why I am not staying at her house.

He could tell from her latest text messages that she hoped to start over. He decided that when she returned, he would meet with Pam and firmly tell her that it was over. He didn't know if seeing her was even a good idea. He had some bitter feelings toward Pam since she was the reason he and Angie weren't together. There is going to be crazy drama when Pam finds out about Angie and me. Whether she admits it or not, what happened between Angie and me wouldn't have happened if she hadn't left the country.

Marcus walked over to the nightstand next to the bed. He picked up the framed picture of him and Angie. Her smile forced a smile to inch across his lips. We were happy that day. The carnival, cotton candy, and her sweet kisses, but now she won't even talk to me. He traced her lips with his fingertip and placed the picture back onto the nightstand. Will I ever kiss her lips again? He grabbed his keys and headed out the door to his car.

CHAPTER THIRTY-FIVE

Angie drove four hours to pick up her grandmother. She wanted to ride along to pick up Pam at the airport the next day. Angie prepared a special meal for them when they arrived at Pam's house that afternoon. They sat down, her grandmother blessed the food, and they both dug their forks into the colorful plate in front of them.

"I almost forgot how talented you are in the kitchen, young lady. This is one delicious meal. It has excellent presentation and is scrumptious." Angie's grandmother licked her lips and forked up another mouthful. "What do you call this?"

Angie wiped the corner of her mouth. "This is honey-glazed salmon with a medley of steamed vegetables and plum parfait for dessert."

"How are your classes going? Your mother told me you changed your major." She turned up her water glass and took two short sips.

"It's Business Administration. I'd like to own a business one day."

"I hope it's a restaurant. You could name it Angie's Fancy Full," she leaned back in her chair, stuck out her stomach, and patted it with both hands. They laughed.

"Fancy Full?" questioned Angie, smiling.

"Yes, because people don't normally get full eating fancy food. But I am stuffed. Your mom is a good cook, too, but I believe you got her beat."

"Thanks, Nana. I like the name. I will definitely keep it in mind."

Something is not right. She's smiling a little, but it's empty, and her laughter seems forced. Mrs. Carter couldn't quite put her finger on it, but she sensed sadness in her granddaughter. "What's wrong, sweetheart? Are you a nervous about picking up your mother tomorrow?"

"Yes, I am a little. I hope everything can go back to normal. I know she's going to be devastated about losing custody of Jayden." Angie got up from the table and took their plates to the sink.

"Yes, that's going to be tough on her. She'll be able to see him. It's just not safe for him to live here right now. Jayden being here would put him in danger. Your mother wouldn't want that. She'll understand. You'll see. She loves you guys," her grandmother said, dipping a spoon into her dessert.

"I know she does, Nana. I just wish she hadn't left us. Everything is different now. If she hadn't left, we wouldn't have had to deal with all this mess." Angie tried to hold back the tears that welled up in her eyes. But they refused not to fall.

Her grandmother abandoned her dessert and walked to the sink. She took Angie's hand and squeezed it. "What's wrong, baby? I thought you'd be glad for your mom to come home. It seems like something else has got you down. This isn't just about Jayden. What's going on between you and your mom? Don't tell me nothing; it's something."

"I guess I'm still a little upset that she left us. I can't believe she did that."

Her grandmother slipped a handkerchief from her pocket and dabbed at her granddaughter's eyes. "Well, I hope that's all it is, sweetie. You would tell Nana if something else was bothering you, right?"

"Yes, ma'am," answered Angie. She'd better stop letting her emotions show through, or her grandmother would ask more questions than she wanted to answer.

Angie was miserable without Marcus. She couldn't shake her thoughts or her love for him. This was the weekend he'd be in San Antonio for his family reunion. She was disappointed that she couldn't go with him. But their relationship was in the past. Yet, her feelings were still front and center in the present.

Her grandmother headed up the stairs to take a nap. Angie took advantage of the time alone to call her friend.

"Hey, Vanessa. Can you talk for a minute?"

"Yep, what's up? I haven't heard from you in a couple of days—just checking in."

Angie leaned against the sink and allowed her true feelings to pour out of her. "I can't believe Marcus and I are not together. I miss him so much, and it hurts."

"You broke it off with him. I knew you would regret it."

Sad-faced Angie twirled her hair around her finger and planted her eyes on the emerald, green-tiled floor. "My relationship with him was too complicated to work through. I didn't want to jeopardize my relationship with my mother. Her feelings come first. "If we hadn't made it as a couple, I would have broken my mother's heart—and for what?"

"Your mom just up and left everybody and everything chasing money.

You found real love. You're giving up on that. Girl, you better think again. Ever since you walked out of Marcus' apartment that day, you've been trying to convince yourself that you made the right decision. But who is happy? Not you and Marcus. When your mom comes home, whether you and Marcus are together or not, he's never going to be with your mom again. So, who gets to be happy in all of this? Not one single person."

"Whatever, Vanessa. I got over Jacoby. I can get over Marcus," argued Angie.

"Jacoby wasn't the love of your life, but Marcus is. I guess we'll see how it all plays out."

"I've got to go. I'll call you tomorrow." Angie punched her keypad to end the call. She started cleaning the kitchen and tried not to think about Marcus. An hour later, she and her grandmother were watching a movie together.

"These movies are all the same. Somebody cheating on their spouse with someone they're related to or someone else's man, and all hell breaks loose. I guess what they say is true. People create storms in their own lives and then cry when it rains," Angie's grandmother proclaimed, clicking the remote to shut off the TV and letting out a noisy yawn.

Angie couldn't help but think of her own situation. A storm was brewing, and if her mother found out about her and Marcus, the storm would turn into a hurricane.

They said goodnight, and both climbed the stairs to turn in for the night. Five minutes after Angie was in bed under the covers, like every night, the usual text message from Marcus buzzed on her phone. **I love you. Pray for us. I am**.

Just as Angie's eyelids gave in under the heavy weight of sleep, a roaring crash of thunder forced her eyelids open. Her head turned to face the window, and just in time, to see the bright flash of lighting that lit up the dark sky. A storm really was brewing. Angie covered her head and sank into the bed, squeezing her eyelids tightly. Sleep had to rescue her and rescue her quickly.

CHAPTER THIRTY-SIX

Finally, in the air, Pam was relieved when the officer exited the plane. The emergency stop had been ordered for a military officer to retrieve some new recruits who were on the wrong flight. The pilot had been ordered to bring the plane to an emergency stop, and Pam had nearly gone into shock. After the false alarm, Pam was delighted to finally head home, after more than eight months of the hardest life experience that she'd ever endured. Japan had been a disaster from day one. Pam thought Dudley must've lied about the whole thing.

Could it have been a set-up or some scheme that was planned all wrong? I feel like I was a pawn in someone's chess game. How could I have left my kids to go to a foreign land, somewhere I had never been, and do something I didn't even thoroughly investigate? Now, all I have to show for it is a scarred face and the haunting memory of a violent rape that claws at my sleep. She fought back thoughts of the rape and emotions that formed a huge lump in her throat. It was a mistake, a big, stupid mistake. I hope my family can forgive me. I can't tell them just yet that I won't get the five hundred grand I deserted them for. I can't tell them anything about the trip. I hope

Marcus has been paying the rent on time, or we're really going to be up the creek.

Pam's attention shifted to the clouds outside the plane's window. Her thoughts rode on those clouds and sailed across the airways back to where she belonged. Marcus is still not texting me back or answering my calls. Who knew he was so darn stubborn? When I get home, maybe I can convince him that I am sorry about the way I ended things and that I want him back. Will he be able to ignore the scars and still find me attractive? If he cares about me, they won't matter. Pam's fingers traced the scars that nagged at her even when she wasn't looking into a mirror. Her thoughts weighed heavily on her as she shifted in her seat and adjusted her travel pillow until weariness overpowered her, and sleep claimed her. She slept for the rest of the flight. It was a peaceful blanket of slumber that had eluded Pam for months.

CHAPTER THIRTY-SEVEN

Beverly Blue, Marcus' mother, was surprised to see that he was not the usual life of the party. She noticed he'd spent most of the weekend watching everyone else have fun. When his sisters or other relatives tried to pull him onto the dance floor to sing and dance to their favorite songs, he'd smile and gently refuse.

His mother looked on while everyone in the backyard ate, danced, sang, and played spades—slapping the cards down on the table so hard they made a loud popping sound. She tapped Marcus on the shoulder.

"Son, help me bring out the boiled corn and frozen grapes."

He followed her into the kitchen. Standing at the kitchen counter buttering up the ears of corn, she probed her son.

"Okay, what's wrong? Don't say nothing. Spill it—what's bothering you? Or no frozen grapes with Welch's Sparkling Cider for you." She handed him a small bowl of grapes.

He popped three into his mouth, determined not to give up too much information. He was his mother's only son, the third of four children. He had three sisters, and along with their mother, they all spoiled him rotten. Marcus knew they all had his back. But this thing with Angie, not even they could fix.

"I'm good, Mom. Just a little tired. I've been working a lot of extra hours lately."

"I think it is a little more than that. Where is Angie?" Her eyes shot up at him, and her gaze settled on his face, waiting for an answer.

"She's busy with school, and her mom is out of the country. She wasn't able to come with me." He popped a handful of grapes into his mouth and chewed slowly.

Something wasn't right. There was something he wasn't telling her.

But for now, she would let it go. "She loves to cook, huh?"

"Yeah, Mom. She can definitely throw down in the kitchen." And between the sheets, too, he thought, holding a naked image of Angie in his mind. "When I save up enough money, I'm going to open a restaurant for her."

"You never know. Maybe Uncle Billy will hit the lottery someday and give you the money you need for that restaurant. He spends enough money trying," she encouraged him.

I haven't seen or heard him on the phone with that girl once since he's been here. His phone hasn't rung more than twice. I won't pry for now. But if he doesn't tell me what's going on soon with him and that girl, he's going to think the F.B.I. is interrogating him. Marcus' mother was determined.

Uncle Billy, the dreamer in the family, walked into the kitchen. Over the years, he'd invested in several get-rich-quick schemes. He'd lost a lot of his own money and other family members, too. Now, his focus was trying to hit big with the lottery. He'd persuaded the family to invest in it at every family reunion until it became a tradition.

Every year, since Marcus was five years old, his uncle would tell everyone that was the year the family would finally hit it big. Each year, every family member would put in one dollar or more for each person in their household. Uncle Billy would collect all the money, take it to the nearest grocery market, and purchase lottery tickets. They'd won money a couple of times over the years. Once, everyone who had chipped in walked away with an extra $400 in their pocket.

He announced to Marcus and his mother, "This year, there's no way we can lose. We've got the Midas touch. Every ticket we touch will turn to gold. We have two hundred and sixty-eight dollars. That means we can purchase a hundred and thirty-four tickets. Alright, Blue family, I'm off with this blessed money to purchase that blessed, blessed ticket that's going to bless, bless, and bless us all."

Kids and adults alike could quote that entire phrase verbatim because he'd said it for so many years. Not everyone there believed that a lottery ticket and blessings went hand in hand, but they went along with it because he was family.

Marcus and his mother cheered him on with the usual family chant, "Go get that blessed money, Uncle Billy." They laughed as he left through the sliding glass doors.

Marcus popped a couple more grapes into his mouth and helped his mom with the food. She led the way, carrying the bowl of frozen grapes. He slipped his cell phone from his pocket and checked his texts and missed calls. Nothing, not a word from Angie. Marcus pushed out an airy breath that spoke to his frustration. He picked up the pan of corn, plastered on a subtle smile, and marched back out on stage to play his role in the next scene of the evening.

CHAPTER THIRTY-EIGHT

Pam's plane landed after an eighteen-hour flight. She unbuckled her seat belt, stood in the aisle, and shuffled slowly toward the exit door. Three more people were in front of her, and she could make her escape. Once she stepped through the door of the plane, she sucked in a breath of sure freedom, glanced back at the plane, and whispered, "Lord, help me leave the nightmare behind me." The thousands of miles between the U.S. and Japan didn't seem to be enough. There will be more questions than I care to answer. Some, I have no intention of ever answering. Pam headed to the baggage area to claim her luggage, attempting to prepare herself for the interrogation that was sure to come from her family.

The double glass door slid open, and a cool breeze swept over her and welcomed her back to Dallas. A voice called out to her, "Mama." Her head jerked to the left to see Angie hurrying toward her. Pam swiftly moved in her direction and closed the distance between them. They embraced and held each other tightly. Pam's mother reached them a few moments later, breathing hard. "It's good to see you, baby." Angie released her mother and allowed her grandmother to give her mom a hefty squeeze.

"Mom, I'm so glad you're finally home. We've missed you."

"Baby, you have no idea how glad I am to be home." A smile spread across Pam's face as her mother released her hold on her.

Angie's smile faded, and the happiness that lit up her face dimmed. Her hand shot up to touch the scars on her mother's face. "Mom, what happened to your face?"

Pam moved her head slightly to keep her daughter's hand from touching the scars she attempted to hide underneath her makeup. "I'm fine, baby. We'll talk about it later."

Pam's mother stepped in closer, "Honey, are you okay? That scar doesn't look fine to me. How did that happen?" She, too, attempted to examine the scar with the touch of her hand.

Pam moved her head again, refusing to allow either of them to touch the raised scars on her face.

"Mom, you can't just tell us we'll talk about it later. We want to know what happened to you."

Mrs. Carter placed her hand on her granddaughter's shoulder. "Baby, your mom's tired. She's had a long flight. We can discuss it later."

A silent breath escaped Pam's lungs as her shoulders rose and fell with a sigh of thanks for her mother's intervention.

"I'm sorry, Mom. Let's get you to the car." She took the handle of her mother's large suitcase and led the way to the car.

As soon as they were about to pull out of the parking lot, the question Angie had been dreading found its voice.

"Where are Jayden and Marcus? Did they decide to wait at the house?

You guys didn't need to plan a homecoming celebration with food and gifts," Pam said, laughing. When no one answered, Pam turned to Angie, who was driving, and asked her directly,

"Where are they?"

"Jayden's with Doug," Angie, responded softly.

"With Doug? What the hell do you mean he's with Doug? Doug doesn't even know that I left. Or does he?"

Silence claimed the car. Pam's eyes shifted from Angie to her mother and back to Angie.

"Do you mean Doug picked him up for the weekend? What's going on? One of you, please start talking."

"Mom, Jayden got into some trouble while you were away."

Pam glanced into the back seat at her mother, then back to Angie.

"Keep talking. It was your job to look out for your brother while I was gone. Why didn't anyone call me about Jayden?" Pam had turned her whole body to face Angie. "What kind of trouble?"

"First of all, he's not a baby, and I couldn't watch him every minute of the day, Mama. He got involved with Jeremy Rungman."

"Jeremy Rungman? Are you kidding me? You know he wasn't allowed anywhere near Rugman's rotten ass!" Pam yelled, slamming the palm of her hand into the dashboard.

Angie jerked the steering wheel, and the car swerved to the left. The driver of the car beside her honked the horn and threw his middle finger up at her.

"Calm down, Pam. None of this is Angie's fault," Mrs. Carter intervened.

Pam's head swung to the left and accused her mother, "I know exactly whose fault you think it is."

Mrs. Carter quietly shook her head and leaned back in her seat while Pam turned back to Angie for answers.

"I didn't know. Jayden never said anything. He lied like he was hanging out with Jeremy Pearson."

"You never checked on him to see who he was with? My God, Angie. What were you doing that kept you from looking out for your brother?"

"I had no reason not to trust him. He'd never lied to us before. I mean to me anyway."

Pam chewed on her bottom lip as she attempted to calm down. "Start talking with all the details."

"Well, in a nutshell, Rungman tried to recruit Jayden into a gang called the Bloods. When he refused to join, they beat him up. He's okay, though. He is going to be just fine."

"Damn it. He knew better than to hang around that thuggish little punk. I knew something like this would happen if he was friends with that piece of trash. What in the hell was Marcus doing?"

"Pam, you shouldn't blame Angie or Marcus. You left your son, and you didn't leave him with his grandparents or his father. You left him with another kid and a man you hardly know. So, you are putting the blame in the wrong place."

"I knew that was coming. I knew it. I left my son with his adult sister and a full-grown man. Both promised to take care of my child. So, yes, Mama, I do blame them. Now take me to my son, Angie."

"Mom, don't you want to go home first?"

Pam twisted in her seat to face forward, folded her arms across her chest, and stared straight ahead. "I want to see my son. Right now."

Angie looked into the rear-view mirror at her grandmother as she pressed her foot down hard on the gas pedal. The ride to Doug's house was an hour and a half. For the next few minutes, only the purr of the engine could be heard. Before my mom left, she was controlling me and everyone else around her. I've gotten used to being my own boss, so that's it. She's no longer going to control me.

"Mom, I'm not driving to Doug's house this evening. I'm going home. It's been a long trip for you. You have to be tired."

"Pam, can't we just go tomorrow? You can give him a call when we get to the house. He may not even be home. No need to drive all that way for nothing," Mrs. Carter suggested.

"I want to see my son today," Pam protested, throwing her hands up in the air and allowing them to flop down onto her lap.

"You know where Doug lives. You can drive out there yourself. You might want to let him know you're coming," Angie advised.

"I don't need you to tell me what I can do, and I don't have to call Douglas Carr and tell him anything. Jayden is my son. I'll go wherever he is, whenever I please." Pam snaked down into her purse and jerked out her cell phone. "And you watch your mouth and what you say to me. You getting jazzy with me is not going to work."

Immediately, Pam called Jayden's cell phone and talked to him until Angie pulled into Pam's driveway. "My poor baby. I just wish I could've been here while he was dealing with this mess."

"But I do thank God that he had all of you. I'm sorry. I overreacted. He's my youngest child. He needs to come home, and he wants to come home. Doug and I are going to have to reach an agreement."

The phone call to Jayden seemed to have calmed Pam down. Angie or her grandmother didn't mention that it would be useless to press the issue about Jayden coming home. They would leave that hurricane of a problem to Doug.

Angie and Mrs. Carter cringed with a wide-eyed look on their faces when the garage door opened, and Marcus' car was not there. All the drama about Jayden had demanded Pam's attention, and she didn't dwell on why he didn't pick her up from the airport. But there would be no side-stepping him not being there to welcome her home.

"Where is Marcus' car? Is he here? Maybe he went to get something for us to eat. I am a little hungry." Just as she attempted to pull up Marcus' name in her phone, her cell died. She stretched her hand out to Angie with an open palm. "Honey, let me use your phone."

Angie dug around in her purse, clutching her phone, pretending she couldn't find it. All hell would break loose if Marcus answered a call from Angie's phone with a greeting of baby or sweetheart. Angie lifted the phone from the abyss of her big purse. "Mom, it's almost dead."

Pam snatched the phone right out of Angie's clutches. "Girl, hand me that phone. I just want to see if he's on his way back to the house."

Angie could not protest without raising red flags. A nervous ball of emotion shot through her as her mother punched in the first two numbers of Marcus' phone number. Shoot, I am glad I have his number in my phone under Marcus and not some sweet pet name.

Pam punched in the last number. One, two, three rings, and a thick masculine voice confessed, "Hey, baby. I am so glad you called."

"Hey, to you too, baby. You knew I would call as soon as I got home," Pam told him with excitement in her voice. She stepped her right foot out of the car and planted her mauve leather heels onto the concrete driveway. "Where are you? I thought you'd be here since you weren't at the airport. I want to see you. I can't tell you how much I've missed you," Pam proclaimed.

"Oh, Pam, you're back. Angie said you'd be home this weekend. Have you guys made it to the house?"

"Actually, we're getting out of the car right now. That's why I'm calling. I was surprised that you weren't at the airport. You're not here either. What's going on?"

"I'm at my family reunion. Let's keep it real. We really haven't talked much over the last few months. Look, I've got to get back to my family. They're calling me. We'll talk when I get home." His words stopped, and the line went dead.

"Did he just hang up on me?" She pulled the phone away from her ear and looked at the screen. "That was crazy. He sounded like he was so glad to hear from me, then his tone suddenly changed. He basically hung the phone up in my face," Pam claimed, heading toward the house.

They all walked through the front door and dropped purses and jackets onto the chairs and sofa. Angie and Mrs. Carter's eyes shifted back and forth between each other. They both knew that Pam would bring up an uncomfortable subject at any minute. They didn't have to wait long before the bomb exploded.

"Ok, enough with the secrets. Somebody better tell me something, and I mean now." Her wide-eyed gaze darted from Angie to her mother and back to Angie. "Wait a minute, just hold on a second."

Pam headed up the steps and took them two by two until she reached the top. She took wide steps and searched her bedroom closet, pulled at dresser drawers, and pushed them shut with a loud bang. Not one article of clothing belonging to Marcus was anywhere to be found. Why? And when did he leave? What have I done?

Pam whipped around and stormed down the stairs, armed with the need for answers. "Did Marcus move out?"

Her mother leaned forward and scooted to the edge of her seat. "Yes, it was after Jayden got hurt because..."

Pam sliced into her words with a cold precision. "Well, I'm not surprised. That's my fault. I'm sure," she admitted. "I went off on him one night and hurt his feelings. I can't blame him. All I can do is try to get him back. Initially, he did seem happy to hear my voice. He's out of town at his family reunion. When he gets back into town, we can talk and work things out."

That ship has sailed, and my man is not your man. Not anymore, anyway. Angie squeezed both arms of the chair she was sitting in so tightly her nails left an imprint in the leather.

"Someone should have told me that Marcus moved out." Pam twirled around in the floor like a child with a bright smile plastered on her face. "But I am so glad to be home. I don't think I'll ever leave the state of Texas again."

"Thanks for letting me come home to a clean house." Pam took in a big whiff of the smell that drifted in from the kitchen. "It smells delicious in here. What did you cook, Angie?"

Pam was pulled into the kitchen by the aroma in the air that teased her taste buds. She lifted the lid of each pot and inhaled its enticing smell. "I will eat until I can't possibly eat another bite. Too bad Marcus isn't here to enjoy this with me. I'll have to fix him a home-cooked meal when he gets back." She licked a spoon that she'd dipped into the pan of candied sweet potatoes. "That is so good," she admitted after licking her lips.

Angie's eyes shot up to the ceiling as she twirled her hair around her finger. I know I broke it off with him. But that sure doesn't mean my mother can have him back. That is just not going to happen.

CHAPTER THIRTY-NINE

Doug and Pam were in the middle of another huge fight about Jayden's custody. Pam had shown up at Doug's house uninvited, for the second time in a week. Jayden sat in his bedroom listening while his parents cursed each other, called each other names, and made threats. Pam's loud voice broke through the walls of Jayden's bedroom, forcing him to hear every word of his parents' confrontation.

"I will get my son back, Doug. You can count on that." Pam shifted the weight of her purse on her shoulder as she stood two feet from Jayden's father.

"Look, Pam, I'm working on some things, and as soon as it's all handled, he can start to visit. For right now, Jayden coming to your house is out of the question. It's too dangerous, and you know that."

"You must be crazy. You think you can just take my son? I can get an attorney, too. We'll just have to go to court. He should be home with me. I raised him." A thick vein on the side of Pam's neck stood at attention and pulsated.

"Talk like that tells me you don't have his best interest at heart. His safety is at risk living with you. Don't you get that, or are you just that stupid? Our son could've been killed. It could still happen if I let him go back there. This conversation is crazy. I don't even know why I'm discussing this with you. The law is on my side. So, from now on, do me a favor, call before you come to my house. You're bringing nothing but stress here, and I'm not having it anymore. The next time you come unannounced, I will call the police." Doug grabbed Pam by the arm and guided her short walk from the center of the living room to the front door.

"Get your hands off me, Doug, before I call the police." She continued to scream and yell, standing on the cobblestone steps outside of the front door. Neighbors out in their yards turned their heads and gave their attention to the loud commotion Pam orchestrated.

"You think putting me out of your house will stop me from saying what I have to say? You can't keep me from my child. That's not going to happen." Pam's gaze scaled the two-story brick home with three tall white pillars that stood guard at the front of the house. "You think just because you live in a big house and you've got money, you're in control. Well, you're not. Why don't you tell your neighbors that you got your money selling drugs? Sure, you are a legitimate businessman now. But that's not how you started." Pam pointed her finger inches away from Doug as she hurled the embarrassing truth at him.

Doug's head moved from left to right as he looked around to see if any neighbors were close enough to hear Pam's news flash. His eyes landed on the elderly man next door who often talked to him about politics. He even kept an eye out for Doug's home when he was out of town. The man shook his head, walked into his house, and closed the door.

Six-foot-three Doug Carr suddenly felt two feet tall as embarrassment and anger flushed his face. He gritted his teeth and growled at Pam. "Get off my property, or I'll have you arrested. The only reason I haven't already called the police is because it would hurt our son. But I am not going to continue to put up with this foolishness. Go home, Pam." The force of the heavy wooden door made a thunderous noise and shook the door frame when Doug slammed it shut.

The loud noise from the door rippled through the house and into Jayden's bedroom. He buried his face into his pillow and yelled, "Mom, stop it. Just stop. You're making it worse." Why couldn't he say that to her? He needed to tell her that the ugly battles between her and his dad made him nervous. His father was right. All her visits were upsetting for everyone, including her. It had to stop. I love Mom. But I don't know how to tell her how I feel. I've already hurt her with all this crazy stuff about the gang.

Jayden was no longer sure he wanted to leave his dad's house. He'd made a few friends and met a girl he liked. The basketball coach approached him to try out for the team. He was confident that he could make it onto the first-string roster. Jayden missed his mother and sister and the old neighborhood. But he'd learned to be content with his new living arrangements. At first, he hated being at his dad's house, and his dad's cooking was terrible. Jayden had learned a few things in the kitchen from his sister and mother and didn't mind using those skills. His dad usually liked whatever he cooked. A heavy knock at Jayden's bedroom door made him sit up on his bed.

"Son, are you okay?" His dad asked as he opened the door and entered the room.

Jayden quickly brushed the tears from his eyes with his shirt sleeve.

"Yes, Dad."

Doug stood over his son and placed his hand on his shoulder. "I know this thing between your mother and me has you upset. Let's talk."

Thirty minutes after Jayden and his father talked, Jayden told his dad he was heading to the park down the street to play ball. In truth, he was meeting a friend from his new school.

He walked onto the basketball court. "What's up, Kaylon?"

The husky boy with dreads bouncing all over his head stopped shooting baskets and faced Jayden.

"What took you so long? I've been waiting for twenty minutes."

"Sorry about that—family drama."

"Then you need that package I picked up for you." He slipped his hand down into his front pant pocket and pulled out a plastic bag of marijuana.

Jayden handed him two bills folded up. "Let's light it up, bro."

They walked over to a tree and sat down to hide from the bright sun. Kaylon fired up the forbidden smoke and passed it to his new friend.

Jayden sucked hard on the strong joint, pulling in the false peace it offered him. Then he pushed out the smoke like a veteran and confessed. "That's some good weed." His attention floated over and landed on the basketball on the concrete court. It had been his excuse to break free from his dad's house and watchful eyes.

He'd been fighting the temptation of getting high. He didn't want to fall into the same trap of bad choices that landed him in the hospital. Yet, the weight of the war between his parents and the scars on his face were both heavy to carry. Today, the load was heavier than usual. It was too heavy for him to stand up straight and say, "No," to temptation. Jayden took another deep pull and sucked in some false courage. Maybe my mom will listen if I try to be honest with her. After a couple of one-on-one games, Jayden headed home.

He turned the doorknob slowly, intending to get upstairs without his dad seeing him by entering through the back door. That didn't work. His dad was standing in the kitchen, blocking his safe passage to the staircase.

"Jayden, I've got some good news for you. The coach just called. He said if you come in for a drug screening in the morning, you can try out for the team that afternoon."

Jayden's eyes retreated from his dad and landed on the floor. "I don't think I can do that."

"Look at me, son. I told him you would be there. I'm proud of you. You've made so much progress since you've been here. Don't allow your mother and me to affect your confidence. Sometimes, grown-ups do foolish things. It's mostly because they love their children. Your mother and I will work things out. I want you to know that you can talk to me about anything. I won't judge you; I promise. I love you. I just want to help."

Jayden turned and glanced out of the window and down the street. He thought of the weed he'd just smoked and the lie that was burning on his tongue to be released. I won't lie. He faced his dad and croaked out, "Dad, you just said that I can talk to you about anything, and you won't judge me. I need to tell you something."

CHAPTER FORTY

Marcus looked down at his watch. He hadn't been home from Dallas for two hours yet, and Pam was blowing up his cell phone. It was her third call. With no desire to talk to her, he knew the needed conversation had to happen. He chose to meet her at a restaurant. Maybe in a public place, she wouldn't try to seduce him, and things wouldn't get ugly. He let his eyes roam up to the ceiling, down to the floor, and then to his cell phone. He pressed the button to accept Pam's call.

"Hey, baby. Are you home?"

"I just got back, and I'm exhausted," Marcus replied.

"I'm glad you made it back safely. I missed you. When can I see you? We need to talk."

"Yes, we do need to talk." Marcus held on to the truth that he wanted to just blurt out on the phone and avoid a face-to-face confrontation. But he had cared for Pam once, and he felt she deserved a real conversation.

"Let's meet tomorrow at Chandler's Deli at 2:00 p.m.," suggested Marcus.

"Okay, that's fine. Maybe afterward, we can go back to your place and have a different kind of conversation. I'll see you tomorrow," Pam said softly and seductively.

Marcus rolled his eyes up to the ceiling and pressed down hard on the button to end the call.

Pam wasn't the only person excited about a meeting. Angie picked up her vibrating cell and read the text message. She hurried out of the house to get the details about an internship that one of her instructors recommended her for. She called the professor on her way.

"Angie, this is a rare opportunity. This business has never offered any of our students an internship. It's a high-end store in Highland Park called Taylored So Fine, named after the owner's daughter, Taylor. I thought you would be a perfect fit. They have ten stores, and each piece is an exclusive design. The governor's wife and her twin daughters have been regulars in the store for years. This will be a great start since you're so determined to have your own business someday. We'll talk more when you get here."

Angie went to the campus to meet Dr. Wilkins to complete the necessary paperwork to be considered for the internship. After receiving all the details she needed, she was told to ask for a woman named Lillian Tome. After a thirty-minute drive, she walked in the door of an elegant upscale store. Angie's eyes lit up brightly, and her gaze drank in the beautiful clothes and the unfamiliar fragrance that tugged at her nostrils. As she shook hands with the clerk, her legs felt weak, her vision faded, and her body dropped to the floor.

"Ms. Lillian, help. This young lady just walked in and passed out," the clerk called to the woman in the back.

Lillian immediately called an ambulance and ran to get a cold towel. The clerk placed Angie's head onto her lap and dabbed her face with the towel. Angie slowly opened her eyelids.

"Are you okay?" asked the clerk with the cold towel. "You gave us quite a scare. You walked in, and before we could speak, you went down. Do you know where you are?"

Angie scanned the room and gathered her thoughts. "Yes, I think so. Taylored So Fine?" She rubbed her right temple. "I came here to apply for an internship. I don't know what happened."

The piercing sirens announced the arrival of the ambulance. Angie refused to be transported to the hospital. After being examined, Angie assured the paramedics that she would follow up with her doctor.

She didn't feel it was anything serious. After the paramedics left, Angie felt well enough to complete the application.

Lillian decided to interview her for the internship on the spot and was very impressed with Angie. "I'll contact your professor, and she'll contact you about the position." Angie thanked her and extended her hand for a firm handshake. She couldn't wait to tell her mom the exciting news. Pam would be a second phone call. On the way to her car, she called her doctor's office. I better take care of it now. "Hi, I need to make a doctor's appointment, please."

CHAPTER FORTY-ONE

Pam looked around the room, where tables were filled with people smiling, talking, and laughing. The life in the room floated in the air and made Pam hungry for a smile and a warm embrace from Marcus. Her glance drifted down to her watch. Fifteen minutes late, and no phone call. What was holding him up? Pam took a quick look at her makeup and headed off to the lady's room. When she strolled back to her table, she noticed Marcus from the corner of her eye. His cologne reached the table seconds before he did.

"Hey, sorry I'm late. Traffic was heavy." He pulled out her chair so she could take a seat.

Okay, no kiss, no embrace, nothing. Not the greeting I expected. Maybe he is still upset with me for how I talked to him when we got into it on the phone when I was in Japan. Why was he still holding onto that? Maybe he'll soften up a bit soon. He would have to let the brick wall down, Pam assumed.

"You look handsome!" She touched the collar of his blue shirt and rubbed her hand across his shoulder.

"Thank you."

Wow, here I am, looking like a million bucks, and this man doesn't even compliment me. Now, I know he must still be pissed.

A waiter brought two menus and two glasses of water and took their drink orders.

"How have you been?"

"I'm good, Pam. How are you?" Marcus answered, forcing a smile.

"I guess I'm okay. I'm glad to be home."

The waiter returned with their drinks and took their food orders. Pam removed a small gift bag from her purse when the waiter left the table.

"This is for you." She smiled as he took the gift from her hand.

"Something from Japan?" Marcus asked.

"No, but it's something you are sure to like." She tapped the table with her perfectly manicured ruby-red nails and directed him to remove the gift from the bag.

"Wow, this is an expensive bottle of cologne, and it is my favorite. You shouldn't have. Besides, I didn't get you anything." He placed the cologne back in the bag and moved it aside. "I assume things worked out for you in Japan to have splurged on such an expensive bottle of cologne." He nodded toward the gift bag.

"Well, not exactly. My mom gave me a loan because she knows I'm in a financial tight right now. I used some of it to get my man a nice gift. I wanted to thank you for all you did while I was away." Pam touched the back of his hand gently.

"Financial tight? What about the half a million?" Marcus sat back in his chair and awaited her response.

"I didn't get it. I can probably count on not getting it, ever. I don't know exactly where to start. I'll tell you one thing for sure. It didn't take long for me to realize that I should've stayed home. Japan was nothing like Dudley said it would be. It was pure hell from the moment I got off the plane. Nothing went the way he said it would." She twirled the ring on her finger around and around. "It was the worst almost eight months of my life."

Marcus tapped the rim of his glass and kept his eyes planted on her lips as her story unfolded.

"I was wrong for taking my problems out on you over the phone when we argued. I was totally stressed out. I hope you can forgive me." Tears caressed her cheeks as they slid down and dripped onto her blouse.

The man sitting across the table offered her no words of comfort, gentle touch, or understanding. He simply remained silent and waited for her emotional storm to pass.

Marcus attempted to change the subject and keep the conversation moving. "I'm sorry about Jayden getting hurt. I did try to keep a close eye on him." He looked directly into her eyes, offering her the truth and hoping she wouldn't blame him.

"My son knew better. I don't know what he was thinking. I'm sorry he gave you so much trouble. I really hate that he had to learn such an ugly lesson so early in his life."

"Yeah, I'm sorry too. I blame myself in a lot of ways. I guess I could've paid more attention to him and at least met the parents face to face."

"Well, in that case, we can both accept some blame. None of it would've happened if I'd stayed home. But you know what they say about hindsight. It is definitely 20/20. My mom told me she was rough on you and gave you a piece of her mind."

"Yeah, your mother is no one to play with. She meant business. I feared for my life." Marcus shielded his face by holding both hands up to prevent a blow to his face.

They both laughed. Finally, a light moment that didn't seem filled with apprehension. Pam took advantage of that crack in the doorway.

She pulled her hair back behind her ear out of habit, placed her hand on top of his, and spoke softly, "I want to talk about us. What are we going to do about us?" Pam waved her fingers between the two of them.

Marcus leaned forward. "What happened to your face? How did you get those scars? What happened over there?"

Pam swept her hair back down over her eye to shield the scars she'd hoped he would not notice. "Nothing, just a little accident. It's okay." She quickly turned the direction of the conversation back to the path she wanted to travel. "So, what about us?"

Marcus didn't respond. His eyes darted away from hers. He glared at the couple across the room, smiling and sharing quick pecks on their lips. Then he planted both eyeballs deep into Pam's stare. "I thought we resolved whatever was between us over the phone while you were in Japan."

"I admit that I made a mistake. I was upset, and I spoke out of anger when I broke it off with you."

Marcus tipped up his sweaty glass of iced tea and sucked down a long drink of courage. Then, he offered up what was in his heart. "Can I be honest with you?"

"Please do." Pam swung her right leg over the left one and sat back in her chair.

Marcus allowed the waiter to place their food on the table and leave before he began his confession. He cleared his throat. "I fell in love with someone while you were away. It was totally unexpected. It just happened."

Pam's visual assault bore into him like a drill driving down into a piece of wood. "You fell in love with someone. Was it two months, three months, or maybe three weeks after I left? If we were dating when I left, and I cut it off between us a couple of months before I came back, how did you fall in love with someone?" She leaned forward and planted her elbows on the table.

"No one can control their emotions. Love just happens. You know that as well as I do." He offered up his response with both palms turned up to the ceiling.

Her voice stepped up in volume. "That's bull. You must have been messing with her all the time, even before I left for Japan." The people at both tables next to them turned their heads in their direction with wide eyes.

"Come on, Pam. Don't make a scene." He motioned with his hands, moving downward toward the table for her to lower her voice. "I wasn't seeing her before you left. We just recently realized how we feel about each other."

Pam pointed both index fingers at her adversary and challenged him through gritted teeth. "You're a lying dog. How in the hell did you stay in my house with my children while you were dating another woman? That's foul, Marcus. So, that's why you moved out like a coward. Is it that crazy-ass Cassie?" She leaned forward, pressing her forearms hard into the table.

"Come on. Let's be real. We weren't in love with each other. We hadn't even dated that long. And let's not forget that you were the one who called it off between us. That means I'm a free man to do whatever I want to do." He pushed his plate of food to the center of the table.

"And let me just put this out there too. Your mother demanded that I leave your house when Jayden got hurt. She blamed me. I didn't move out by choice. So, yes, I moved on. I suggest you do the same." Marcus got up, tossed the cloth napkin onto the table, and marched toward the exit door.

Pam followed him with her eyes. "Where the hell do you think you're going?"

He fled the restaurant with wide strides and did not look back.

Pam hopped up and planted her six-inch heels in Marcus' tracks. Her shoes sounded off each time her heels stabbed the marble floor. When Pam got to the door, Marcus was four steps from his car.

"You didn't even have enough class to pay the bill, you bastard!"

Marcus got into his car, cranked up the engine, and let it roar several times. He pressed hard onto the gas and jetted up to the curb where Pam stood. He reached into his pocket and stretched his arm out the window toward Pam.

She snatched the money from his hand. "You're a trip, and you have a lot of nerve to walk out on me."

Marcus left tread marks on the pavement as he sped toward the parking lot exit. The growl of his engine could be heard as the sleek sports car changed gears.

Pam grabbed a rock from the ground and threw it at Marcus' speeding car.

He stomped his foot down hard onto the brake. The car jerked, and the tires screeched as smoke climbed up from the pavement. Marcus jumped out of his car to check the window and discovered a small crack. He looked in Pam's direction with a piercing stare, jumped back in his car, and sped away quickly before his temper pushed him to do something else.

Pam pushed the anger out of her body with a scream. Seconds later, back inside the restaurant, she handed the money to the waiter placing the check on the table.

"Sorry, but we can't stay. Keep the change."

Pam sat in her car in the parking lot, pounding both fists into the steering wheel. Her fists were red and sore, and she continued to pound the steering wheel with a clear image of Marcus in her mind.

CHAPTER FORTY-TWO

Tears clouded her view as Pam pulled out of the Deli parking lot. She brushed them away with the palm of her hand as they streamed down her cheeks. She steered the car mindlessly, barely aware of her path, until the squealing sound of a car horn shook her attention. Pam slammed on her brakes to avoid a car when she plowed through a red light.

Pam saw Marcus' car parked at a gas station two blocks down the street. She eased her car over to the side of the road and watched him pump gas. Once he pulled away from the gas station, she couldn't fight the need to follow him. Yeah, Mr. Big Shot, I want to see where you live. She was surprised that he'd moved such a long distance from her house. He pulled into an apartment complex. Pam stayed out of view and slowed down to watch which apartment Marcus went into.

Memories and anger flooded her thoughts as she watched him. She wasn't in love with him, but the fact that he could just toss her aside and claim to be in love with someone else gnawed away at her.

Marcus walked into his apartment and flung his jacket on the bar stool. His keys missed the bar and landed on the floor. He walked down the short hallway that led to the living room. He wasn't alone in his apartment. And it couldn't be her standing there in front of him.

Angie closed the distance between them and laced her arms around his neck. He held her close and inhaled the scent of her soft, sweet perfume.

Marcus released his hold on her and stepped back. His eyes met with hers. "Oh my, God. What are you doing here?"

Her bottom lip trembled as a tear slipped over her eyelash and made its escape.

"What's wrong, baby?"

Angie hugged him again tightly and still said nothing.

"Come over here and tell me what's going on." He led her to the sofa and kneeled in front of her.

"I've missed you, baby," he whispered.

"I've missed you too, but..." and before she could utter another word, he kissed her lips.

She tried to fight it. "No, Marcus, this is not what I came here for," she said, pushing him away. The scent of his cologne weakened her desire to struggle against his embrace. She leaned away from him to strengthen her resolve.

"What do you want from me? You can't just show up here out of nowhere and expect me not to want to kiss you or hold you." He stood up and looked down at her. "Being away from you is hard."

"It's been hard for me too. I've missed you like crazy, but..."

"Then what are we doing? Just tell me what you want me to do. How can we make this thing work?" His arms flew up in the air and dropped back down to his side.

Angie stepped closer to him and took in the drift of his cologne. "I love you. But I'm afraid of what us loving each other will do to other people."

He planted soft kisses on her neck, parted her lips with his strong tongue, and reminded her of what his passionate kisses tasted like. His fingers unbuttoned her blouse, and his lips sucked her plump nipples into his mouth.

An airy gasp escaped Angie's mouth as she moaned. She pulled his shirt over his head as they continued to kiss and touch each other's bodies. Marcus slipped his finger between her legs and searched out her wet core. He planted his tongue deep inside of her mouth while his long finger explored her depth and wet dripping nectar. He pleasured her and made her want him more.

Angie cried out in ecstasy, "I love you, and I missed your touch."

On the other side of his apartment door, almost an hour passed, and Pam was still sitting in the parking lot. I guess his woman is not showing up tonight. Pam decided to scan the parking lot for headlights.

She needed a reason to knock on his door. She wanted to get inside his apartment and see what was happening. "I don't care anything about who he thinks he's in love with. I'm knocking on his door, and if he lets me in, all I can say is too bad for her," Pam spoke her confidence out loud to herself and flipped down the mirrored visor, painted on another coat of lipstick, and pulled her hair down over her eye.

She grabbed her purse from the bucket seat, stepped out of the car, and trekked across the parking lot and up the two flights of stairs in her high-heeled shoes. Just as she raised her hand and formed a fist to knock on the door, erotic sounds of lovemaking came straight through the door and pricked at her ears.

This jerk is in there screwing some woman. Pam leaned closer to the door.

"Marcus, I missed you so much. Oh baby," Angie moaned.

Pam bit down hard on her bottom lip. Her eyes narrowed with a hot gaze that bore into the door that separated her from the woman who was sexing the man who used to be hers. I really wanted to try to make things work with Marcus. Obviously, there's no chance of that happening now.

The moans and groans of passion got louder, and then a cry of pleasure delivered a blow of jealousy that landed smack dab in Pam's face. "Who does he have in there? She better not be someone I know," she challenged herself with a whisper in the dark. Coming here was a bad idea. What the hell was I thinking? He told me it was over, and I should've listened.

The female voice taunting her was faint, but the act of sex was clearly what was going on. Pam removed her shoes and retreated from the victory celebration behind the door of Marcus' apartment. The battle was lost to another woman. What was next? She'd come home with scars inside and out that would never leave her. She didn't get the half a million, and now, no man.

After their intimate encounter, Angie and Marcus showered and dressed. He intended to take her out for dinner, unaware that things wouldn't go as smoothly as he hoped.

"I thought we could go out and get some dinner, then come back here and relax. Before we do that, I still need to know why you were crying when I got here?"

He turned and faced Angie, who sat beside him on the long leather bench at the foot of his bed.

"It's no big deal. I'll be okay. I shouldn't have bothered you. I'll work it out." She stood and picked up her purse.

Marcus shot up from the bench, took it out of her hand, and laid it down on the bed. "Please, don't leave like this. You came here for a reason. I need to know what's happening. If you want to move back in with me, just say the word. You know I'm down for that. There's nothing I want more."

"You're right, Marcus. There is something wrong. I don't know how else to say this. I should've been more careful. You're probably going to be angry." Angie turned her back to him and dropped her head.

He touched her shoulder and guided her to turn around to face him. "I won't be angry. Whatever it is, just tell me."

"Okay, Marcus, if you say so." She licked her lips, took in a deep breath, and looked him straight in the eyes. "I'm pregnant." The words hung in the air and demanded silence.

Say something. She shifted her weight to her other foot. Say something. Lord, why is he so quiet?

Marcus dropped down onto the bench without looking behind him. The bench rocked forward since he sat so close to the edge.

His silence poked at Angie's nerves and her voice. "Did you hear me? I'm five weeks pregnant. Please say something. I'm sorry. I didn't mean for this to happen. We used protection most of the time, and I was on the pill. I can't believe this is happening." Angie's shoulders jerked up and down when her cell phone squealed. She glanced over at her purse.

A wide smile inched across his face, and he scooped Angie up in his arms and spun around in a circle twice. Her feet touched the floor lightly as he put her down. "I'm happy. I'm excited. I'm going to be a father. How could I be angry? This is wonderful."

Angie took a step back from him, shaking her head. "No, I'm not having it. I can't. We can't afford a baby. You work too much as it is. Besides, I'm not ready for all of that. I'm too young to be a mother. My life is just starting."

He turned and stomped over to the window, planted both palms hard against the window frame, and hung his head.

Angie stood in the same spot, gazing across the room, shaking her head left and right and rubbing the fingertips on her right hand together.

The newly expectant father spun around, took four wide steps, and stood in front of Angie with a wide-eyed cold stare. "What do you mean you're not having it? Then why did you come here?"

"I came here because I need money to pay for an abortion."

Marcus paced the floor and pounded his fist into the palm of his other hand. "You can't seriously think I'm going to allow you to do that." His voice got louder. "You have the nerve to ask me to pay for you to kill my child. That's out of the question. What in the hell is wrong with you?"

Angie snatched her purse up from the bed and tossed her firm words at Marcus. "I'm not your wife. You can't tell me what to do. This is my body, and I am in control of my life. If you think you'll be giving me orders, you've got the wrong one."

Angie marched out of the bedroom, through the living room, and out the front door. She marched to the beat of her own drum, leaving the door standing wide open.

Marcus stood in the doorway, yelling after her, "That's my baby, too. I should have some say in what happens to it. This conversation is not over."

Angie slammed her car door, cranked up her engine, and fished her cell phone from her purse. "Are you busy, Vanessa? I need to come over." She whipped her car out of the parking stall and hit the gas. She glimpsed into the rearview mirror, needing distance between her and Marcus Blue.

CHAPTER FORTY-THREE

On the way home, Pam tried to push the thought out of her mind for the third time. Was that Angie's car in the parking lot of Marcus' apartment complex? She'd zipped out of the lot quickly. Maybe it wasn't. Yet, the thought continued to nag at her like a fly buzzing at her ear.

Pam made a call to her mother. She had no right to put Marcus out of her house, and she planned to tell her so. My mother may be to blame for all of this. That's probably what made him run into another woman's arms. Her mother didn't answer, and Pam didn't leave a message. Just as she ended the call, the phone rang. Pam answered without checking to see who was calling.

"Why haven't I heard from you? You've been in town for at least a week, and I should've been the first to know it."

"I'm sorry, Dudley. I've been dealing with some things with my kids.

My son's father went to court and took custody of him while I was in Japan."

A cryptic laughter crept through the phone. "You don't think I care, do you? I want to know one thing. Where is my merchandise or my money?"

"Dudley, I went through hell and back in Japan, and nothing was how you said it would be. I took the darn thing to the shop you sent me to, and those people stole it from me. I ended up with a warrant for my arrest when I stole it back. Chu hid me in some rat den to keep me safe until he could find a buyer for it, and I could leave, but..."

Dudley cut her off and sliced into her words with a cold precision. "Then where the hell is it? Chu said you left the house that he hid you in, and he couldn't find you," he growled with a thick voice.

Suddenly, nothing Dudley said mattered. She totally tuned him out to focus on the sirens and flashing lights in her rearview mirror. As she pulled into her driveway, two police cars pulled in behind her and blocked her car. She pressed the button on the phone hard, ending the call with Dudley yelling at her. She stepped out of her car and stood with the door open. Two police officers stepped out of their car and walked toward her. The tall, husky officer rested his hand on the handle of his holstered handgun.

"May I help you, officers?"

"Yes, ma'am. We hope so. Are you Pamela Carter?" asked the shorter officer.

"Yes, I am. Is there a problem?"

"A Sasebo-based American sailor, Petty Officer Mario Woodard, was killed on May 25th of this year. Authorities in Japan seem to think you're responsible for the sailor's death."

Pam felt like her tongue was glued to the roof of her mouth. She was silent for a few seconds. Finally, words passed her lips. "What, what, why would they think that?"

The officers exchanged glances. The officer, with his hand on his gun, stepped closer and asked, "Ms. Carter, do you mind coming down to the station with us? We need to ask you some questions. It shouldn't take too long."

"Am I under arrest?" Her eyes shifted from one officer to the other. "I haven't done anything wrong." Her palms were sweaty, and beads of sweat sprouted out onto the tip of her nose.

"No, we just need your cooperation to answer some questions," the short officer assured her. He escorted Pam back to the police car and opened the door so she could climb into the back seat.

Suddenly, Pam couldn't breathe. Her chest felt heavy, and she hyperventilated and fell to the ground. The officer caught her before her head hit the pavement. "Relax, ma'am, and breathe in and out slowly," he told her.

A few minutes passed, and Pam's breathing was under control. The officer, who still had his hand on his gun, gave Pam a hard look accompanied by a doubtful smirk.

The officer slammed the door shut after she got into the backseat. To Pam, it sounded like the crash of a cold steel prison door slamming shut. She looked straight ahead with tears streaming down her face. Only God knew what would happen next.

CHAPTER FORTY-FOUR

Angie walked into Vanessa's apartment, chatting away the second the door opened. "Girl, it's been a week since I told Marcus about the baby, and he has called me every day. I am so tired of him hounding me about keeping this baby. I don't care what he says and how many messages he leaves. I am not ready to be anybody's mother." The two sat down on the sofa, and Vanessa reached for the remote and turned down the volume on the TV.

"Angie, you need to talk to him. You won't be happy until you are with the man you love. Having his baby would be special. Don't do something you'll regret later. You have a handsome and hard-working man who really loves you." Vanessa touched Angie's arm gently.

Angie leaned back and allowed her head to roll from side to side. What did she have to do to work out the knot of tension in her neck that had been poking at her for the last few hours?

"I know you keep thinking about your mother. You're even willing to risk your own happiness for her. That's sweet and noble of you, but it's also reckless and stupid. Everybody loves their mother. This situation can't be about making your mother happy. It's too late for that." Vanessa flung her hands into the air. "Let's keep it real. You did have sex with your mother's man more than once. You even fell in love with him before you were intimate with him. It's too late in the game to be noble."

"Yeah, Vanessa, I hear you calling me a hypocrite. You're saying I didn't think about my mother then, huh? And you're right. I was selfish and thoughtless. I feel terrible about it. I should've never let it happen."

"I'm not calling you a hypocrite. I'm calling you a slut." Vanessa snickered. "No, I'm just kidding." She pushed her knee up against Angie's, and they both heaved up a cleansing laugh.

"Everything is going to be alright. You keep blaming yourself for falling in love. You didn't tell your mom to leave that man. This is not your fault. Honestly, I know it is a crazy situation, but I think you and Marcus were meant for each other. We never know when and where love will happen."

"Vanessa, you just don't get it. It goes so much deeper than just being in love." Angie fumbled with the car keys still in her hand.

"Well, I'll make it easy for you. I'll take that fine brotha right off your hands. If you don't want him, toss him my way." Vanessa walked away laughing.

Angie tossed her a tight-eyed, admonishing stare that said more than words could.

"Seriously, I know it's hard, Angie. I feel that if you give up this baby, you will regret it for the rest of your life. You really need to give this thing more thought. Pray about it. God will lead you to the right answer if you allow him to." Vanessa walked into the kitchen, returned to the living room with a glass of ice water, and stretched out her arm toward Angie.

"Find a way to talk to your mother and tell her she has a grandbaby on the way. She'll be alright. She should have stayed her butt in Texas instead of leaving that sexy piece of chocolate for anybody's taking."

Angie looked at Vanessa and shook her head.

"Don't look at me like that. You know I'm right!"

Angie drank half the glass of water, reached for her purse, and stood up to leave. "I can't talk about this anymore, not to you or Marcus. I just want to get this over with. My appointment is Saturday morning at 9:00. I'll call you after I leave the abortion clinic. This pregnancy has made me weak and tired. I've got to deal with this."

"That's what pregnancy is supposed to do. I sure hope you change your mind. If you don't, I will go with you."

"Thanks! I love you for that and for not judging me. Now is not a good time for me to have a baby. I didn't tell you about this but brace yourself." Angie clenched the handle of her purse as she prepared to spill her mother's secret.

"What?" Vanessa inquired, stepping closer and looking over the rim of her glasses.

"Some sailor was killed in Japan. The police think my mother did it.

She's being extradited back to Japan soon."

"What? Are you serious? Girl, that is crazy. Why haven't you said anything? They're saying your mother killed someone?"

"Yes, but I know better than that. Now you can see why my mother has to be able to count on me. She needs me."

"Angie, you are not a lawyer. How can you help her, especially if they take her back to Japan and you're pregnant?"

Angie's nostrils flared in and out while beads of sweat painted her forehead. She poked the palm of her left hand with her index finger as she made her pledge to Vanessa. "I'm not having this baby. I'm done talking about it." Angie whipped around so fast that she dropped her purse. She bent down and scooped it up in one motion, fled the apartment, and slammed the door with a thunderous crash.

Vanessa hurled loud and angry words at the door, "You are going to regret that."

CHAPTER FORTY-FIVE

A frustrated Marcus threw the last four darts that landed as a bullseye on the dart board. He struggled to yank them out since they were wedged deep into the board. "This is crazy. I will have to tell Pam that I'm the father of Angie's baby. There is no other way. The truth has to come out," he declared to the walls in his empty spare bedroom.

Angie wouldn't answer his calls, and he couldn't believe she had just cut him off after telling him she was pregnant. He'd been to Pam's house to talk to her and Angie. He'd decided to tell Pam the hard truth that he knew would be hurtful. He was the father of Angie's baby. Angie was the woman he loved, and no amount of anger could change that.

He had it all figured out. He would apologize to Pam for how things went down between them at the restaurant. The conversation would be difficult at first, but if she knew that another life was involved, her own grandchild, that could soften her heart. If Pam could put her feelings aside, Marcus thought she could help him talk Angie into keeping the baby. Since no one answered the door each time he'd dropped by, Marcus wasn't sure what to do next.

He took a shower and got into bed. Rest was required since he had to work the next day. Sleep did not find him. Unable to push thoughts of Angie and the baby out of his mind, and the frustration gnawed at him. He got up and hunted through his closet, then out to the kitchen, yanking open cabinet doors and slamming them shut. A thought came to him, and he remembered where he placed them.

Marcus went to the refrigerator, and in the vegetable bin out of sight were the last pack of unopened cigarettes he'd purchased six months ago before he decided to stop smoking. He picked up the pack and ripped off the thin cellophane seal. He turned the pack over and over in his hand. He licked his lips, lifted the pack up to his nose, and inhaled a whiff of cool menthol. One more whiff and Marcus decided to toss the cigarettes back into the drawer. He considered something else that would give him some relief from the pain he was feeling.

She had taken a baby away from him as well. The only difference was that little girl was not his baby. Depression had consumed him back then and climbing out of that emotional hole had been difficult. He couldn't let himself go back there. He needed a warm body, the touch of a woman. It would only be sex because his heart belonged to Angie. He dressed, grabbed his keys, and made a quick phone call on his way to the car.

"Cassie, you busy?"

"I thought you had forgotten about me, and I was trying to move on and forget about you too. Every time I do, here you come, drifting back into my life. You know I can't say no to you. The kids are at my sister's house for the night," she purred. "That is why you're calling, right? That special little treat down between my legs that loves it when you come to visit?"

Marcus rolled his eyes and started his car. "I'll be there in twenty minutes. Make it thirty." I better stop at the drugstore. I definitely don't need two baby mamas.

His conscience, which rode along in the car, tried to tell him he was wrong for going to Cassie's house. Didn't he still love Angie?

Angie sure wasn't acting like she loved him or his baby. He muted the small annoying voice in his head and slowly pressed down on the accelerator.

CHAPTER FORTY-SIX

Angie went to the county jail to visit her mother earlier that evening after leaving Vanessa's place. The stench of the visitor's quarters nearly made her sick. She raced to the bathroom more than once, hurling up the contents of her stomach. Pam watched her daughter pinch her nose and grab her stomach as though she were resisting the urge to throw up.

"Girl, are you pregnant? I meant to ask you that a couple of weeks ago. I thought I heard you throwing up in your bathroom one morning." She observed Angie's reaction closely to see if she would tell the truth.

"Uh, no ma'am, I'm not, and I wasn't throwing up. Maybe I was coughing or something."

"Well, it didn't sound like it to me. I know the difference between a cough and vomiting. You do look a little heavier. Are you sure you're not pregnant?"

Angie's gaze shot to the right, fleeing her mother's firm accusation. No words passed her lips, just a deep breath she held silently before exhaling.

Pam decided not to press the issue. She knew they would discuss it when Angie was ready. She reached out to hug her daughter until a guard stopped her.

"No touching," the guard scolded.

Angie decided it was a good time to see if her mother could spit out the truth herself. "Are you going to tell me how you got those scars on your face that you try to hide with makeup every day?" Angie strummed her fingers on the steel table.

Pam's hand shot up to her face to touch the scars that refused to be hidden and haunted her daily. Pushing out an airy breath, she swallowed down the lie that she had been prepared to tell everyone eventually. She exchanged it for the truth as she stared directly into her daughter's eyes and told her every ugly detail about her rape.

They both cried as the words were released into the air. It was the closest they'd felt in months. The horrible, ugly thing that Pam tried to hide forever built a wall between her and her daughter. The truth tore it down. Pam swore Angie to secrecy. She was never to tell anyone the nightmare that her mother had entrusted her with. Pam also didn't want her mother to know that she was in jail and being extradited back to Japan. They prayed together that Pam could make a jury see that it was self-defense.

"I'll be here every day to see you before they take you away. I love you so much," Angie proclaimed.

Pam wiped tears from her eyes and hugged her daughter goodbye. What did it matter if the guard saw them? She was already on her way back to hell, back to Japan, to stand trial for murder. What could the county jail do to her that would be worse than that?

Her eyes followed Angie as she exited the visiting room while her heart cried out to God. She whispered, "Lord, I feel like I am losing my mind. Have you turned your back on me? I need you. Please, forgive me for what I've done, or take me. I can't do this. You promised that you wouldn't put more on me than I could bear. Please, help me. I'm not strong enough to deal with this. Please, Jesus! I need you." She sobbed audibly at the visiting table, waiting for the guard to escort her back to her cell. She didn't care who heard her.

When Angie made it to her car, she checked her cell phone. She had missed several calls from Marcus. She read his text message that tugged at her heart.

Please call me. I need you to hear me out before you throw us away for good.

It wasn't that she didn't love him. Having a family with Marcus would crush her mother. "I just can't do that to her," Angie said aloud as she put her car in reverse.

When Angie got home, she planted herself in bed and slept for over two hours. When she awakened, thoughts of Marcus had not abandoned her. I need you out of my head, man. This is just too much. Just when I think my mind is made up, I think of how much you don't want me to have an abortion. She rolled out of bed and schlepped over to the full-body mirror in the corner. The ten extra pounds she noticed on her belly and hips mocked her. Her jeans fit snugly around her waist and pinched her. The truth was looking back at her. Those jeans didn't fit that tightly a few weeks ago.

CHAPTER FORTY-SEVEN

Immediately after sex, Marcus lay in bed with Cassie, wishing he had stayed home.

"I'm sorry to say it, but I would rate that performance a zero," Cassie drew a big zero in the air with her index finger.

Marcus lay on his back with his eyes fixed on the ceiling. "Yes, I know. I have a lot on my mind. I should've just stayed home."

Cassie rubbed his chest and planted quick, moist pecks on his neck with her full lips. "No, it's okay. I'm always glad to see you. I will tell anyone who listens that I love you and you only, Marcus Isaiah Blue. I'm still hoping you and I will have a future one day. I know I hurt you a few years back. I am so sorry, and I've said that over and over again. But you just won't forgive me."

Marcus could hear her, but her words didn't touch his heart. His eyes roamed the room, and his thoughts were with Angie.

"Hell, I don't even know where you live. You act like I am the enemy. I really love you. Every time you drop by for one of your infrequent visits, I cry myself to sleep, knowing it will be a long time before I see you again." Cassie stroked his cheek and waited for Marcus to respond.

Marcus could feel cold and wet tears landing on his chest.

She gently kissed his chest again and then his lips. "You know you like it."

Still, he didn't respond. It wouldn't be right to make her think things between them would change. He wanted to leave, but Cassie knew how to make a man stay put. Her hands and her mouth went to work on Marcus. His long, thick rod responded to her touch and stood at attention.

Cassie moaned, loving every inch of his deliverance that drove deep inside of her.

"Is this still a zero performance, Angie, baby?"

Cassie froze, and ice-cold words latched onto Marcus. "Who the hell is Angie, Marcus?"

"What are you talking about?"

"You just called me Angie."

"No, I didn't. That's not what I said." He tried to convince her with his firm glare and deeper strokes.

"Get off me." She struggled beneath him, pushing his shoulders at the same time. "Move! I heard you as plain as day."

"No, you didn't; I said Cassie."

"Okay, Marcus, let's get this straight." She leaned back against the wooden headboard. "You're saying you had no reason to call me Angie because there's no Angie in your life? Don't lie to me. You know I don't play games. Just answer the question. There's no Angie in your life, right?"

He could not confess his feelings for another woman while lying in Cassie's bed. She'd just pleased him sexually and pledged her love for him.

Cassie got out of bed, threw on a robe, yanked the belt tightly around her waist, and tied a hard knot. "Then don't give it another thought. I believe you. If you say there's no one named Angie, then there's no Angie. It's all good."

Marcus' wrinkled brow spoke to his confusion. It wasn't like Cassie to be so calm when it came to him and another woman. He swung his legs over the opposite side of the bed Cassie was sitting on and slid out of the bed. His eyes were fixed on Cassie as he plucked his clothes from the floor and stepped into his pants. With his shirt tossed over his shoulder and Timberland boots in hand, Marcus made a swift exit.

Cassie held her silent visual pursuit of him as he fled her apartment.

"It is something wrong with that chick. I can feel it." Marcus fired up his engine and let it roar. He couldn't leave fast enough.

CHAPTER FORTY-EIGHT

Angie headed to the store to pick up butterscotch ice cream to satisfy her craving. The thought of the baby growing inside her pricked at her heart. She steered the car toward Marcus' apartment instead of home. She knocked on the door several times with no response. After waiting another minute, she put her key in the door and turned the lock. She put the ice cream in the freezer and headed straight to the bedroom.

The empty bedroom mocked her. I wonder if he went out of town. I don't even know why I'm here. He's probably out with some other woman. I can't blame him if he is. I have definitely rejected him, and I gave him no reason to think that would change. I can't expect him just to put his life on hold. She took off her shoes and crawled up into his bed. Angie took a deep whiff of his cologne-laced pillow and snuggled under the covers. "I miss you," she whispered into the pillow, and in minutes she was asleep.

A streak of light broke through the blanket of night when Marcus opened his apartment door. He walked into his bedroom and found her lying in his bed. The woman I just denied to Cassie is here in my bed. Why? Did she have the abortion? If she did, there is no way we can reconcile. The thought of Cassie and how spooked she made him when he called out Angie's name during sex flashed through his mind.

Marcus sat on the bed beside her and brushed hair from her face. "Hey, wake up."

Rubbing her eyes and with a noisy yawn, Angie's eyelids popped open.

"Hi," she said, smiling.

"I'm surprised to see you here. What's going on?"

"I think we need to talk. You weren't here. I let myself inside. I didn't think that you'd mind. Did you go out of town?"

The truth would hurt her, and a lie could haunt him. He chose to ride the winds of a lie. "Yeah, something like that. It was a quick trip. What did you want to talk about?"

She cleared her throat and allowed her glance to shoot past him to the window and back again. "I thought I would hear you out about the baby."

"Hear me out? You heard me. What's the point of hearing how I feel again if you've already decided you are the only one who can make the decision? I don't know what you want from me. I'm not going to beg if that's what you think. I told you where I stand, and that hasn't changed."

He sprung up from the bed, put some distance between them, and shoved both hands into his pant pockets. "Did you already have the abortion? If you did, we're completely done, and there is nothing else for us to discuss."

She drew her knees up to her chin and wrapped her arms around them. "Why is having a baby so important to you?"

"Damn it, Angie. Did you have the abortion?" His hands flew out of his pockets, and he shook both fists in the air.

"No, not yet, but I have to do it. I keep thinking about my mother. Why can't you understand that?"

"Really? Your mother again? It's your life. Be an adult and decide based on what's in your heart, not what someone else will think." His voice was louder, and the veins on the side of his neck had swollen and resembled worms crawling up his neck.

"Be an adult... I was adult enough to conceive your child." She slid out of the bed, and her feet hit the floor. "Why can't you understand that I don't want to hurt my mother? I feel like the worst daughter in the world. I wasn't supposed to fall in love with my mother's boyfriend. She may never forgive me for this. One day, when you decide to leave me, for whatever reason, this will all be for nothing. I don't want to end up raising a child by myself."

"Is that what you're worried about?" He took a step toward her. "If you don't leave me, we'll be together forever. I've told you before that I have never loved anyone like I love you. You're carrying my child. I told you I would take care of you, and I meant it. You and this baby mean the world to me." He pointed his finger at her belly. "Why can't you see that?"

A tear slipped down Angie's cheek, and she raked her teeth over her quivering lip.

Marcus stretched out his hand to her. "Come here, baby." He swallowed her up with his arms and squeezed hard.

She wanted Marcus, but the thought of it not working and her mother hating her was a heavy burden. Her love for him softened her heart and compelled her to relax in his embrace.

He lifted her chin with his fingertips and pressed his lips against hers. They kissed long and hard as he attempted to satisfy his hunger for the taste of her lips.

Angie eased out of his embrace and led him into the kitchen.

Marcus followed happily. Maybe the crisis was over. Could there be a chance they could be a family, the three of them?

Angie cut up onions and scallions on a chopping block. "I need to know. Why do you want this baby so much?"

Marcus spilled his heart and was candid about the hurt that Cassie had caused him about the little girl he believed to be his daughter.

Angie could feel his pain as he shared his story, and she could see that he was still affected by it. "You were willing to marry her just because she was pregnant?"

"Well, honestly, yes, that was the reason. I believe that both parents should raise their children together."

"So, when you found out the baby wasn't yours, the two of you just broke up, and never saw each other again?" She cut down hard on the onion as the knife slammed against the chopping board.

"It's a little more complicated than that. But for the most part, we just ended it." He kissed the back of her neck, hoping the lie he'd just told didn't come back to bite him in the butt.

For the next hour, they ate omelets and talked about everything from parenting to their own childhoods. The laughter and conversation brought the apartment that had been quiet and drab back to life.

Marcus stopped talking and gave Angie a long gaze.

Angie put her fork down and tilted her head. "What's wrong?"

"Nothing, not one thing." He got up, scooped her up from the chair, and carried her to his bedroom. He kissed her slowly, enjoying the sweet taste of her lips and body. He made love to her slowly and passionately. With every stroke, Angie moaned with pleasure, sending quick tremors of ecstasy through her body.

When they both reached the height of their lovemaking, Angie trembled with pleasure as the core between her legs erupted and sweet nectar oozed out of her. She only had the strength to confess one thing before drifting off to sleep. "I love you, Marcus. I'm having your baby."

CHAPTER FORTY-NINE

Angie and Marcus woke up the following day, snuggled in bed, and caught up on what was going on with each other since they had been apart. Angie reluctantly confessed to Pam's current stay behind bars and the fact that she was about to be extradited back to Japan to stand trial for murder.

"That's not all. She doesn't want Jayden to know anything about it. How can I keep it from him? He wants to know why she hasn't been to Doug's to see him and why she is not answering his calls." Angie rolled over onto her back. "This whole thing is a mess. Doug tried to visit her to get some answers, but she wouldn't see him. He's pissed off." She kicked her feet up and down on the mattress. "I can't believe this is happening."

Marcus placed his fingertips on her temples and massaged gently. "I know you're concerned about your mother. Try to relax, baby. We've got to watch your stress level. Stress is not good for you or the baby."

Marcus brought up the subject of marriage and wanted to know how Angie felt about them getting married. They talked about it for almost an hour. Angie wasn't sure getting married was a good idea.

Her mother would have a hard enough time accepting that she was having Marcus' baby. Marrying the man might send her over the edge. They were happy and secretly trying to plan their life together. But a swollen belly would soon blow the lid off the secret.

A baby and a potential husband weren't the only new things in her life. Later that day, Angie got some unexpected great news. Her internship was going well. The owners were very impressed with her dedication, hard work, and innovative ideas. Angie had suggested their retail store carry a maternity line. The District Manager, Ms. Lillian, loved the idea, set up a meeting with the owners, and invited Angie. With her cost-effective research, she suggested merchants for the line, and ways to get the customers excited, and the owners.

"Well, Angie, the owners want to add you to the payroll. How does that sound to you? They know that you'll be graduating in December. They don't want you to slip through our fingers. They're offering you $80,000 yearly and a salary increase after graduation. They're willing to negotiate if you're not completely satisfied with the offer." Ms. Lillian leaned back in her high-back leather chair and waited for Angie's response.

"You cannot be serious. They want to hire me. Oh my, God. Please tell them yes. Are you kidding? I don't know what to say," Angie squealed enthusiastically. A smile claimed her face and showcased her pearly whites. "Negotiate, I don't need to negotiate. I am more than satisfied with the $80,000. This is such a blessing. Thank you so much for this opportunity." She popped up from her seat, thrust her open palm out, and vigorously shook Ms. Lillian's hand. "Please excuse me. I need to make a phone call. I can't hold in this great news. I've got to tell Marcus. This is unbelievable."

Perhaps this news would take some of the stress off Marcus as he prepared to take the state RN exam? Hopefully, he would be proud of her and not expect her to stop working before or after she had the baby. The unknown would make itself clear soon. When Angie walked through the door that evening, Marcus was studying at the breakfast bar.

"I'm so proud of you. You're going to ace that test this time. I can feel it," she said, kissing the back of his neck. Angie wrapped her arms around him from behind and squeezed.

He turned around in his chair to face her. "Proud of me. You're the one that will be bringing in the big bucks. I knew you would do great things. This is just the beginning for you," he told her with multiple kisses on her lips.

The excitement on her face drained as she told him about her plans for the next day.

"I meant to tell you earlier, Friday, I have to help my brothers pack up my mother's house. I'll be gone most of the day. She's being evicted."

With wide eyes and a wrinkled brow, Marcus inquired, "Why is your mother being evicted? I paid the rent every month, and it was on time. Didn't your grandmother say she paid up the rent for at least three months? It hasn't been quite three months, has it?"

"No, it hasn't. And, yes, she did pay it. The landlord sent a portion of the money back and put the eviction notice on the door. Apparently, he sold the house without telling her, and the buyer will be moving in soon. My grandmother keeps calling me to find out why the rent money was returned to her. I don't know what to tell her. I haven't answered any of her calls. I will tell my mother what's happening when I see her tomorrow. She can tell me what I need to tell Nana. Somehow, we'll figure it all out."

Marcus stood to embrace her and kissed her gently. "Do you need my help?"

"No, we can handle it. I won't be carrying anything heavy."

"You better not pick up one item. Your brothers will probably give you a hard time for not doing any grunt work."

She placed her hand on the slight bump in her belly. "We're all going out to dinner after we get the house packed up, and I plan to tell them about you and the baby. This is one secret that won't be a secret much longer." She patted her belly and glanced down.

The expectant father picked her up and swung her around in the middle of the floor. "That is great news. We can be out in the open about our feelings for each other."

"As soon as this crazy thing with my mother is all worked out, I'll tell her about us, too. I'm never going to apologize for loving you. You are my soul mate."

"Well, I wish I could be there to support you tomorrow. I hope all goes well with your brothers, especially with the bomb you will drop on them."

"Don't worry, it'll be fine. Anyway, I don't care who doesn't like it. I'm happy. I am happy," she yelled and danced in the middle of the floor. "I'm so happy."

It was Thursday, and Nelson came to town a day early to help his sister pack up Pam's house. He wasn't exactly sure why they were moving, where their mother was, and why she wasn't helping. He knew Jayden had gone to live with his father, and his mother and sister would need to find somewhere else to live. Why? He planned to get the answer to that question pretty darn quickly.

His wife, Patrice, had come along with him to help get a jump start on things. They arrived at the house that morning and got straight to work. They packed up boxes and went to a place he knew nearby and rented storage space. He waited for his sister to come home. Where was Angie? He planned on surprising her by arriving early to help. The surprise was on him since she wasn't home, and he hadn't heard from her.

Later that evening, after a lot of hard work packing boxes, Nelson called his sister's cell phone for the second time.

"Hey, Angie. Where are you? Patrice and I have been waiting for you to get home. I left you a couple of messages. I was trying to surprise you. We've been here all day working. What's up?"

"I'm sorry. I didn't know you were coming today. I moved out a few weeks ago. I'd come over tonight to see you guys, but I don't live that close. Besides, I have to work in the morning. I promise to be there as soon as I get off tomorrow. I'll be off by 11:00 a.m. Tell Patrice I'll see her tomorrow. Love you. Bye."

"Where's our mother?" he asked, but Angie had hung up the phone. He looked over at his wife, who was wrapping up the last of the dishes in newspaper. "Something is not right here. You better believe that I'm going to find out what's going on."

CHAPTER FIFTY

Angie sat in Kelly's Seafood Grill the next day, waiting for her brothers to join her. It wasn't a long wait. The siblings all greeted each other with wide smiles and a warm hug. The warm family reunion might soon turn ice cold. It's too bad that Patrice would have to be exposed to family drama. She was still kind of new to the family.

They ordered their food and got all the small talk out of the way. It was time Angie opened her bag of secrets. She told them their mother was in Japan handling some business. They talked about it briefly and got their questions out of the way. Angie exhaled quietly, glad she didn't have to do battle trying to explain where their mother was and why. It was time to tell her own truth. No more cover-ups on her end.

"Okay, everybody." Angie tapped her water glass with a fork to get everyone's attention. "Does anyone notice anything different about me?"

"Yep, sure do," Jayden proclaimed. "You're pregnant. We can all see that. I thought you and Jacoby broke up."

"We did end it. He's not the father. I'm not sure if you'll all be okay with this, but it is what it is. Marcus is the father. He's the father of my baby, and I love him." Angie snatched up her glass and sucked down a long gulp of water to moisten her suddenly dry throat.

Glances danced around the table from person to person and then back to Angie.

"Hold on. I know you are not talking about the same Marcus that our mother was dating and left at the house with you and Jayden the first time she left for Japan." Nelson's eyeballs had grown the size of a half dollar.

"Yes, the same one," Angie admitted, slumped back in her chair, and folded her arms across her chest.

"Just because you think you've found love doesn't make this right. I think it's downright disgusting. You do realize the man had sex with your mother, too, right? What kind of man does that? And what kind of daughter would stoop low enough to sleep with a man her mother slept with?" Nelson scooted to the edge of his seat and clenched his fists underneath the table.

"It wasn't planned, Nelson. It just happened," Angie tried to explain.

Nelson slammed his right fist down onto the table. The dishes clattered, and his water glass fell over, and water soaked through the tablecloth.

Heads turned toward them, and a hush fell over the room. "You shouldn't have let it happen. That's the kind of crap that sluts do. What in the hell were you thinking?"

"Nelson, lower your voice." Patrice placed her hand on top of her husband's rock-hard fist. "You shouldn't judge your sister," she said.

"My grandmother was right. She felt like something like this was bound to happen."

Jayden tried to say something, and Nelson talked right over him as if only he and Angie were at the table.

"I knew something was going on. His car was at the house when I drove up unexpectedly with Nana. But he was nowhere to be seen. Where was he, hiding under your bed like the coward that he is?"

"Enough, Nelson. I'm grown. I can do as I please, sleep with who I please, and make my choices, right or wrong." She grabbed the edge of the table with both hands. "You're not my daddy. You can stop talking to me like you are."

"Does Mom know that you screwed her man? She can't know, or she would have kicked your butt."

"Nelson, that's enough. You're talking to your sister. Don't be rude," Patrice counseled, touching her husband's arm.

"She'll know soon enough. Don't you worry about it." Angie placed her hand on her stomach.

"Man, this ain't cool. I can't go along with this bullshit, and now you are knocked up by the dude. He'd better be glad he didn't come here with you. I would beat his..."

"Calm down, Nelson," said Jayden. "You shouldn't talk to Angie like that. Marcus was good to us while Mom was away. He took care of us. I can see how it happened. I don't even think Mom was in love with him or anything."

"I don't care. It's still wrong, Jayden. They're both wrong; something is wrong with you and Patrice if you can't see that. Cancel my lunch. I'm out of here." He shot up from his chair, causing it to rock from side to side before all four legs were firmly back on the floor. "Let's go, Patrice." His head jerked to the right in her direction.

"You can leave. I'm staying to talk with Angie."

"Whatever. Do what you want to do." Nelson stormed out of the restaurant.

Angie sat sobbing while Jayden tried to comfort her.

"I'll talk to Nelson. Everything will be okay," Jayden offered with a hand on her shoulder.

"It's the initial shock that's got him worked up. It's going to be okay, girl. Try not to be so upset. It is not good for the baby," Patrice advised, squeezing Angie's hand.

"Thanks, Patrice. I'm so glad you came," Angie mumbled through the wad of emotion that clutched at her throat.

"Everything will be okay, Angie. Just give it some time," Patrice advised, glancing at the exit door Nelson used to escape.

Three weeks had gone by since the blow-up at the restaurant. Angie hadn't heard a word from Nelson. Three phone calls and four text messages, and he had not responded to either. If her brother shut her out completely, her mother's reaction would be much worse when she learned about Marcus and the baby. Angie shook her head from side to side as if she could shake the thought right out of her mind as she walked through the double doors of the county jail to visit her mother.

They sat across the table from each other with the hum of voices in the visiting room nipping at their ears.

"You're sure Nelson and Jayden believed I'm returning to Japan to take care of some business? They have no idea of the charges I'm facing?"

"Mom, relax. I promise. I didn't tell them anything about it." Angie dared to touch the tip of her mother's fingers with hers and drew her hand back quickly.

"You know I won't see you again until this mess is all cleared up. They're sending me back to that hellhole Japan tomorrow." Pam lightly touched her daughter's hand and jerked it back before the guard could reprimand her.

"Isn't there something that you want to tell me?" Her eyes landed on Angie's stomach.

Angie swallowed hard and decided to follow her mother's example and only cough up half the truth. "I didn't want to tell you because you're dealing with so much right now." Anxiety challenged her to stop there. But she leaped off the edge with, "I'm pregnant."

Pam offered a smile and soft words. "I didn't want to pressure you about it before, and I still don't. I know it's not easy for you. Be strong. Everything will work out, and you will be a great mother. Somehow, babies change us. You'll see. You're having my first grandbaby. How does Jacoby feel about becoming a father?"

A blatant lie wasn't cool. No need to dig a bigger hole she would have to climb out of.

"We only have a little time. I don't want to talk about that. Is there anything you need? One of the officers said I could get all the information I need to get money to you once you get to Japan."

"You've done enough. Don't worry about me. Take care of you and my grandbaby. I pray to God that I am back home before you have that baby."

They talked a bit longer, then cried and prayed together before Angie had to leave her mother. She walked away slowly with teary eyes, the unspoken fear of what was next for her mother, and a lie of omission between them.

As Pam walked in a long line of inmates waiting to be approved to leave the visiting room and be escorted back to her cell, she heard a familiar voice. That's him. I know it is.

"Why do you keep calling me Brianna? My mom is not going to be nice if she answers the phone and it's another collect call from you, especially from jail. When I wanted you, you had a thousand excuses for not having time for me. Your three-month rule was the main one. Yet, you took money from me like I was some sugar daddy or something. You drove my car until you finally decided to steal it."

Finally, the line moved enough for Pam to look around the corner to the next row of tables. "Jacoby, is that you?"

He turned to see who else in the jail would know him. "Yes," he said, glaring into the face of the person that called his name. "Miss Pam?"

"Yes, it's me."

Jacoby hustled up to her and stood a foot away from her. "What in the world are you doing here?"

"It's a long story, Jacoby. I suppose I could ask you the same question. Who is the girl you're visiting?" Why are you here visiting some girl while my daughter walks around pregnant with your baby?" Her right hand shot up to rest on her hip.

"Pregnant!" Jacoby took a step backward. "Miss Pam, your daughter is not pregnant by me. I promise she's not." His hands flew up in the air as he surrendered the truth. "Ask that dude you left at your house who the baby daddy is. I'm sure he'll know more about it than I do."

"What? How would Marcus know who...OMG! Are you saying..."

There was a river of distance between her and the inmate in front of her who had just left the waiting room.

"Lady, move. You're holding up the line. You've got to get back to your cell," the husky guard barked.

"Sir, I need to finish my conversation with that young man." Pam pointed her finger at Jacoby.

"That's not going to happen. Visiting hours for you are over."

Jacoby took two more steps back. "You better go, Miss Pam."

"Can I at least make a phone call? Please! It's an emergency. I need to talk to my daughter. I leave first thing in the morning. I really need to make a phone call." She pressed her palms together in front of her face in a praying motion as she pleaded.

"No! Now, let's go," the guard said, motioning with his hand for her to move toward the door.

"Please," Pam pleaded all the way back to her cell. No way Jacoby could be right. It just wasn't true. He had to be wrong about her daughter's pregnancy. But how could she get the answers she needed when the bars of a jail cell held her captive?

"Is it true, Jacoby? You and Angie got back together, and now she's pregnant?"

"Didn't you just hear me say that I am not her baby's daddy?" He sat back down across the table from Brianna. "That's her problem. I only came here to find out why you keep calling me. You used me, Brianna. I lost a great girl because of you. Tell me something." He leaned closer. "What did you do, and why did you try to get to Mexico? My car was found at the border after you borrowed it, correction, stole it—and abandoned it."

"It's a long story, Jacoby."

"You obviously don't have anywhere to go. So, talk."

"Well, you know that I have a son. I lost custody of my son to his dad a couple of years ago when he was an infant because of something I didn't do. The judge ordered only supervised visits. I love my son more than life, and it was killing me not to rock him to sleep at night. I was missing out on my baby growing up."

"Why didn't you just get a lawyer and try to get custody?"

"We did. I can't tell you how much money my parents have spent trying to get my baby back home with us. His paternal grandfather is a powerful politician, and he is obsessed with keeping my baby away from me. I couldn't take it anymore. I changed my identity and tried to take him away from them. I'm sorry that you got caught in the crossfire. I was desperate, and that's how I got here. They found me and arrested me. I've been here for weeks. I met Pam in here, but I had no idea she was Angie's mother."

"I kept calling to apologize and to thank you." She rubbed the back of her neck. Tension rested there.

"Thank me for what? Ruining my relationship with Angie?"

"Jacoby, you have to understand. It wasn't personal. You were the kindest person I'd met in a long time. I needed someone like you to help carry out my plan. Thanks to you, I was able to spend a month with my son. I'll cherish that time forever. I don't even know if I will ever see him again."

Jacoby looked past her eyes and deep into her. His heart began to soften for the hurt and empty young girl in front of him. "How much time did you get?"

"I have a two-year sentence. When I get out, I will fight for my son again and do it the right way." A single tear slid down Brianna's cheek.

As Angie made her way to her car, the cell phone in her purse rang, demanding her attention. She scooped it out in frustration. The name that flashed on her screen was an unexpected one. She stopped in her tracks and considered not answering. Seconds later, she pressed the button to take the call.

"Nelson, I don't want to hear ..."

"Clam down, hold on. I didn't call to fight. The bottom line is you're my sister, and I love you. It's your life; my job is to be your big brother, no matter what."

Angie pulled open her car door, climbed inside, and talked with Nelson for half an hour. Thank God, one storm in her life had passed.

CHAPTER FIFTY-ONE

Will she be safe? God please don't let my mother be afraid. She'll be there all alone. Tears burned Angie's eyes as she walked through Marcus' apartment door.

"Hey Baby," Marcus greeted her and kissed her lips with a peck. "I'm glad you got a chance to see your mother. I know you're worried about her. Everything is going to be fine."

"I hope so. I really hope so. I need her to be okay and free." She stepped out of her shoes and sat down in a chair at the table.

"I've got something that I know will make you smile," he assured her while placing a black velvet box in her hand.

She moved her fingers over the soft velvet that adorned the small box and then lifted the lid slowly. "Oh my, this looks expensive. Are you sure you can afford this?" Her eyes surveyed the bracelet as the light danced against the colorful prisms owned by each diamond.

"I don't want you to think that everything I buy for you is a strain for me financially. I work two jobs so I can do some things other than pay bills with my money." He nodded at the bracelet. "Hopefully, I will only be working one job soon. I'm taking the RN test for the second time tomorrow. I'm going to pass it this time."

She placed both hands on his face and kissed him gently. "I know you'll pass that test, baby. I have faith in you."

"I'm excited about getting my license. I will be able to do more nice things for you." Marcus bent down and kissed her growing belly. "And I'll be able to take care of our baby."

"I don't need expensive things to make me happy. I just want you. I never want you to stress your financial situation for me. It's not necessary."

"I understand that. I need to be in a better financial situation in general. I have a family now. I'm the provider, and I mean to be a good one. In the meantime, can you just enjoy wearing a diamond bracelet from your man?"

"Absolutely, I can." A grin claimed her face and lit up the dimples in her cheeks.

Marcus placed the bracelet around her wrist and secured the clasp.

Angie tugged at the clasp. No way was she going to lose the unexpected treasure she'd just been given. "I love you," she declared in a soft voice.

"I love you more," Marcus declared with a kiss.

Pam was no longer on U.S. soil. The steamy stench in the air in the jail welcomed her back to Japan. She finally remembered Hanai's phone number and contacted her with the first phone call she was allowed to make. She needed her to go to the shop where Dudley's weight loss device was taken from her on her first trip to Japan. She figured that since she was stuck there, waiting to go to court, that she should try to somehow connect with a buyer. Hanai agreed to help her and that gave her a glimmer of hope. She had to stay positive and encourage herself in order to keep from sinking into a pit of depression.

She would have to be found innocent of the murder charges she was facing because she was innocent. It was self-defense. The truth would have to come out and be believed, one way or another. Once she was free from the charges that dared to steal her life from her, she was determined to find a buyer for the device. Pam saw no reason to rush home. The hurtful reality that she couldn't push from her mind was the reason why. The thought of it pounded at her until her head hurt. Angie is having a baby with Marcus. The same man I was dating and had sex with. How crazy and disrespectful is that?

Three days later, she was able to make another phone call. This time it was a collect call home.

"What on earth are you doing back in Japan?"

"Mother, I had to come back to take care of some unfinished business. It's just something that I have to do. I should be back in Texas soon. I'm calling to tell you..."

Her mother's voice stepped on top of her words. "Pam, I really think you have lost it. Why on earth would you go back to Japan, and how did you get that kind of money? You are just doing too many things, girl. I received a portion of the rent money back from your landlord and he wouldn't even give me an explanation for sending it back. I heard he sold the house. Are you in some sort of trouble, Pam? Be honest, baby." She took a brief breath and continued.

"You refused to talk about the scars on your face. I know something terrible happened while you were there the first time. Why would you go back? What is really going on?"

"Nothing, Mama, like I said, I'll be back soon. This is an expensive call, and I don't want to run your phone bill up. I called to tell you that your granddaughter is pregnant."

"Pregnant? Oh, my Lord. I had a talk with that girl while I was there. I told her that she should be careful and not to get caught up like that."

"Mama...

"Darn it, Pam. This is a result of you being gone for all those months, and apparently for nothing. That girl didn't have her mother with her because you were in Japan chasing money like..."

"Mama, you..."

"Pam, you have to..."

"Mama, stop and listen to what I'm saying. Maybe all of this is my fault. But that does not excuse the fact that she is pregnant with Marcus' baby."

"What? Marcus? That's not true. Who told you that? Did he spread that dirty lie about my granddaughter? I put him out of your house when Jayden got hurt. I don't believe it. Angie wouldn't do anything like that."

"She would. She did, and it's done." Pam pulled hard on the steel cord to the phone.

"If she did, you can still blame yourself. You're the one who opened that Pandora's Box. How did you think this would all play out? I told you going to Japan would be a disaster."

"Mama, I don't need this right now. I know this is a big mess."

"Then tell me why in the hell are you back in Japan?"

"Okay, I will tell you. I had no choice. I'm in jail, Mama."

"Jail, you're in jail? What in heaven's name for?"

"You want the ugly truth? Here it is. I was raped in Japan by two sailors, and I stabbed one of them, and he's dead. I have to prove that it wasn't murder. Hopefully, they will see that it was self-defense."

"Pam, my goodness. This is just too much. Do the kids know?"

"Angie knows. She visited me while I was in the county jail at home. That's how I found out she was pregnant. She lied and told me the baby was Jacoby's. I saw him at the county jail while he was there visiting someone, and he told me the truth. The baby isn't his. Marcus is the father."

Her mother's voice trembled, "Lord, have mercy. What can we do?"

Pam heard her father's voice. "Pam, are you okay?"

"Yes, Dad, I was talking to Mama. Where is she?"

"She's here crying. She handed me the phone. What's going on? We're worried about you, and we love you. What can we do?"

"Pray, Dad. Just pray!"

CHAPTER FIFTY-TWO

Marcus cranked up the engine of Angie's car and looked down at his watch. The unexpected meeting at work had taken too much of his time. It was too late to get the tires rotated, and the oil changed. He figured he'd make a stop on the way home. After driving a short fifteen minutes, he whipped the car into the only empty parking stall, walked into the building, and planted himself on the bar stool next to his friend.

"What's up? I was shocked when you called and said you wanted to go to a bar. You know that's my thing. You've never been a drinker. It must be something serious going on if you want a drink." Marcus' friend D.—short for Darius—tipped back his beer, took a long gulp, then gave the bartender a quick nod to bring Marcus the same.

"Yeah, I know I just needed to hang out for a minute. I'm just dealing with some challenges on the job." Marcus tapped his fingers on top of the bar loudly.

"Aren't you still a nurse?" Darius asked as his attention shot up to the big screen TV to check out the score of the football game.

"Yeah, I'm still an LPN. I failed the RN test again. On top of that, I just lost my part-time job. They said they had to cut back. At first, it was down from five to three days a week: now, nothing. I just got the news today that they don't need me anymore. Does your old man still own that medical supply store?"

"Yep, he's still there. I go in and help him out every once in a while, just to give him a break. I don't know too much about medical supplies, though."

"Well, I definitely do. Let me know if he ever needs some help. I could use the extra cash." Marcus turned up his bottle and nursed it like he was dehydrated and sucking down water to save his life.

"Slow down." Darius motioned with his hand for Marcus to put the bottle down. "You don't want to make this bar scene a part of your life, even for unwinding. You have a great girl, and you are about to be a dad. Drinking and hanging out in bars is the last thing you need. It can only lead to bigger problems."

"I'm going to have a couple of drinks and see if that makes me feel a little better. Then I promise to take your advice, my brother, and head home."

"How's Angie?" A tall guy walked by Darius, stumbled, and almost knocked him off the bar stool. "Hey man, you need to watch where you are going," Darius warned.

"She's good and busy turning my extra bedroom into a nursery," he said, chuckling.

The proud father took his second beer from the bartender and wet his lips with it. "I'm going to have a son."

"Oh, that's great. Congratulations!" They tapped their beer bottles in salute of Marcus' announcement.

Another hour, two more beers, and two shots of gin later, Marcus decided he'd better stop turning up the bottles and head home.

"I'm really looking forward to being a father." Marcus stumbled over his words slightly, then admitted, "I think I've had enough."

"I think so, too. When is the baby due?"

"February seventh. I feel a little guilty about being here drinking, and she's probably home and tired from working today. I need to get out of here."

"Man, you got it bad. Angie got your nose wide open." They laughed.

"Yep, and I'm not ashamed to admit it either."

"You'd better keep her away from that crazy Cassie." Darius twirled his index finger around in circles, then pointed it at his head and crossed his eyes.

"Man, you're right. That broad does have some issues."

"Yeah, some Marcus issues. If you haven't been swinging that way lately, maybe everything has blown over by now."

Marcus gripped his beer bottle tightly and decided to keep his latest rendezvous with Cassie to himself. Hopefully, like Darius said, it had all blown over. "Two more over here, please, bartender."

"Slow down, buddy," Darius warned. "I thought you were leaving. Cancel that; we won't need any more drinks," he advised the bartender.

Angie walked through the door of Marcus' apartment with a shopping bag of the latest maternity fashions from the boutique that employed her. No way was she going with Marcus to his mother's for Thanksgiving and not look jazzy. Her round belly just wasn't going to stop that.

She dumped the bag of clothes onto the bed and schlepped to the kitchen and took a pot out of the refrigerator and placed it on the stove. The ringing cell phone interrupted her.

"Hey, big mama. What's happening?" Vanessa teased.

"Girl, just these pots and pans. I'm trying to get dinner done before Marcus gets home."

"Dinner, he should be cooking for you."

"He failed the nurse's licensing exam again, and he's been a little depressed ever since. He's worried about making sure we're okay financially when I go on maternity leave."

"Girl, if God couldn't afford this baby, he wouldn't have formed him in your belly."

"I know and I believe you, but you know how men are. It's a pride thing with Marcus. He wants to know he can cover everything without an issue."

"This baby will have the best of everything and the main thing he'll have is love." Angie put the lid back on the pot of steak and potatoes that was still simmering in brown gravy and rubbed her belly with both hands.

"Speak that thing, girl. With me as his godmother, you bet he will."

"I love you, girl. Thanks for all your support. I better get off this phone before I burn something up."

They wrapped up their conversation. Then Angie checked every pot and turned the burners down low on each one. She waddled over to the couch to rest for a few minutes. She closed her eyes. Thoughts of her and Marcus sharing their life with their baby painted a smile on her face. She was happy. Yet, there was a shadow of guilt that nagged at her daily. This could be the most exciting time in my life. I have a man who adores me, I am having his baby, and on top of that, I have a successful career. I'm winning, but I don't feel like a winner.

Angie was still troubled that her mother was in the dark about her relationship with Marcus. She hadn't kept secrets from her mother in the past. They'd always shared everything. She had finally confirmed with the jail in Japan that her mother had arrived safely and was there in custody. But that was all she knew. Had she been to court? Did she need money? Mama, why haven't you called me? Are you okay? Angie stewed in her pity pot of emotions. Minutes later, she pushed herself up from the couch when the doorbell rang. A blonde-haired officer with blue eyes stood face to face with her when she opened the front door. A second officer stood next to him.

"Ma'am, do you know a Marcus Blue?" The blonde-haired officer questioned with a firm unemotional tone.

"Yes, I do. Is he okay? What's wrong?" Angie took a step closer and held onto the doorknob so tightly that her racing pulse could be felt in her hand.

"He's been in an accident."

"Jesus!" Angie pressed her hand against her chest, as if trying to steady her heart. "Is he okay? What kind of an accident?"

"It looks like he hydroplaned, and his car flipped several times. You probably need to hurry. We retrieved his driver's license from his wallet and found this address. He's been taken to Dallas General Hospital," The blonde-haired officer advised. "Would you like us to drive you there?"

"No, thank you. I appreciate you coming to tell me. I can get there on my own." She hurried inside, turned off the stove, and rushed off to the hospital.

A few days after Marcus was released from the hospital, his depression was obvious. He tried his best to be positive when Angie was around. His left leg was broken in two places, and it made a smile for him almost impossible. The weight of his depression was dragging him down day by day. He was angry at himself for drinking and driving. It rained the night of the accident. Wet pavement and alcohol combined could have caused him to kill someone or himself. He should have listened when Darius insisted on driving him home.

He lay on the couch with his leg propped up with two pillows. Raindrops traced slow paths down the windowpane, and the darkened sky turned the Friday afternoon somber—fitting his mood: pure gloom. He replayed the accident over and over in his head. What if he'd killed himself and never had the chance to see his son? On top of that, the trip to San Antonio to visit his family for Thanksgiving had to be canceled.

He tossed the tenth wad of paper at the laundry basket of clothes sitting at the end of the couch. Two had landed in the basket, and eight were on the floor.

Angie strolled into the room, stretching her arms up to the ceiling and releasing a soft yawn. "I needed that nap. Your son is wearing me out."

Marcus' guilt and insecurities introduced themselves to Angie right away. "I just got off the phone with my supervisor at the hospital, and she told me there would need to be a hearing before I could return to work." He pounded his good leg with his fist. "It was just my luck to end up in the emergency room of the hospital I work for that night."

Angie sat on the arm of the sofa next to him and massaged his neck. "Baby, don't stress yourself about it. It's done and over with, and things will be alright." She planted a gentle kiss on the side of his face.

"Now I know why I don't drink. Me drinking that night just made matters a whole lot worse. I was upset about losing one income, but now I'll likely have no income at all. On top of that, I totaled your car. I'm so sorry, Angie," Marcus admitted it, his eyes holding her gaze but his foot tapping nervously against the side of the sofa.

"It's okay. I don't mind driving your fancy sports car for a while," Angie teased with a weak smile. "Just be patient and let your leg heal properly. I'm still working and tucking away some money to get us by while I am on maternity leave." She kissed his lips softly.

However, the sweet taste of her lips didn't hypnotize him this time. "That's the problem. That's exactly the problem. You're tucking away money to support us, not me. That's my job. I'm the man, and it's my responsibility." He snatched up the crutch that leaned against the back of the sofa and hurled it across the room.

CHAPTER FIFTY-THREE

Jayden had completely turned things around—both in school and in his attitude—and was now on the right path. Doug got a good report from each teacher as he moved from classroom to classroom, meeting his son's teachers and discussing his performance.

Doug's attendance at the parent-teacher conferences had rendered more than a good report on his son. He'd also met someone he believed to be a good woman, who had just happened to be Jayden's science teacher, Ms. Lang.

The attraction was immediate. The two started dating shortly after they met. A couple of months had gone by, and things were going well. Maybe it was time to let Jayden know about his involvement with Ms. Lang. Sitting at the mahogany dining room table across from his son, who was studying his next chess move, Doug decided to test the waters. "So, Jayden, how do you like your science teacher?"

"She's cool. I hear she's gay, but that's none of my business. Why do you ask?" Jayden inquired without taking his eyes off the chess board.

Each player was left with a king, a bishop, and seven pawns on the board. Jayden's focus was intense as he plotted a way to win the second game in a row.

"What do you mean you hear she's gay?" Doug's line of view landed directly on Jayden's mouth, waiting for his reply.

"Well, that's what most of the kids say about her, especially when they get upset about their science grade. I know that doesn't mean it's true. Why, Dad, did you meet her?"

"Yeah, I met her a few times at the last parent-teacher conferences. I told you that. Don't you pay attention to anything I say?"

"I guess I do remember that now. If you think she's cute, throw some of that thug thizzel on her, Dad. Who knows, old Lesbo Lang might change her mind."

"Hey, don't be disrespectful," Doug admonished, tapping his knuckles on the table.

Jayden looked up at his father. "Sorry, I didn't mean to be."

Maybe I better dig a little deeper into this woman before I announce that we're dating. Pam would never let me live it down if she found out I was dating a lesbian. Doug rubbed his stomach to soothe the sudden pang of concern that nudged at him.

On the other side of the world, Doug was the very least of Pam's concerns. Visiting time was almost up. Pam tried to give Hanai as much information as possible. "Be careful asking questions about the device and the names on that piece of paper." Her eyes searched the room as she passed the paper to Hanai underneath the table. "Those are the two names Dudley told me Chu would deal with regarding the device."

"I will see what I find. Have friend that maybe help me."

"When I get my money from the sale of this thing, you and your mother will be compensated for you kindness and your help. I promise. I won't forget you."

The chatter in the room was busy and consistent. There were lots of inmates and visitors, but the guards had full control, and they let it be known the second the noise level got too loud. The lonely, sad spot in her heart drove Pam to confess Angie's betrayal to Hanai and the hurt it caused her.

"I have to figure out a way to accept Marcus, my ex-lover, my grandchild's father, and possibly, someday, my son-in-law. I don't know if I have that in me."

"You have it. It's called forgiveness. He was your lover, not your husband. Your love for your daughter overrides everything. You will see. You will love each of them," Hanai patted Pam's hand and offered her a confirming nod of her head.

"Inmates line up," a husky voice commanded.

It was confirmed. It was time to go back to the dark, dusty cell that confined her.

CHAPTER FIFTY-FOUR

While her mother struggled with how to accept the little family that Angie was building, Angie and Vanessa were in the middle of a secret shopping trip. The white flowing gown in the big display window of the Bridal shop beckoned to Angie.

Vanessa sat back in the plush high-back chair, nibbling on fancy chocolates as Angie tried on one wedding dress after the other. When she walked out of the dressing room for the twelfth time, Vanessa rose to her feet to meet Angie.

"Girl, that is the one. You can stop right now," Vanessa proclaimed with bright eyes and a grin across her face.

The white gown was embellished with a lace overlay, a sweetheart neckline with intricate beading. It flowed from the bust outward. So, the fact that Angie was pregnant didn't matter since the waist was loose and flowing.

Angie reached for the dangling price tag. The four numbers that screamed back at her drained the excitement from her face. Marcus wasn't working, and her income had to cover everything. Maternity leave was in her near future, and she had to spend her money wisely.

"How much is it?" Vanessa demanded.

"Vee, it doesn't matter. I can't afford it. I don't know why I even came in here. Thanksgiving is only four or five weeks away. I have a lot of people coming into town. I can't afford to purchase anything this expensive." Angie lifted the long-laced train and draped it over her arm.

Two women strolled by the bride-to-be. "What a gorgeous dress. You look stunning," the young woman carrying a wedding dress to the dressing room told Angie.

Vanessa clutched the swinging price tag and held it in her hand. "Ma'am, we'll take this dress." She waived the salesclerk over with her free hand.

"I can't let you buy this dress. $2,500 is way too much money."

"Listen, girl, that is the perfect dress, and you look amazing. It's my treat. I want to do this for you. You deserve it."

"Are you sure? That's a lot of money."

"I have some money saved up, and I think you, Marcus, and my godchild will be a great investment." Vanessa whipped around, snagged her purse up from the chair, and whipped out her credit card. "We'll take it."

Angie covered her face with both hands and let them slowly slide down her face. "I cannot believe you. This is an unbelievable gift. You've been my best friend since sixth grade. You have always had my back." She pressed her fingers against her bottom eyelids to prevent the tears welling up in her eyes from falling. "Thank you! Thank you!"

Vanessa hugged her friend. "No problem. It will be worth it to see you pull off a surprise wedding to a man who doesn't know he's getting married."

"Let me get out of this dress, and we'll go to lunch, on me. I'll give you all the details."

After Vanessa paid for the dress and Angie was measured for the alterations to the dress, they headed off to lunch. They talked about the wedding and the fabulous gown that Angie would dazzle everyone with, especially Marcus.

As soon as Angie parked Marcus' car, they climbed out and noticed a curvy, attractive woman boring into them with a hot gaze that moved up and down their bodies and back to their faces.

"My goodness, what did we do to get her attention?" Vanessa asked, annoyed and loud enough for the woman to hear her.

"Oh, was I staring? I didn't mean to. It's just that your friend looks so familiar. What's your name, if you don't mind me asking, sweetie?"

"Sweetie?" Angie said with a wrinkled brow. "My name is Angie."

"Oh, I'm sorry. You're not at all who I thought you were. You, ladies, enjoy your day," said the tall woman with flawless skin and hazel eyes. She walked over to a burnt orange Camaro with a woman waiting in the passenger seat.

Angie explained to Vanessa that Marcus' sister and her husband were renewing their wedding vows. Marcus and Angie would stand with them but do more than be a witness at their wedding ceremony. Marcus had mentioned marriage to Angie several times. She always changed the subject. But things were different now, and so was her heart.

"Since his accident had spoiled our visit to San Antonio, his parents and sisters agreed to come to Dallas to visit him for Thanksgiving. This will be the best surprise ever."

"Girl, that is so cool. I hope Marcus appreciates you. You know how to take care of that man. Speaking of your man, how's your mom? Oops, sorry, girl," she said, laughing.

"Very funny, Vee, but seriously, I have no idea. I haven't heard from her. I have to keep busy, so I don't go crazy worrying about her. I miss my mother. If I could talk to her, I would be honest about everything. Something I should have done before she left."

"Is she still in jail?"

"As far as I know, she is. Like I said, I haven't heard from her." Angie wasn't the only one worried about her mother.

Patrice answered the landline and handed the phone straight to her husband. The Caller ID helped her avoid the drama smoldering on the other end of the line. "It's your Nana, honey."

"Nana, what's going on?" Nelson asked as he stood looking out the bay window in his living room. Two squirrels struggling over food on the ground held his attention.

"Darn it, boy, I don't know what's going on. You kids have totally left me in the dark about everything. Did you know that Marcus guy was sleeping with your sister when we went to put him out of your mother's house?"

"No, Nana, I didn't know," his attention fled the window and the two squirrels.

"Well, I guess it's Angie keeping all these secrets. She didn't call you or me and tell us that your mom was in jail and had been forced to leave her house?"

"JAIL? What do you mean?" Nelson demanded as he walked to the chair and planted himself on its arm.

"I knew my mom had to go back to Japan to take care of some business, and I knew she had to move. Patrice and I went to help Angie pack up her house. No one said anything about jail. Why is my mother in jail?"

"Your sister knows about all of this. She was the only one that your mom confided in. I'm sure she will tell you if you ask her. I talked to Pam last night. That's how I found out that Angie got herself pregnant by the man your mother left to watch Jayden. I knew that was a bad idea to begin with. Pam's poor decisions have gotten everyone snagged up in a big net of mess. I hope your mother is mistaken about this pregnancy thing. I just can't see Angie being that careless. This thing just can't be true."

"It's true. She is definitely having a baby." Nelson slammed his fist into the air, landing a silent blow. "Unbelievable, my mom is in jail."

His loud voice had summoned his wife back into the room. Patrice embraced him and pulled him into her thin arms that offered him strength. Silence filled the phone line, and the spacious living room suddenly felt very small.

"Baby, can I get his phone number from you?"

Nelson searched through his phone until he located a text message from Marcus and chanted the number off to his grandmother. "Now, Nana, tell me what's going on with my mother?"

"You need to call your sister. She's known all along. I have to go now. Pray for her and try not to worry too much. I have to believe that she will be home soon. I love you."

"Love you, too."

They couldn't end the call fast enough. Nelson called Angie, and his grandmother called Marcus.

CHAPTER FIFTY-FIVE

Over the next few weeks, Marcus had physical therapy daily for his leg. Doctors assured him it was healing properly. Yet, his consuming depression mounted daily, and the verbal tongue-lashing he'd just endured added to it. He glared at the cell phone still in his hand. Angie's grandmother's words crawled through his mind and set his nerves on edge as considered the bitterness of her statement.

You can't take care of my granddaughter. You are not the man for her. You had the nerve to sleep with my daughter and my granddaughter and then think that you will be accepted into our family. It will never happen. Her words stung and nipped at his heart. They were all words he'd said to himself.

The front door swung open and the gush of wind and leaves that were whirling around outside barged right in with Angie. Marcus stepped out onto the balcony and closed the door behind him. He couldn't face Angie at that moment. He needed a moment to steady himself—he couldn't let Angie see how worried he really was. Soon, he would have to make a hard decision. He couldn't come between a mother and her daughter—or tear a family apart. He couldn't afford a girlfriend who he thought would be his wife and a baby. He couldn't even pass the test to become an RN. So, what made him think he could afford a baby—or that his relationship with Angie wouldn't eventually tear her family apart?

Angie didn't notice him as she walked toward the bedroom, since she was engulfed in a conversation with Vanessa. "Does Marcus know you're bringing his family here next week?"

"Girl, no, it's a surprise. I think he could use a pleasant surprise after what he's been through lately. Through it all, he still puts me first. He's been so sweet. He even sleeps in the extra bedroom, afraid that he might hurt me with the cast on his leg. It's been a while since we've slept together. But it's okay. He's so worried about money that he just hasn't been himself." She tied the bow to a gift she bought for Marcus' mother.

"Goodness, he's still sulking about money."

"I've tried convincing him that I can manage our finances. It does no good at all. He believes a man should take care of his household financially. He thinks I will eventually resent him. He's said that to me more than once. The call from my grandmother didn't help. I told you about her calling and going off on him, didn't I?" She stretched her legs out across the bed and shoved two pillows behind her back.

"Yes, you did, and I felt so bad for him."

"Well, last week, she and I had a long talk. She told me Nelson was okay with Marcus because he could see I've never been happier. I think she's having a change of heart, too. She kept saying that she loved me and that it was important to her that she and I were close. I got a check in the mail from her a few days ago for five thousand dollars. Her note told me to take care of things until Marcus gets back to work." The sun burst through the clouds for the first time that day, and the bright sunlight seeped into the dim bedroom.

"Girl, are you serious? Can I have your grandmother?" They both burst into laughter.

"I paid the rent up for a couple of months and took care of all of the bills, and I still have money left over."

"That's awesome girl. It's about time your folks came around. This baby does not need all that drama."

While Angie enjoyed the cease-fire between her and her family over Marcus, her mother was in a definite battle for her life on the other side of the world. Pam's trial date was fast approaching, and her sleepless nights ate away at the little hope she clung to. She talked to her mother whenever possible, who kept her abreast of what was happening in her kids' lives. She pushed the thought from her mind that tugged at her to call Angie. Nothing she could do about all the things that were unraveling at home. Freedom had to be her focus.

Had Hanai been lucky enough to track down the man with the scar on his chin? He was the man who had tried to give Pam a ride home and protect her from the likes of the two men who'd raped her? Did she know how to find him? The man who she had been rude to, the one she'd shown no appreciation to for his concern for her. The only clues Pam had given her were his name, Andre, he had a scar on his chin, he was tall, he might be found on the Navy base, and he looked like he could take down a giant. Lord, please give her a little help.

The next day, Pam was told to go to the visitor's room. It had to be Hanai coming to visit her because there was no one else on her side in this foreign land.

At Pam's request, Hanai had located another person who could help with her case. Pam asked her to look for him on the Navy Base. Hanai received help from a Navy friend who was willing to assist her in locating the six-foot-six stranger with the keloid scar. It was the mystery man who was waiting for her in the visitor's room.

His name was Andre Crayton. Right away, Pam realized a strong attraction between the two of them. He was just as kind and patient as she remembered. She felt ashamed about the way she'd treated him, but he obviously didn't hold it against her. Surprisingly, when he saw her, he smiled and said, "So, we meet again." He not only wanted to help get her acquitted, but he also wanted to help make sure the other sailor who attacked her was arrested. He was the one who had injured Pam's jaw.

Soon after their first meeting, his mission was complete. The other assailant was identified and arrested. He went back to the jail to inform Pam. She was barely able to choke out the words, "Thank you." There was no way for her to know, the night they met, that he was not only a naval officer but also an attorney. Andre and Pam talked and got to know each other through his visits with her. He, too, had experienced drama and heartbreak. He shared with Pam that his ex-wife informed him by mail that she was divorcing him. He'd been stationed in Japan for a little over two years. After eleven years of marriage, distance and the demands of serving both his wife and his country had torn their relationship apart. They had two daughters. However, Andre found out later, after demanding a DNA test, that the second child wasn't his. His daughter and only child was now thirteen years old.

Once he had delivered the good news to Pam, he didn't want to leave—and found himself sharing things he had never intended to divulge. "The first night I met you at the club, I found you very attractive and enticing. Your hardcore exterior was even amusing to me." He leaned back in the wooden chair and gazed hard across the table at Pam.

"I'm not even sure why I wanted to help you out of the mess you've gotten yourself into. When Hanai found me and told me you needed my help, I immediately remembered you and how you refused to let me help you in the first place. I knew those guys were up to no good."

Pam's eyes shot down at the rusty table and attempted to stay there. But his handsome face and kind voice drew her gaze back to his.

"I started to tell her no. There was nothing I could do. You didn't want my help when I offered it that night at the club. You were reluctant to even let me ensure you got home safely. I wanted to say that you should know how to treat people who are trying to help you." He tumbled a coin between his fingers. "But I just couldn't do it. Something compelled me to do all that I could to help you convince the authorities of your innocence."

He shoved the coin down into his pocket. "How did you know that I was an attorney?"

"I didn't. I just hoped you could be a witness or something since you knew I went home drunk, and those guys were there at the club that night." Pam offered him a half smile. "Now, I have a question; what is the sadness behind your eyes? You've been here to see me, help me drive this case, and call in favors with people you know. But no smiles, and you don't even know me. What can I do for you?"

He was honest with her. Something he'd asked her to do when he first agreed to help her with the case. At forty-five years old, he would retire in another month and go home alone to the house he'd bought in New Mexico. He had suffered a great deal of heartache and pain because of his divorce, and from finding out that the child he loved was not his daughter. His mother had met and married a man fifteen years older than her. She'd married him for his money but eventually fell in love with him. After a few short years together, he became very ill. When he died, he left most of his wealth to her. Sadly, his mother died a year later of a massive heart attack. His mother left all her inherited wealth, twenty million dollars, to her only child, Andre.

After he'd told Pam of the heartbreak in his life because of his divorce, learning the daughter he'd raised wasn't his, and then the painful loss of his mother, he gambled with a raw truth. "I can't explain it; I've tried to fight it. But something about you makes me not want to see you walk out of my life. You asked what you can do for me. My answer is let me get to know you. Let's not let the end of this case be the end for us."

Pam thought God had forgotten about her. She was sure she'd done too many things wrong to expect God to do anything good for her. She knew now that she was wrong. Andre offered her hope that love, happiness, and even freedom could be hers again.

CHAPTER FIFTY-SIX

Marcus was excited and surprised that Angie had gone through the trouble of getting his family to Dallas for Thanksgiving. Maybe he shouldn't leave Angie. Just try to put his pride aside and hope that his lack of finances won't choke the life out of their relationship. He loved her, and she got along well with his family. Those thoughts would be short-lived. Marcus looked on as his mother handled the cooking with plenty of help from his sisters.

"Angie, honey, you go over there and sit down," Marcus' sister, Gabe, directed. "We don't want your feet to swell up like grapefruit," she chuckled, pointing down at Angie's plump ankles.

"That's right. We have a big day tomorrow," said the youngest sister, Carmen.

"Shhh. It's a surprise," Gabe snapped.

"What surprise?" Marcus inquired, scooping down into a pot with a spoon.

"Okay, since big mouth over there just let the cat out of the bag, Harrison and I are renewing our vows tomorrow in the Botanical

Gardens Ballroom. He wants you to be his best man. He won't be here until morning, but I brought a tux for you both. Will you do it?" Gabe pleaded with both palms pressed together in a mock prayer.

"Of course, sis. I would love to. Why is it a surprise? You guys are celebrating ten years, right?"

"Yep, that's it. We just wanted to surprise you, and do it while we were here for Thanksgiving, and you and Angie could be a part of it." Gabe released a wide grin and tossed a wink over at Angie.

"How do you know if my tux will fit?"

"You can thank Angie for that, baby brother."

"Man, this girl leaves no stone unturned. I didn't even know she knew my measurements." Marcus lifted Angie's feet and slid a pillow underneath them.

"Never underestimate a woman in her third trimester," Angie giggled.

Laughter rippled through the kitchen and living room.

Marcus scanned the room filled with family and the woman who'd stolen his heart. He would have a son soon. He and Angie would start their own holiday traditions. Maybe even have more than one child. What she wanted was what he wanted. For that to happen, his money had to get right. He had to pass the test to be licensed as an RN.

His dad's voice snatched him from the fog of thoughts that made him wonder how he could pull it all off.

"Are you keeping up the tradition and naming my grandson Marcus?" His dad sat on the couch amongst all the women turning his head from the sports channel to receive his answer.

"Well, Dad, that's up to Angie. I'm letting her choose the name."

"Son, are you okay? You've been acting a little preoccupied since we got here."

"I'm good, Dad. I just have some things on my mind. Got some tough decisions to make, that's all."

"You're right. You're about to be a dad. Being a parent isn't easy. Playtime is over. Another life more important than your own will be counting on you. Our children are the greatest gifts we could ever receive. It definitely takes two parents to raise them. You're on the right track. I'm proud of you, and I'm looking forward to the wedding."

Marcus was puzzled by his father's statement. He had to be referring to his sister renewing her wedding vows the next day. "Yeah, so am I," he replied.

The next morning, Marcus headed off to get his cast cut off. The examination went well, and the doctor was pleased with the way his leg healed after he removed the cast. Perfect timing since he had to wear a tuxedo for his sister and her husband at the ceremony. On the drive home, he felt some pain. But nothing he couldn't deal with.

Marcus wanted to get back to work as quickly as possible. He called the hospital to schedule his reinstatement meeting for Monday. He'd let Angie continue to use his car until he could buy her one. He felt he owed her that much because he'd totaled hers the night he'd gone out drinking.

CHAPTER FIFTY-SEVEN

Mia read the wedding invitation that Doug placed in her hand. Mia and Doug had found love. Occasionally, they'd share a laugh at the thought of Doug thinking she was gay. Mia was glad she didn't give up when Doug tried to push her away. She knew something wasn't right when he'd started to be distant with her. When she confronted him about it, he told her about the gossip going around that she was gay. She couldn't help but tease him. "You sure you want to walk in the room with a gay escort on your arm." She tapped the invitation with her index finger.

He peered into her honey-colored eyes. "Please, all that good loving I'm throwing down on you; if you had been gay, you would've had to come over to the other side by now."

Their laughter brought brightness into the room that wasn't there on a cool, dim winter day, even with the skylight overhead and every blind in the room open. Jayden trotted into the kitchen, headed straight for the pot that simmered and released a compelling smell that pulled him to it.

"Miss Mia, I've gained five pounds since you started cooking for me and my dad." He lifted the top off the pot and inhaled the intoxicating aroma. "What were you guys laughing about?"

Doug and Mia both responded at the same time, "Nothing."

"Hey Dad, Nana said my mom will be home soon. I can't wait to see her."

The water seemed to have settled on all fronts with Jayden, Angie, and even Pam, hopefully. Some things were about to change. Not all of them would be good.

CHAPTER FIFTY-EIGHT

The response from the hospital regarding Marcus returning to work had delivered an unexpected hard blow. His supervisor informed him that since the incident that caused the injury to his leg was alcohol-related, the board felt it would be unethical for Marcus to continue his employment at a hospital that prided itself on hiring staff that the community and families could trust their care and lives to. "I'm sorry, Marcus. I really I tried." The words of his supervisor were stuck in his head. He had no other options. His fate was sealed.

Marcus went home to change into his tuxedo. The apartment was empty. He tried to reach Angie on her cell phone. No answer. After fully dressed, he opened his closet door, snatched clothes from hangers and dresser drawers, and stuffed them carelessly into two suitcases and a duffle bag. He would have to grab the rest another time. He couldn't stay there and allow Angie to take care of him while he had no income to contribute. He was in no mood to go to a wedding, much less participate in one. Yet, he had no choice. He'd promised his sister, and there was no way he was going to let her down.

Marcus loaded his bags into the car and drove to the nearest and cheapest motel. He slipped the key card into the slot and pushed open the door to his room. His eyes assessed the dingy carpet, the worn linen on the bed, and the dim lighting that left the room dark in the middle of the day. He showered, got dressed, and headed to the Botanical Gardens Ballroom to play the role of a best man who was happy and excited about the day. He would have to find the strength to play that character.

The family members spilled into the room for the ceremony. The place was nearly filled to capacity. Music played throughout the hall, serenading the guests with "Ribbons in the Sky" by Stevie Wonder. Various hues of purple and beige adorned the room's decorations. The caterers and other staff members put on the finishing touches. The room was small and intimate, prepared for a party of sixty people. The bubbling champagne fountain in the corner teased Marcus. A drink was just what he needed.

The groom took his place at the altar shortly after Marcus arrived. He saw his best man and gestured for Marcus to take his place at his right side. No one could've guessed by looking at Marcus that a wedding was the last place he would've chosen to be. He was handsome, wearing a beige tuxedo with tails. His hair was cut low, and his mustache and beard were groomed to perfection.

He shook hands with the groom. "You're looking good. You sure you want to say those vows for a second time?" Marcus nudged his shoulder.

"Wouldn't have it any other way. I got a wife that I love, and she completes me."

I know the feeling. Marcus sucked in his own truth with a quiet breath. "My sister deserves the best. You definitely seem to be giving her everything she wants because I know it wasn't your idea to renew your wedding vows. Aren't people usually married for at least twenty-five years when vows are renewed?"

Harrison shrugged his shoulders and responded with a weak grin.

Marcus patted him on the back. "Just love each other, brother, and be happy."

Soft music commanded the start of the wedding ceremony. A hush swept over the room. Marcus scanned the crowd as more guests entered. Where is Angie? She's probably somewhere helping the bride. He peered over at the door again, but still no Angie.

The overhead music slowly faded, and the organ player began the traditional wedding march. One of Marcus' sisters slowly walked down the aisle, followed by another. The sister who was to renew her vows, Gabe, came down the aisle next. To Marcus' surprise, she was not wearing a wedding dress. His eyes searched for Angie. Where was she?

The guests all stood to receive the bride. Marcus nudged his sister's husband and whispered, "All right, you're on."

He glanced over at his parents and got a goofy grin from his dad. It was then that Marcus noticed Angie's family. Why would Jayden, Doug, and his girlfriend come to see his sister renew her vows? They didn't even know her. Why would Nelson's wife and Vanessa be sitting in the front row? Both flashed Marcus a puzzling grin.

Marcus looked beside him and behind him. What in the hell was going on? Were they smiling at him or Harrison? Where was Angie? Why was Gabe at the altar with them while the wedding march was being played as if the bride had yet to stroll out?

Harrison stepped to Marcus' right and gently pushed him into the spot next to the minister. Just as Marcus was positioned in the correct spot, Angie appeared in the doorway, dressed in a beautiful white wedding gown. Nelson escorted her down the aisle, past family and friends. Cameras flashed, and tears dropped across the room.

Angie's eyes and bright smile were locked on Marcus. Her bottom lip trembled slightly even as she smiled. With no concern for her makeup, the glowing bride allowed tears to slide down both cheeks. The tears were bittersweet. She was marrying the man she'd fallen in love with. Her mother hadn't been so lucky. She was in jail in another country and couldn't share in her happiness. Would she even be happy for her if she knew the man her daughter was about to marry was the same man that she'd shared a bed with?

The pastor's strong, baritone voice stirred Marcus from his daze.

"Who gives this woman to be wed to this man?"

"I do," said Nelson. The big brother kissed his sister's cheek and took his seat next to his wife.

Marcus did what came naturally to him whenever he was nervous. He bit his bottom lip and scratched his chin. Then he looked out at the smiling faces in the audience. Apparently, he was the only one in the room who didn't know he was about to get married. He latched onto Angie's eyes with a burning look that spoke to his anger. He leaned over and whispered to her, "Angie, what the hell are you doing? Whose dumb ass idea was this to blindside me with a surprise wedding? Why would you do this without talking to me first?" His lips were tight, and his eyelids so narrow that his eyeballs were barely visible.

"I don't want to get married. Not like this, not right now."

She shook her head slightly. "What? What did you say?"

"You heard me. How could you do this to me? This is some bull. Did I ask you to marry me, and you accepted? Tell me because maybe I forgot."

Time stood still as she wondered how to deal with the most embarrassing moment in her life. The music stopped, and a complete blanket of silence had fallen over the entire room. The pastor wore a wrinkled brow and tapped two fingers on the Bible he was holding.

Angie cleared her throat and turned to face her guests. "I'm sorry. The man I love just informed me that he doesn't want to get married." Angie tried to spit out the next word, but emotion wouldn't allow it. She burst into uncontrollable tears and whimpered like a wounded puppy.

Marcus opened his mouth, and before one syllable was uttered, Nelson jumped up and ran toward him with both fists clenched. He punched Marcus in the face with a quick left and right combination. Marcus fell to the floor, and Nelson got down on one knee, continued punching him in the face, and cursing him. The two men wrestled across the floor, then tumbled off the podium and right down to the feet of the first row of guests. Nelson's wife leaped up, screamed his name, and pleaded with him to stop. A wave of people headed to the front of the room.

"Stop it. Stop it right now. This is a holy ceremony," the pastor admonished, with a rumbling voice as he lifted the Bible into the air.

Men from both families finally pulled Nelson off Marcus and stopped the fight. But not before Marcus' left eye was swollen shut, his lip busted, and blood painted his white shirt red. Both families were confused about how the wedding could have become such a disaster. Marcus' mother had been restrained by his sisters. She stood nearby, confused and furious. "Marcus loves this girl. What could cause him to act this way? This is ridiculous," she said aloud while launching a lethal visual assault in Nelson's direction.

"Maybe she shouldn't have surprised him," suggested one of his sisters.

"What difference does it make? He calls her the love of his life. So, what if she surprised him? What is he waiting for? What he did was stupid and selfish. They're already having a baby. What's left to do but get married? He even told me he wanted to marry her." Marcus' mother snapped back with a sharp tongue and a swivel of her head.

Angie's grandmother shook her head in frustration and tried, along with Jayden, to comfort Angie.

Marcus pushed himself up from the floor and stumbled out of the building. A trail of blood followed him.

Darius arrived late after changing a flat tire on the way to the surprise ceremony. Marcus shoved his way through the sea of people right past him without making eye-to-eye contact. Darius tried to help Marcus and was pushed away with a hard shove.

"What in the world is going on here?" Darius questioned the crowd.

"Just let him go for now. I'll talk to him," Marcus' dad told Darius.

Less than twenty minutes later, Marcus slammed shut the door of his motel room. His head was pounding. Pain crawled through his leg. Each step he took felt like his leg was being cut from his body. He limped to the bathroom and hung his head over in the sink. The cold water from the faucet pooled in the palm of his hand. He buried his face into the water. Marcus did that three times, then stood to face the man in the mirror.

His reflection mocked him while his voice was laced with pain. "Stupid, stupid, stupid! What the hell did I just do?" Marcus stared at the angry man in the mirror with one eyelid closed shut. His finger gingerly assessed the swollen eyelid. His lip was sore and swollen, too. The tears that swelled in his eyes burned and slipped over his eyelashes and down his cheek. He couldn't stand the sight of the man staring back at him. He broke the mirror with one thunderous blow, and pieces of glass crashed down into the sink. With a bloody hand and a broken heart, Marcus retreated to the bed and collapsed.

The shrill of his cell phone exploded in his ear, antagonizing his brutal headache. He silenced the cell phone but was unable to silence his thoughts. *Angie will probably never speak to me again. Damn! What the hell just happened? My life is a mess.* The miserable man let out a loud yell that sounded like the growl of an angry bear. He then pushed himself up from the bed, snatched the lamp from the bedside table, and slammed it into the wall.

Marcus' phone had squealed several times in the last hour. He hadn't answered anyone's calls. He thought about turning it off. But if by some miracle Angie called, he wanted to know about it. He finally answered a call from his father. He gave him directions to the motel and waited for the sound of his father's voice, which he was sure would be laced with anger and disappointment.

A firm knock at the door caused a jolt of tension to move through him. He opened the door and met his father's stern gaze. Marcus Blue Sr. reached out and wrapped his muscular arms around his son. He held him close for a few moments. Then, he walked through the door and sat down in the chair by the bed.

"Have a seat, son," he directed, patting the edge of the bed. "What happened back there? Is that what you were talking about yesterday? Was that the tough decision you had to make?"

Marcus rubbed his sweaty palms together. "I had no idea Angie was planning a wedding. I'd asked her to marry me, but she hadn't agreed for more than one reason. The wedding was a complete surprise to me."

"I thought you knew all about it. Don't you remember me saying I looked forward to the wedding?"

"Yes, but I didn't think you were talking about my wedding. Both people need to know when they're taking such a huge step in life. Don't you agree, Dad?" He needed someone on his side.

"Yes, I do agree, but you love her, though, don't you?"

"Of course I do—very much! She knows that. I guess that's why she thought this would be a good idea. Still, she should've talked to me first."

"If you really love her, what's the problem? I don't understand," his father stated with a firm pat on Marcus' shoulder.

"I lost my job, and I am still not an RN yet. I don't have a way to take care of a wife and baby right now. Because of me doing something stupid, I may not even be able to keep my LPN license. I don't know what else I can do if I'm not a nurse."

"Why? What did you do?"

"I didn't tell you and Mom what caused the accident. I had been drinking."

"What? But you don't drink." His father leaned back and tilted his head to the right.

"I know; I got frustrated when my part-time job laid me off. I know it was a dumb idea, but I called a buddy to go out drinking, of all things." Marcus dropped his head into his hands and allowed his palms to slide up and down his face as he pressed his elbows into his knees. A wave of pain sparked through his leg.

His father's cell buzzed in his jacket pocket. He fished it out and checked the caller ID. "It's your mom. What should I tell her? Are you going back to the apartment?"

"No, Dad, I'm the last person Angie wants to see. I think I'll just stay here for a while and maybe come over to the Hilton and hang out with you guys a little later."

"You owe Angie an explanation. If you really love this girl—then show her. Let her know. Don't make her wonder where your head is about you guys. Besides, she doesn't need extra stress. Know this above everything; your child needs his dad, and his mom does too."

Marcus nodded, walked his father to the door, and wrapped his arms around him. "Thanks, Dad. I appreciate you and your wise counsel."

CHAPTER FIFTY-NINE

Marcus wasn't the only one unsure of what was happening with him and the woman he loved who was about to have his baby. Angie rode back to the apartment with her grandparents and Jayden. Her voice was heavy with emotion. "Nana, I'm sorry you guys came all this way for nothing."

"I just don't understand that man, Angie. When I called to chew him out about being with you, he went off on me just a few weeks ago. He talked about how you loved each other and would be married, whether I liked it or not. Then he does this. What is he, bipolar? Didn't you guys plan this together? Why would he change his mind at the altar?"

Angie lifted her head from her grandmother's shoulder, which was heavy with thoughts. She shifted her weight to face her. "He didn't know about the wedding. I wanted to surprise him. I've been planning this ever since his accident. He'd asked me to marry him more than once. I said no, not until my mother could accept our relationship and be there for the ceremony. He's been so depressed and worried about money because he couldn't work. I just wanted him to know that I love him no matter what."

Angie sniffed hard as her grandmother dabbed at her tears with her handkerchief. "I asked his family to come here for Thanksgiving. I told them about the wedding. His mother was excited. I just don't understand, Nana," she admitted, sobbing and sniffling.

Mrs. Carter pulled Angie into her embrace and spoke softly, "It's going to be okay. Maybe he was upset because he was in the dark about everything. If it's meant to be, then all of this will work out. If it wasn't for my great grandbaby in there," she said, gently rubbing Angie's full belly, "I'd be hunting Marcus Blue down like a bloodhound. And, when I found him, I'd give him a piece of my mind and a clunk upside his head with my purse. You know I can't stand for anybody to mess with my babies." They both chuckled.

CHAPTER SIXTY

Angie was alone. All her guests, including her brothers and grandparents, had returned home. For days, she came home to an empty apartment. She cried herself to sleep each night, wondering where she had gone wrong with Marcus and why he hadn't called. Maybe she shouldn't have tried to surprise him with a wedding. Who does that? Her hormones must have made her brain take a brief vacation. The fact that the wedding was a surprise couldn't have been the only reason he didn't want to get married. They'd talked about it. He'd asked her to marry him, and she was the one who had refused. What was going on with him? The big bed was empty without Marcus. His pillow teased Angie in the dark. Silent whimpers kept her company until sleep claimed her sadness.

Marcus struggled to sleep as well. Against his better judgment, just like the night he almost got married, he found himself at Cassie's, where else but in her bed. She looked a little different. Her hips had spread, and a pudgy stomach peeked over the top of her jeans. Definitely, some extra pounds had found her. He lifted his wrist to study the face of his watch. Two hours had gone by, the deed was done, and he still had his socks and watch on. There had been no reason to get too comfortable. He hadn't come there to make love. It was all about sexual healing. Now, it was time to make a quick exit.

Marcus hoisted himself up straight and, swung his legs over the side of the bed and reached for his pants.

Cassie spoke to his back. "The look on Angie's face was priceless. I should have snapped a picture," she laughed.

"What do you know about Angie?"

Cassie told him about the day she'd met a pregnant woman named Angie and her friend outside a restaurant. "Angie, your little girlfriend; you know, your almost wife. The day I met her, she was driving an expensive sports car, just like the one I helped you pick out."

Puzzled, Marcus twisted his body to look over his shoulder at the woman who knew more than she should have.

"If you still say you don't know anyone named Angie, then I'm sure that was just another coincidence, right? Just like the wedding she planned for you. You did almost get married, right?"

Marcus bolted from the bed and stepped into his pants. "What are you talking about? Who told you that?"

"I saw it for myself. It's okay. You proved that you love me. I'm not even tripping. You lied about her the last time you were here in my bed, sexing me up and down and calling out her name. I did a little investigating. I was at the wedding, and I realize you chose me when you humiliated her in front of everyone." She circled the bed and stood in front of him. "You finally came to your senses. When you called me the evening you were supposed to get married, that was confirmation that you chose me over her." Cassie poked him in the chest with both index fingers. "You know you saved that girl's life, right?"

He stepped both feet down into his Jordans and didn't lace them up.

"What the hell are you talking about?"

"If you had married Angie that day, you would've had to bury her the next day. You can't seriously think that I'm going to let her just take you from me. I told you, this thing between you and I, it's for life." Cassie placed the palm of her right hand onto Marcus' chest, then put her other hand on her own chest. "I gave you my heart, and you know that. You will not play in my face, walk over, or use me. And that tramp can't have my man." Cassie stepped back and allowed her eyes to roam his body, starting with his penis, down his legs, and up to his cinnamon-brown eyes. She tilted her head and snapped her fingers twice. "All of that belongs to me. You better remember it."

Marcus yanked his shirt down over his head and snatched up his keys from her nightstand. "Cassie, I have to go. That day had nothing to do with you. You stay away from me, and I promise to stay away from you. I was wrong to come here. Stay away from me and stay your crazy butt away from Angie."

"What did you just say to me? Crazy, you think I'm crazy. You're the one that better stay away from Angie. I'm going to show you crazy." She lunged forward like a lion attacking its prey.

Marcus grabbed her arms in midair and flung her down onto the bed. "You are crazy; I was crazy not to see it." He retreated to the front door with wide strides pursuing an exit from the lion's den.

Cassie got to her feet and chased him down before he could turn the front doorknob. "You liar, you're a cheat," she screamed and scooped up the lamp from the table and launched it at his head.

Marcus spun around to face her. "Hey, you almost hit me with that. What is wrong with you?"

"I meant to hit you with it. I'm crazy, remember?"

"Stay away from me," he demanded with flaring nostrils and gritted teeth.

He fled with Cassie following him down the steps and to his car. He yanked the car door shut, locked the doors, and fired up his engine. He snatched the gear shift into reverse. Something hit the car before he could shove it into drive. A loud noise came from the rear end. Looking in the driver's side mirror, Cassie had kicked a dent in the back door of his car.

Marcus slammed both fists into the steering wheel twice, shoved the car into drive, and tried to stomp his foot through the gas pedal. The car's rear end jerked hard, knocked Cassie to the ground, and jetted off like a missile.

"You are a lying dog. This is not the end. I will have the last word. Your beloved Angie will for sure take her last breath." She stood to her feet and yelled at the sports car that left a trail of dust behind that slapped her in the face.

CHAPTER SIXTY-ONE

The sound of a judge's gavel shook Pam from her daydream. Her head jerked from side to side. Where was the judge? Her attorney wasn't sitting beside her. She wasn't even in the courtroom. But it seemed so real. Yet, the female guard sitting next to her in the back of a squad car was indeed real. She was being transported to the courthouse. It was the first day of Pam's trial.

The breeze that commanded the movement of the few leaves still clinging to the trees was brisk. Tussles of leaves and paper sailed down the sidewalk. As the police car rolled to a stop at the red light, a woman latched onto Pam's face as she gave her attention to the woman sitting in the back of a police car. Pam willed her to move on down the street and stop judging her with her eyes.

Pam's right leg had a mind of its own and would not stop shaking. She pressed the weight of her arm down onto her leg to control the noticeable trembling. That didn't help. Her nerves were on edge, and her leg felt like it was being attacked by a thousand little needles stabbing away at it. Pam squeezed her eyelids tightly and began to pray. Lord, I finally get it. I have made so many mistakes. I was disobedient, arrogant, rebellious, controlling, and I've been living in denial. Now, I can see my bad choices and foolish thoughts. This crazy situation that I've gotten myself into has forced me to really see myself. I don't have all the answers; I can't do it all on my own. I need your guidance, and I have to put my children first and not let my desire for money and worldly gain consume me.

Thank you, Lord, for loving and protecting me amid the insanity that has been my life over the last year. I understand now that you know what is best for me, and I need to trust you. During the raging storms that have been my life, a blessing came out of it all, Andre. Whatever happens in court today, I know that you are with me. In Jesus' Name, Amen!

Pam's eyelids popped open when the squad car hit a bump in the road. She glanced out the window and focused on the words on the Tokyo High Court building.

After a four-day trial, the sound of the gavel crashing onto the wooden block was real. It sounded like a freedom bell to Pam. Her body shook when the gavel made its powerful impact. She rubbed her palms together under the table as she sat beside her attorney. She was frozen in her chair, and it felt like time stood still. It wasn't until her attorney spoke that she exhaled.

"It's over. You are free to go. Congratulations!"

The trial was over. Pam was acquitted. The verdict was self-defense. She faced her attorney and whispered, "Thank you. Thank you." Emotions made her voice weak and tremble. Gratitude forced her arms around her attorney.

She cried as she hugged Hanai and then Andre, who had helped her attorney tremendously in the fight for her freedom. Hanai and Andre were why she was free and not lost in a foreign prison system.

Andre pulled a credit card from his wallet and suggested the two ladies enjoy a spa day on him. "I'm sure a day of pampering yourself and shopping should be relaxing for you," he told Pam, giving her hand a gentle tug. "I'll meet you both at the Wei Chan Restaurant at 6:00 p.m. Have a good time. It will be therapeutic for you, Pam."

"This is unbelievably generous of you. Thank you so much." Pam folded her arms around his neck and inhaled the scent of his soft, masculine cologne. "I can't believe it's over. The nightmare is over." Her head fell back, and she glanced up at the ceiling. "Thank you, Jesus!"

Andre stepped back, took her hand, and placed his cell phone into her palm.

"What's this for?" Pam questioned.

"Call your family. I have international calling. Let them know that you're coming home."

The word home slayed her. That did it. She let go, and the floodgates opened wide as she leaned into his chest and wept. Home, she was going home to her family.

Hours later, Andre scanned the crowd, searching for Pam and Hanai as he sipped the strong, dark cognac to calm his anticipation. The ladies walked in laughing like children toting several bags each. The Auburn highlights that dusted through Pam's silky mane swept across her shoulders and danced with every stride she took toward Andre. He drank in her beauty and held his breath without thought of any other woman in the room. Her hot gaze made the burn in his mouth travel down his throat, set fire to his body, and then stroked the desire building between his legs. She stopped within a breath's distance from him.

"You're absolutely stunning," he declared and turned up his glass, sucking down all its contents before his thoughts became words. He needed to be hosed down, but the liquid that slid down his throat would have to do for now.

"Thank you. You certainly can take the credit."

"Not at all. It all belongs to you," Andre proclaimed, willing his eyes not to roam her body and latch onto her bosom, which was full and disturbing his manhood. "Would you ladies like a drink?"

They drank, talked, and laughed for over an hour. Hanai prepared to depart. Her excuse was that she needed to get home and see her mother. Pam swung around and hugged her new friend with a strong embrace and assured her she would visit her before leaving for the States.

She turned around to face Andre and met a familiar shaped box he held at eye level. The quiver of nerves that stole her voice would only allow her to stand motionless and question him with her eyes.

The man who had helped her to gain her freedom slowly opened the lid of the box.

Pam's eyes were swollen with surprise. It was Dudley's weight loss device. "Oh, my God. Andre, how did you get this? How did you even know about it?" The people talking and moving around them, the music and noise from the room filled with lots of people were suddenly all silenced. Pam only heard Andre's voice.

"Hanai, she told me everything. I had to strongarm a couple of guys, but I set up a surveillance system in the house you stayed in next door to Hanai. I knew they would return to that house until they found the device. I connected with the guy that designed the chip that needed installing to make the device fully functional." He opened the small compartment underneath and pointed to the chip.

"Are you saying that the piece I came here for has been installed, and all I have to do is return it to Dudley and collect my money?"

"That's it. Now, I have to get you out of here before those guys looking for this thing find out you've been released. After we meet with Dudley, you will need to stay with me in New Mexico until it's safe. I want to make sure the last two guys that were paid to get the device at any cost are behind bars."

"Where do we meet, Dudley?"

"In China. We'll fly out this weekend to Tibet. We'll only be there long enough to deliver the gadget and pick up your cash."

"You don't know Dudley. He may refuse to pay me and try to take the device. He did say the buyer he had lined up had him on a deadline to deliver. We're months past that time frame."

"Trust me. He won't. He's already been contacted, and everything is taken care of. I'll be with you, and you'll get your money, or he won't get the device. You'll be five hundred thousand dollars richer when it's over."

Pam could not believe her ears. She was in awe at the turnaround her life had made in just a short while. Things had been bad for far too long. She cried, laughed, and she cried some more. "What about my kids? My daughter is graduating college next week, and I can't miss that. I want to see my children and my parents." Her hands were moving along with her lips to express her excitement.

"Slow down. We will work it all out." The tall man stood over her and gently placed his hands on her shoulders to assure her things would be fine.

Pam traced the scar on his chin with her finger. "You are perfect, kind, gentle, and so giving. I keep pinching myself to be sure that this is real." She kissed his lips softly. "Why are you doing all this for me? You don't even know me."

"I really can't explain it myself." He stepped back to lean against the bar stool and realized someone had slid into his seat. "Excuse me, sailor. I didn't see you there."

He and Pam had been standing on an island in their own space and time, and no one was present but them.

"I guess we've been standing here talking for a while now." Andre slipped his hand into hers and laced their fingers together. "I don't really have an answer for you that makes any sense. All I can tell you is the truth. You deserve to be happy, and I want to be the man to make your heart smile." He lifted the back of her hand to his lips and pressed a warm kiss against her soft skin.

The unstable waters of life seemed still now. Yet Pam would soon realize the raging storms and harsh winds in her life had not all settled.

CHAPTER SIXTY-TWO

Angie was reading a text from Marcus when Vanessa rang the doorbell. She folded the long-laced train of her wedding dress and gently placed it into the box.

"What are you doing?"

"I want to get your money back. I am so sorry it went to waste for a botched wedding."

"I don't need my money back. I told you that you and Marcus are a good investment, and I still believe that." Vanessa gently shoved her friend's shoulder.

"Girl, stop; that ship has sailed." Angie chased the comment away with shifting eyes that rolled up to the ceiling and back down to the dress.

"No, it hasn't. You still love Marcus, and he loves you."

"Oh, yeah. What gave it away? When he refused to marry me while we were standing at the altar?"

"Angie don't be so hard on him. Some of this is your fault, too. Sit down and get off those swollen hooves of yours," she advised, pulling out the chair at the kitchen table for her.

Laughter eased the thick haze of tension that was mounting.

"Surprising him with his family was a wonderful gesture, and I know he appreciated that. But a wedding is not something you surprise a man with."

"Maybe you're right. I've been thinking about that, and my grandmother said the same thing."

"Well, you know that old bird is full of wisdom." Vanessa bent over laughing.

Angie's laughter turned into hiccups, which demanded that she nurse the eight-ounce glass of water in front of her.

"I was wrong to do that and even told him so. But he could have handled things differently that day. He's been sending me text messages all morning. He said he loves me but can't financially support us since he lost his job. I keep telling him that doesn't matter to me."

"I know what you're saying. But you scared the heck out of the man." Another text message sang out with a buzz to Angie's phone. Angie handed her phone to Vanessa so she could read the message.

I still love you. Someone out there can take better care of you than me. I didn't pass my test, and my nursing license might be revoked because of the accident in your car. I have no income at all. I'm at a dead end in my life, somewhere I've never been before. I refuse to bring you down with me. You deserve to be happy.

"Where's his faith? That's stupid. I cannot believe that he would be willing to let another man raise his son because he fell on hard times. Girl, you guys need to talk. You and Marcus are both messing up a good thing." Vanessa twisted in her chair, placed both palms flat on the table, and leaned close to her friend. "I know people who would kill to have what you two are throwing away. I'm out of here. Call your man, straighten out this mess, and let him come home."

Angie snorted out a light snicker. "I don't know about all that, girl. What did you really come over here for?"

"I came to tell you I have the most fabulous baby shower planned for you. I have a list of people to invite. Take this list and add to it or take away from it." Vanessa pushed the list toward Angie.

Angie latched onto the corner of the list. Vanessa didn't let go. "Get the list back to me soon. Don't forget to tell your man to come home." Angie pushed the door closed behind her friend and pressed her palm hard against the wall. Her feet hustled to the table, and she snagged up her cell phone. Her fingers stroked the keys hard and fast with a sincere text message.

I just wish you'd been honest with me. I'm sorry that I surprised you. I know now that I was wrong. Can you forgive me? I don't want another man to raise our baby. If you're in a storm, I want to be in the storm with you. It's called for better or worse.

Angie dropped the cell on the table, startled when it rang out. She grabbed it up and wasn't sure if she would answer. What was he going to say? Was he breaking it off for real and just wanted to say the words aloud to her and not send it in a text? What? Only one way to find out. She swallowed her fear and slid the green icon on the screen to the right. His voice climbed into her ear.

"Did you read my entire text message? I said that my nursing license might be revoked. I am not in a good place right now. I don't even have a job."

"I understand that, Marcus. I don't care. Do you hear me? It doesn't matter. It won't always be like that. You'll get a job; we will have this baby, and things will be better than good. But right now, I need you." Her right hand landed on her round belly as she stroked the baby, doing summersaults and making her nauseous. "Come home, baby. Just come home."

A few moments of silence taunted the line. Then, his heavy voice dismissed her concern. "I'm on my way, baby."

CHAPTER SIXTY-THREE

Pam and Andre sat side by side at the American Airlines departure gate. Japan was their destination. It would be a brief trip and a joyous occasion this time since his retirement was one of the reasons for the journey. After that, a one-way ticket to New Mexico would be a happy purchase.

Pam tried to finish up her conversation with Angie before her final boarding call. "I'll be home soon. I can't wait for you to meet Andre." Her gaze shifted to him sitting beside her, reading the New York Times. "I know we've talked about it. I still have to ask you again to forgive me for my harsh thoughts about you and Marcus. I am very sorry for shutting you out. I was hurt and blamed you and Marcus for my own mistakes. I wish you the best in every area of your life, including your life with Marcus."

Her daughter swallowed the ball of emotion in her throat and croaked out, "I love you, Mom. Thank you for understanding about Marcus and me. I can't wait for you to be a grandmother."

The final boarding call announcement overhead ended their conversation.

"I will see you soon. Got to go, honey. Love you."

The couple of days they spent in China couldn't have gone fast enough. Now, they were in sunny New Mexico, drinking in all the privacy and warm weather and get-to-know-me time they could handle.

Foothills and mountain views, an open floor plan with floor-to-ceiling windows, glossy hardwood floors, and skylights in every room, including the bathroom, had cast a spell on Pam. She didn't see how a retired Navy officer could have such a lavish lifestyle. She slept in late each morning and woke up to fresh fruit, croissants, eggs, bacon, coffee, and fresh flowers. The handsome man who labored for her freedom was attentive and kind.

They had grown close quickly, and the unspoken sexual tension between them was understood. As much as Andre wanted to make love to her, he hadn't pushed it. He knew she'd lived through a nightmare with the rape and trial. He wanted her to feel comfortable and safe. She would have to be completely ready to give herself to him. There could be no regrets afterward. The woman he cared for had slept in his arms but hadn't given him her body. He was willing to wait for her heart.

Scented candles offered a sultry ambiance on the lanai. Soft music played in the background while Pam and Andre shared life experiences over a bottle of Merlot. Their conversation took a turn down some dark paths that unveiled heartbreak and regrets. His honesty, soft kisses, a warm embrace, and the sway of her hips to the rhythmic beat of the music confessed her readiness to give him her body. The dim light of a new morning found them spent having met each other on the mountaintop of ecstasy, and now they rested in the valley of satisfaction. Their private time together went by too quickly. They promised to run off together again soon. But just a few days later, they had to leave paradise.

Angie's University of North Texas graduation wasn't as smooth as she hoped. Her mother and Andre were the life of the party that day. Pam was happier than Angie could ever remember seeing her. The family took to Andre quickly, and that had been a relief. There had been enough drama circling the family that year. Pam and Marcus were cordial, and there didn't appear to be any bitterness lurking overhead.

Nelson, however, was another story. He was still very angry with Marcus and didn't even want to hear his name whenever Angie tried to talk about him. Though he had made an effort for Angie's sake to make peace with her about Marcus, it would take more time for the air to be clear between Marcus and Nelson. That's what Angie hoped for. The Christmas Holiday was next, the baby shower, and then a baby boy would hopefully make all the rough spots smooth in her family.

It would take a job to make things right for Marcus. His nursing license had been revoked. He would have to find work in another field until he could get his license reinstated. He struggled to find a job that paid decent money. Marcus leaned his back against the wall across from the balcony door and dialed the number on the back of his debit card to see if his unemployment check had been deposited into his account. He pulled at the short hairs of his mustache and tapped his foot while he waited for the balance. The expectant father couldn't stand still.

He stepped out onto the balcony in the brisk weather, needing a few minutes to get his head on straight if that money hadn't hit his card. What would he do? He needed to take care of some things and didn't want to ask Angie for a dime. She was about to have his baby and would be on maternity leave in two weeks.

Marcus considered the slow-falling white snowflakes that colored the ground. A new year was fast approaching, and it needed to bring new opportunities. He glanced up at the sky and told the bright stars that belonged to God the promise he'd made. "I will keep my word.

As soon as I find a job, I'll propose to Angie. My son will have my last name, and so will his mother." He offered up a few words of prayer when the recording announced that his unemployment funds were now available for immediate use. Marcus pushed back the sliding glass door and stepped into the warmth of the living room.

"What are you doing out there in the cold?" Angie inquired, entering the room.

"Just getting some fresh air and thinking."

Angie stood in front of the glass door next to him and studied the clean white snowflakes that were falling. "I can't believe it's snowing in Texas."

"You know it will be gone in the morning. This is definitely a rare occasion. Let me ask you something. Is there anywhere else you would like to live? Maybe somewhere that it does snow every year. Tell me where you would like to make a home for our children."

Laughing, Angie said, "Children? Let's get this one squared away first." She considered his question for a moment. "I don't know. I've always thought Florida would be a wonderful place to live. Why do you ask?"

"Well, one day, I want to build us a house. It doesn't have to be in Texas if you would rather live elsewhere."

Angie released the anxious smile that parted her lips. "I love you. I believe you will do just that." She took his face into her hands and kissed him softly and slowly.

That's what he would give her this year for Christmas, hopes and dreams. But one day, he would hand her keys to the house he promised.

CHAPTER SIXTY-FOUR

In twenty-four hours, the baby shower would be in full effect. Angie and Marcus' family would be front and center for the action. This time, no punches would be thrown. Angie remembered the brawl at the altar during her almost wedding. She shook her head to toss out the image of Nelson punching Marcus.

"You okay, Angie?" Pam probed, touching Angie's shoulder as her daughter steered the car.

"I'm fine. Your grandchild just keeps kicking me." No need to get her mother upset about the battle between Nelson and Marcus.

The grandmother-to-be rubbed her daughter's stomach in a circular motion. A pear-shaped 2-carat diamond ring sparkled at Angie with its majestic prisms of color, which teased her.

Angie sucked in a big breath and lifted her mother's hand to within inches of her face. The car swerved. A screeching horn called Angie's attention back to the road, and she steered the car over into her lane. "Are you...are you engaged? That ring is stunning."

Andre's strong voice climbed into the front seat with them. "Your mother has accepted my marriage proposal, and I am such a lucky man." His hand found Pam's shoulder and squeezed gently.

"We haven't set a date. We thought we'd wait and set one while we're here with everyone. The ceremony will be held in New Mexico, and we want the whole family to come."

"Really, Mom?" Excitement stood up in Angie's face and then plummeted with the thought of the expense. "That's going to be expensive. With a new baby and Marcus just starting a new job, I'm not sure we will be able to swing the cost of a trip like that. Can't you get married here? I don't want to miss it." Angie's wide eyes shot up to the rear-view mirror as they pleaded with Andre. Here, get married here.

"You're not going to miss anything. Everyone is coming for a whole week. The flight, hotel, and food are all on me. I want everyone to have a good time," Andre promised with a grin as he popped a stick of gum into his mouth.

"Oh, my goodness, that is wonderful and so very generous of you. Thank you, Andre. Thank you so much for making my mother happy." They talked about the wedding the rest of the way to the hotel.

Marcus' family arrived earlier the same day. They'd gone out to dinner and were just finishing up. Between the travel to get there for the baby shower and their full bellies, the Blue family was ready to nestle into their hotel rooms.

Mr. Blue Sr. massaged his bulging stomach and confessed, "I drove too many miles today, and I've eaten too much food. I need to find a pillow and a bed."

His daughters chimed in with agreement. Marcus' sisters left the table first to visit the restroom just as the waitress deposited the bill onto the table. Mr. Blue whipped out some cash. "Keep the change."

The young girl thanked him and trotted off with a nice tip.

"Go ahead, honey, give it to the boy," Mr. Blue, Sr. instructed his wife.

With a wide Cheshire Cat grin, she removed a small black box from her purse and deposited it onto the table in front of Marcus.

"Open it," she told him, giving the box a nudge closer to him.

"What is it?" Marcus swept up the little black box and lifted the lid. A shiny diamond ring glared at him.

"It was my mother's. It's an antique that was made in 1930. I wanted you to have it. When you're ready to propose, you won't have to worry about buying a ring. I know you'll eventually get Angie a ring you choose, especially for her. Then that ring can be a family treasure that continues to move down the Blue family line, maybe even with your son."

Marcus drank in the ring's beauty. The European cut diamond center stone was accented by two-channel set baguette cut diamonds on both sides. The ring was unique, with sixteen genuine single-cut diamonds that circled the other three stones. The ring was crafted with a solid platinum band.

"I don't know what to say. It's gorgeous and unique. You're giving it to me? How did you know that I plan to propose to Angie soon? Now that I have a pretty good job managing one of Darius' father's Medical Supply stores; I can plan for marriage." The overwhelmed son glanced over at his dad. "I'm so grateful to have a job."

"Son, I know. A man has got to feel some worth about him. That's a hard thing to do when you can't take care of your family."

Marcus stood up from his chair, pulled his mother up from hers, and folded her into a grateful embrace that swallowed up her short, small frame. "Thank you, Mom; this ring is such an incredible thing for you to give me. I love you."

His mother hadn't seen tears fall from her son's eyes in many years. He was a man. But today, he was her baby. She kissed her son goodnight. Everyone left the hotel ready for a good night's sleep.

The next morning, Marcus stretched his long arms up toward the ceiling while his wide-open mouth bellowed out a loud yawn.

"Goodness, the way you were tossing and turning last night, I'm not surprised that you're still tired," Angie declared.

He sprayed on Angie's favorite cologne as he looked into the mirror in their bedroom. "Yeah, I didn't sleep too well. I've never been to a baby shower, and everything is so expensive. We're going to owe Vanessa a fortune. I can't imagine what she spent putting this baby shower together." He turned to face Angie and swept back the strands of hair that dared to dangle over her eye.

She kissed his lips softly, then parted them with her tongue, distracting him from his needless worries for a few seconds. Angie sealed the kiss with a gentle nibble on his bottom lip.

"Okay, you keep kissing me like that, and you and I will be late for the baby shower."

"You just finish up so we can go. And you're right, Mr. Worry Wart. We couldn't afford it, but my mother said to spare no expense for her grandson. Vanessa took her up on it. She paid for everything. She went all out."

"Wow, so your mom hit the jackpot with that Andre dude, huh?"

"Well, I think he's pretty wealthy, but my mom collected the money Dudley promised her for going to Japan."

"No way!"

"Yes, and we are reaping the benefits of some of it, today. Now, I need you to do me a favor, babe," she painted on lip gloss and stepped back from the mirror.

"Anything for you, beautiful."

"Are you sure about that? I know how you hate going to the mall. I promise I'm not going to shop. I have a makeup appointment at the cosmetic counter, and I'll pick up the diamond bracelet you bought me at the jewelry store on the second floor. I snagged it on something last week and broke the clasp. We need to leave now if we're going to get to the shower on time."

"Yes, ma'am, let's do this. I'll sit in the car and listen to music while you get your face put on. It shouldn't take that long, right?"

Angie snickered and shook her head. "Let's get going."

Marcus' cell phone rang in his pant pocket. He slid it out and checked to see who was calling. The familiar number and name stared back at him, challenging him to answer. No time for drama. I don't know why she keeps calling me. I haven't answered her calls, and I'm not going to. He silenced the phone and shoved it deep down into his pocket.

"Who was that?" Angie wanted to know.

"Just some fool that I don't have time for," he responded, hoping he wouldn't be interrogated.

An hour passed, and Angie was still inside the mall. The makeup consultant handed a mirror to Angie, who could not believe how smooth and beautiful her skin looked after the makeover. "I look pretty good for someone almost nine months pregnant," she told her reflection.

"You look great. I'll bag your makeup selections and get you out of here in just a couple of minutes," the consultant promised.

Marcus waited patiently in the car, his head laid back, his earbuds planted in his ears, and he listened to music. He searched hard for the song he wanted to play at the baby shower during what would be an unexpected proposal to Angie. There was nothing to hold him back now. He had a job and a beautiful ring to offer the woman he loved.

An incoming phone call interrupted his music. He answered without checking to see who was calling. A loud, frantic voice pounded in his ear.

"We did it. Everybody's life is about to change. We did it. I told all of you that it would happen. Nobody believed me."

"Wait a minute, slow down," Marcus said. "I can't understand you."

"It's me, Uncle Billy. We finally hit!"

"Hit what? What are you talking about?" Marcus inquired, sitting up tall in his seat.

"Boy, we finally hit the lottery. I have a ticket in my hand worth a hundred and seventy-five million dollars. Hold on. I'm getting another call."

Marcus hustled out of the car and headed toward the double doors of the side entrance to the mall. He felt a jolt of adrenaline spurt through his body. His heart rate was elevated, and he was sweating. He yanked the cap off his head and wiped at the beads of water on his forehead. He had to tell Angie. She wouldn't believe it. Money, the family had money. He had money.

Just as he reached the doors, his cell phone vibrated in his hand with a text message. He'd almost forgotten that he was still on the phone with Uncle Billy, who had him on hold. A second text message hit his phone. He pulled the door open, stepped inside the mall, and summoned up the text messages.

So, you got two baby mamas, huh? You must think I'm a fool. Her name's Angie, right? She just happened to be the same Angie I saw outside of a restaurant driving a car just like yours. The same Angie that you almost married. Yeah, that was me behind the tinted windows of the car that you were trying hard to look into.

I hate that bitch. I told you to stay away from her. I want her to die. And why should you care? You denied her. There is no Angie, remember? You are a lying, no good dog. She won't have your baby. I'm the only baby mama you're ever going to have. There are minutes between that bitch and death.

CHAPTER SIXTY-FIVE

Marcus stared at the words in the text message until they were blurry. Desperately, he stabbed at the keys on his phone to punch out a response when Uncle Billy's voice screeched through the phone line.

"Marcus, are you still there? Can you hear me?"

"Uncle Billy, I'll call you back. Angie's in trouble."

Cassie's threatening words that drove Marcus out of her apartment weeks ago flooded his memory. You saved that girl's life when you rejected her at the altar.

"Hey man, you're blocking the door," a male voice advised Marcus.

Marcus was still frantically texting.

"Hey dude, you need to step out of the way."

This time, the louder, firmer voice penetrated Marcus' brain. He stepped aside, never looking up, as he punched out the last words of his text message to Cassie, **I'll kill you**.

Marcus ran through Macy's with wide eyes, his jacket flapping open and his head jerking from side to side, searching for Angie. He passed the empty make-up counter and ran out into the middle of the mall, knocking over anything and anyone that got in his way. He sucked in a deep breath that stung his chest as he slowed to check both ends of the mall. He searched deep into the sea of people moving around and stopping at store windows. No Angie or Cassie in sight. She was in the mall somewhere. He needed to lay his eyes on her quickly before he collapsed and gave over to the panic attack that was coursing through his body like poison.

He ran up the escalator to the jewelry store on the second floor. Angie had to go there to pick up the bracelet. Once inside, he described her to the lady standing behind the counter.

"She picked up the bracelet but left her purse on the counter. Her sister came back and grabbed the purse."

Angie doesn't have a sister. Cassie, it had to be Cassie. Marcus slammed his fist into his right hand and dashed out of the store. It appears he'd covered the mall. Where could Angie be? He was afraid he was running out of time. Maybe she had gone to the car. By the time he made it downstairs and back out to the parking lot, his phone buzzed with another text message. He swallowed the lump of fear lodged in his throat as he opened the message.

Well, this is just perfect. Little Miss Angie and I are about to get on the escalator. Guess what? She's going down, literally. LMAO!

Marcus grabbed his head and screamed, "God, help me," and sprinted back inside the mall. He reached the middle of the mall on the ground floor and saw Angie approaching the escalator. He yelled her name repeatedly. The mall was flooded with people, many of which were watching the dance troop perform. There was no way she could hear him over the loud music.

Cassie was nowhere in sight. Maybe he could get to Angie first. He hustled through the waves of people, tossing out an "Excuse me, let me through," here and there.

As he got closer to the bottom of the escalator, his eyes met Angie's. A smile crawled across his face when she lifted her wrist and tapped on the repaired diamond bracelet.

Angie stepped onto the escalator, heading down to Marcus. He held onto her with his eyes. A small sense of ease attempted to rest upon his mind until Cassie stepped onto the escalator behind Angie. Fear claimed Marcus' heart and stabbed at it like the sharp end of a knife.

Cassie lifted her hands slowly, tossed Marcus a wide, toothy smile, and mouthed, "I told you." She shoved Angie with the force of a bulldozer and let go of a hearty laugh that she was sure Marcus would feel in his soul.

Angie tumbled down the escalator moaning and clenching her stomach. People screamed as the pregnant woman crashed at the bottom of the escalator.

Cassie turned and ran up the escalator that was moving downward. Her cryptic laughter bellowed through the air as she fought against the escalator to get away.

Marcus hurled curse word after curse word at Cassie and pointed his index finger at her like it was a weapon. "I am going to kill you." Cassie turned fast and disappeared into the crowd.

When Marcus reached Angie, she was unconscious, and red blood stained her white pants.

"Call an ambulance, somebody. Please call an ambulance. We need help, now, right now," his voice bellowed into the swarm of people.

The phone in Marcus' jacket pocket rang out. He ignored the call as he held onto Angie's hand peering through the crowd of people. Where were the ambulance and the paramedics? They weren't getting there fast enough. He looked down at Angie's legs. Blood had completely soaked through her pants and was now inching down her legs onto the floor beneath her.

Marcus didn't know which way to turn. The voices of the people looking on at this tragedy clawed at him.

"Oh, my God," a female voice yelled out.

"What happened? This is terrible." A young girl close to him questioned.

Marcus shot up to his feet. "Where's the ambulance? She's going to die. There's too much blood."

"There is no way she or that baby is going to make it," the woman standing next to Marcus said to him, not knowing who he was.

That was it. He couldn't take it anymore. Whaling pangs of fear and anxiety beat at his ear drums as the voices around him predicted death for Angie. Finally, both hands flew up to cover his ears, and he fled the crowd, sprinting toward the glass exit doors in search of the ambulance. Where was it? His breathing was rushed, his head was pounding, and every step felt like he was pulling his feet out of quicksand.

Just outside the mall doors, Marcus bent over and heaved up the breakfast that was gnawing at his insides. The paramedics were just rushing through the other set of double doors a few feet away from him. He wiped his mouth with the sleeve of his shirt. He raced inside reaching Angie seconds before the emergency team.

Two paramedics wheeled a gurney right up to Angie's still body that seemed lifeless to Marcus. They felt for a pulse, listened for a heartbeat, and assessed the amount of blood that she'd lost. "We've got to move," one of the paramedics demanded. After lifting her onto the gurney, the paramedics followed the path cleared by the mall security officers to the exit.

"Will she be okay? She's still breathing, right?" Marcus needed to know as he held her hand, called her name, and trotted alongside the gurney. She gave him no response. He could barely focus through the plump tears that pooled in his eyes.

"Sir, are you a family member?"

"I'm her fiancé," he proclaimed. He would be if they had made it to the baby shower and he'd gotten a chance to propose.

"Can I ride along in the ambulance with her?"

"Sorry, we can't allow you to do that."

"Please, I don't want to leave her," Marcus pleaded.

"Sorry, it's against regulations," the paramedic advised jogging alongside the gurney.

"I will follow the ambulance."

The ambulance sailed through traffic with the siren screeching and lights flashing while the big vehicle ran every red light. It was on a mission to save two lives, and every car and truck had better pull over to the shoulder of the road and let the ambulance barrel past.

"This is not happening," Marcus yelled, chasing behind the speeding ambulance. His cell phone cried out for the third time begging to be answered. The nervous expectant father plucked the phone from his pocket. His mother's voice leaped into his ear before he could say a word.

"Where in the world are you two? You guys are an hour late for the baby shower."

"Mom, she's not waking up. She was pushed down an escalator at the mall."

"What? Marcus, what are you talking about?"

He gave his mother the frightening details and advised that he was following the ambulance headed to the Methodist Dallas Medical Center.

"Oh, my God! We're on the way. Pray, baby, pray!"

CHAPTER SIXTY-SIX

Fear haunted the waiting room, which was packed with both Marcus and Angie's family. Several people schlepped out of the waiting room and down the hall to the elevator. Their destiny was the fourth floor, where the chapel would hopefully be a source that would welcome their prayers and send a miracle their way. Tear-stained faces, red puffy eyes, sobbing, and wads of Kleenex seemed to be the constant that bonded the Blue and Carter family on one accord, who were still sitting in the waiting room.

Echoes of disbelief drifted from one side of the room to the other. "How did something like this happen? This can't be real. Why would someone want to hurt a pregnant woman?"

Pam leaned over on Andre while Marcus' mother held her hand and her son's. She sat between them, encouraging each as best she could. Minutes crawled by, and no word on Angie.

A stern female voice stirred the group, "Code Blue, Code Blue, ICU." Marcus looked at Pam and bolted from his seat.

"No, that can't be my baby," Pam eked out.

Jayden and Nelson rushed to their mother's side.

Before Marcus could reach the door handle to exit the waiting room and head to the ICU, a nurse pushed open the door.

"I promised that I would keep you abreast of what's happening. I'm sure you heard the Code Blue call that just went off overhead. Angie did stop breathing."

A heavy cloud of sighs and, "Oh, my God, No, she can't be ..." escaped into the air.

"The doctors are working on her right now. The chaplain is on his way down to sit with the family. I promise I will be back shortly to give you an update."

"I need to go back there. I need to know for myself what's going on," Marcus demanded with a slam of his fist into the palm of his hand.

"Sir, I know this is hard. The doctors are doing their very best. You won't be able to go back until we have her stabilized." She touched his arm and assured him, "I will be back as soon as I know anything. I will come right back."

Marcus dropped his head and gave her his back as he departed from the doorway. His father stepped closer to him and wrapped him up in his big, heavy arms.

"She'll make it. You've got to believe that."

Marcus plopped down into the chair next to Pam. His father remained by his side. Silence cast a cloud of gloom over the room and sucked the life right out of it. The room was still and sullen for more than a few minutes.

Marcus shot up from his chair, bumping the table beside him, causing the lamp to wobble. "Where is that lying nurse? She said she would be right back. Somebody better tell me something, and I mean right now." His arms were flailing in the air as he stomped back and forth with fire in his eyes.

The door opened slowly, and the hospital chaplain entered. He introduced himself and asked if he could pray with the family.

"I'm going back there, and nobody is going to stop me," Marcus declared after the prayer. He barged toward the door. Four wide steps and the door swung open, almost crashing into the wall.

Three family members and Pam got up from their seats to march to the beat of Marcus' drum. They'd waited long enough, and somebody needed to tell them something about Angie.

A male doctor in a long white lab coat and blue scrubs stepped into Marcus' path and would soon feel his whirlwind of emotion. They both stopped suddenly within inches of each other.

"I'm sorry, sir. Please excuse me."

"Are you treating Angie? We've been waiting for the nurse to come back with an update on her condition. She never came, and no one has told us anything."

Pam's shaky voice cosigned Marcus' demands. "Please, tell us something, doctor. How is she? Is the baby, okay?"

"Let's step into the waiting room, please," the doctor motioned with his hand.

Marcus and the others followed the doctor into the same waiting room they'd just bolted out of.

"Is everyone here, family?" The doctor questioned with his eyes scanning the crowd that circled him.

"Yes, yes, now tell us what's going on," Pam ordered.

The doctor's glance dropped to the floor and quickly shot up to rest on the questioning faces in front of him. "Her internal injuries were severe. There was trauma to the brain, spleen, and heart. Internal bleeding caused a blood clot to form and travel to her heart. I'm so sorry. We did everything we could. She and the baby didn't make it."

The air in the room was heavy, and sorrow immediately swept in and hung overhead as if it owned the entire room. Pam's mouth moved, but no words escaped from her lips. She sucked in a slow breath and fainted in Andre's arms.

Tears streamed down the faces of every person in the waiting room. Disbelief and anger stood up and spoke out in shaky voices, whimpering and sobbing.

Marcus was still standing in the middle of the floor with a far-off look on his face. His cheeks were wet, and his hands trembled.

"Why don't you sit down for a minute," someone said to Marcus.

Marcus ignored the suggestion. He gritted his teeth, clenched both fists and declared, "I'm going to kill her," and stormed out of the waiting room, leaving behind a gaping, ten-and-a-half-sized hole in the wall from the thunderous kick he delivered on his way out.

The chaplain stayed with the family, attempting to console and encourage them. When Pam awakened, she wept constantly and complained of shortness of breath and chest pains. She was examined in the emergency room and admitted for observation. The difficult task of seeing her daughter lying dead would have to wait.

Throughout the night, Pam repeatedly awakened with words tumbling out of her mouth, "I can't do it. I just can't do it."

Andre never left her side knowing the days ahead would be filled with sorrow and pain that he wished he could wash away for her.

CHAPTER SIXTY-SEVEN

The sky was dark and frequently lit by sparks of lightning, that crashed overhead and crawled across it with a haunting, thunderous roar. Rain poured from the clouds like an angry waterfall determined to drown everyone in its path. Andre pulled up to the front entrance of the hospital. Pam's mother got out and ran for cover beyond the double-glass doors. Andre parked the car and then braved the waterfall as he dodged the puddles of water that sprung up like land mines on his path to the front door.

Once inside, he shook the umbrella and snatched off his soaked jacket. Pam had been released from the hospital shortly before her mother and Andre arrived. Her blood pressure was down, and her heart beat out of the danger zone. She hadn't had a heart attack, but a blow to her heart had caused her to collapse when she was told that Angie was dead.

The three of them met at the information desk. Andre wanted to absorb the pain he could see on Pam's face, put it all on his shoulders, and tote it around like a boulder of grief that was too heavy for her to carry. But all he could do was hold her hand and help her to walk the green mile. On the elevator, down to the lower level, across two different departments — there it was: the long hallway described by the woman at the information desk. Not one word was spoken before reaching the corridor.

"Can you wait for us here?" Pam's eyes pleaded with Andre to understand.

"I'll be right here." He kissed her forehead and pulled her into his broad chest for a few moments. Then he released her to face the inevitable.

Mrs. Carter pressed the button on the wall and gave Angie's name. They were there to identify her granddaughter's body. Would they be able to bear it?

The double doors opened when the buzzer sounded off. A man stepped into the hallway. His voice was soft, "I'm very sorry for your loss. Please follow me, ladies."

Pam didn't want to hear the usual words, "I'm sorry for your loss?" Was he sorry that her daughter was murdered? Did he know why she was murdered? Pam didn't even know. Those were just words. And she had already heard them too many times. If one more person says that to me, I will just scream.

Pam was numb as she walked with her mother's weak arms around her. They followed the man in a white coat. She doubled over every few steps, unsure if she could do it. Sorrow clutched at her chest, stole the even rhythm of her heartbeat, accelerated her breathing, and pushed out a flood of tears and a scream that tore through her mother's heart. "I can't do it. I just can't do it."

"Baby, I know it's painful. It's killing me, too. Let me do it for you. I will go and see her." Her words were clear, but her voice trembled, and so did her hands.

Pam slowly stood and swabbed at her eyes with the back of both hands. She eked out, "She's my daughter. Why, God? Why?" With her head tilted back and her eyelids closed tightly, she whispered, shaking her head, "I can't do it."

A tightness gripped at the grandmother's lungs that felt like a vice squeezing life out of her. She wanted to turn and run back down the hall, through the double doors, and not stop until she woke up from the nightmare she had to be living. The strength she needed was difficult to summon up, but her love for her daughter and granddaughter pushed her forward.

Pam pressed her back into the wall and slid to the floor as her mother released her hand to walk through the doors of the ice-cold room. Mrs. Carter rubbed her arms as the chill in the air stung at them. There it was, the long steel gurney that held the body of her only granddaughter lying there on display, waiting to be identified.

Mrs. Carter sucked in a cool breath. The white sheet that covered the body intimidated her. Didn't white represent purity, clean, happy things? Not that white sheet. It represented sorrow and unbearable heartache.

The man's soft-spoken voice seemed loud in the stillness of the room, "Are you ready, Ma'am?"

Who could be ready to do such a painful thing? She held his gaze, not wanting to let go. She had to. There was no going back. No denying her grandchild's body waiting for her beneath the white sheet. She clenched the handle of her purse as her head bobbed up and down.

Slowly, the man pulled the white sheet back. She stared at the body in front of her. The still-cold body before Mrs. Carter stole her breath and her thoughts. It was like time stood still. Was she having an out-of-body experience? It felt as though she hovered above her own body looking downward. Mrs. Carter struggled for words, but her throat wouldn't obey.

She stepped closer to the body as she balled up her fists and felt her nails dig deep into them. Her voice sliced through the silence, "It's not her."

"Ma'am, is this your granddaughter?" His voice questioned the denial.

She closed her eyelids one more time. Okay, is this real? Did I really see right? Her eyelids peeled back slowly like the curtain being drawn for the opening act of a play. But this wasn't a play. It was real life.

Mrs. Carter leaned closer, and her voice found her. "No, it's not her. Jesus, how? This is not my granddaughter. Where is my granddaughter? Where is she?"

Pam entered the room and stood behind her mother. Her strength faded from her body as she sank to the floor again. "Cassie, it's Cassie. That's not Angie."

CHAPTER SIXTY-EIGHT

Marcus schlepped through the sliding glass doors of Methodist Dallas Medical Center. His father marched beside him. They shook the rain off their jackets and headed to the same information desk that Pam and her mother sought out for directions. They met with a different attendant.

"I need to see Angie Carter." Marcus couldn't say the word body or dead. It would make the loss of her real. He was there to see her one last time before the funeral home would do the dirty deed and remove all evidence that she had once been alive. His body was limp, heavy, and tired. He could barely focus on what the male attendant was saying.

"Son, come on; the elevator is this way." His thick hand landed on his son's shoulder as they walked. "I'm not sure how you're still standing after running all over the city last night looking for the crazy woman who pushed Angie. We've got to get you back to the house. You need some rest."

Marcus stopped abruptly, and his father's hand fell from his shoulder. "I can't sleep. I have to find that insane demon that killed my family and make sure she pays for it." His eyeballs were infected with sprouts of tiny red blood vessels that crawled across both eyeballs.

His father took his big, strong son into his arms and allowed him to weep. "Let it out, Marcus. Just let it go. I know the hurt is heavy."

Marcus wept silently, with tears dripping down his face onto his father's shoulder. More than a minute of silent sorrow overwhelmed him. He lifted his head and swabbed his face with his father's white handkerchief. Mr. Blue Sr. pressed the up button for the elevator. They stepped inside, and he pressed the button for the fifth floor. The elevator jerked and started its climb. Once the doors opened, they stepped out and were immediately touched by the bright lights, nurses walking down the hallway, and the activity at the nurse's station.

Marcus' head shifted to the right and left then up to his dad. "This can't be the right floor." Wouldn't a morgue be dark and quiet? There wouldn't be any smiles or laughter, Marcus told himself.

His dad stretched out his arm, pointing to the nurse's station. "Let's ask there."

Slowly, they approached the desk. Marcus rubbed his hand against his pant leg. The sweat on his right hand wouldn't seem to go away. He shoved his hand down into his pant pocket as it started to tremble. He rested his other hand on the desktop. "Angie Carter, we need to see her, please. His gaze shifted to his dad, then back to the blonde-haired nurse in front of him.

"Sure, she's in room five twelve, next to the last door on the right of this hallway," the nurse directed with a lifted hand, pointing the way with a smile.

Would her body still be in the room that she died in? Wasn't she in the trauma area when she died? There that word was: died. He'd allowed himself to think it twice. It wasn't true until he saw it for himself. Though his heart didn't want to face the dark reality as his feet moved toward the room. Marcus walked the last few steps at a slower pace.

His father's heavy hand landed on his shoulder once again. He squeezed hard. "I'm here. I'm right here."

Puffy eyes and a scruffy, unshaven face painted with sprouting black stubbles of hair faced the closed door. Marcus pulled in a deep breath, held it for four seconds, pushed it out hard, and pushed the door open.

The room was dim, the blinds closed, and the light over the head of the bed was off. Only the trail of light that spilled into the room from the hallway landed on the body lying in the bed. Marcus stood in the doorway for a moment, willing his feet to move toward the bed. Why would she be here and not in that cold, dark morgue? Still confused, the closer he got, certainty hit him. It was Angie, the mother of his child. It was her lifeless body that lay still before him.

The room was quiet. Neither he nor his father had said a word. Just as the grieving fiancé took a step closer to the bed, a nurse entered the room, and light barged in along with her.

"I'm sorry to interrupt. It's time for her to nurse, and I need to wake her."

"Wake her?" Marcus' voice was heavy and hoarse. Water was welling up in his eyes. "She's gone. How can you wake her?" He stepped closer to the side of the bed.

The nurse glanced over at him with a wrinkled forehead. "Are you a family member?"

Before Marcus could respond, Angie's eyelids opened, and she shifted her head to face the nurse.

"It's time for you to nurse your baby. I'll bring him to you in just a few minutes. You have some visitors." She nodded her head in their direction.

Angie turned her head, and her eyes found Marcus.

Marcus couldn't move. Was he dreaming? It all felt so real — the drive to the hospital, the rain pouring down on him, the elevator ride, and the nurse who directed them to the room where they now stood.

"Marcus, baby, are you okay?" Angie stretched out her arm and offered him her hand.

He latched onto her warm palm; he could feel the life in her body. She was alive, he wasn't dreaming, and Angie wasn't dead. Tears trickled down his cheeks as he struggled to push his voice out.

"How? How is this possible? They told us that you were..."

"Shhh. Don't say it. I know what you believed to be true. I know what the doctor told you."

Marcus held onto her hand as she spoke. His father stood by his side with no words, eager to listen.

"There were two of us brought into the emergency room with the same first and last name. The other woman used my name, and she was pregnant, too. The nurse said she was hit by a car running out of the mall. She was the one who died. She even had my purse and wallet. I guess she took it when I was at the mall. I must have walked off and left it when I got my make-up done or stopped at the jewelry store." She rubbed her forehead. "I could hardly believe it when the nurse told me about the crazy mix-up."

As the fog in his head started to clear, Marcus collapsed onto Angie's bed and covered her with his upper body. "This is a miracle. Yesterday, no one could have told me I would be this happy. You would be alive, and my life wouldn't be upside down." His lips found hers, and with the passionate kiss he delivered, he offered her the joy that filled his heart.

Abruptly, his lips departed hers. "My son, he's okay, right?" His eyes were wide and pleading for the answer to be yes.

"Yes, baby. He is two weeks early, but perfect." She pushed herself up in bed. "Speaking of the youngest Mr. Blue, here he is now."

The senior, Mr. Blue's eyelids popped open as he ended his prayer just as the nurse rolled the baby into the room. She lifted the baby and gently placed him into Angie's arms.

"Would you like me to try calling your mother and the baby's father again?" The nurse inquired of Angie.

Angie cradled the baby close to her. "No, my family just got here." She offered Marcus a smile as she kissed the little boy's tiny fingers and took a whiff of his soft skin. "Little Marcus, meet your father and your grandfather. Guess what? They are also named Marcus." She gestured to Marcus to take the baby.

The new father cradled his son close to his chest. He kissed his fingers and forehead. "Dad, this is my son."

The proud grandfather's head rolled back, and his eyes found the ceiling. "Dear God, you are more than good. Thank you."

"Marcus, where is my mother?" Angie wanted to know.

"Oh, my God, I need to call her and my mother." He marveled at his son, not wanting to leave him for one minute.

"Stay here with your family. I'll step out and call them both," his father assured him.

Marcus leaned over and kissed Angie's lips softly. "Thank you. Thank you for my son." With one hand, he touched the bruises on her face. "How did you survive such a horrible fall?"

"Only God could have done something so miraculous," she proclaimed with a smile.

Two hours later, family members on both sides stood in front of the nursery window. They smiled, pointed, and peered at little Boy Blue, kicking and screaming at the top of his lungs as he greeted his family. Pam, Angie's brothers, her grandparents, Vanessa, Marcus' parents, his sisters, and every other possible family member who could get to the hospital, including Uncle Billy, stood with their faces glued to the window of the nursery, just taking in the wonderful miracle God had performed.

Marcus pulled his dad to the side. "I need you to go to my apartment and get the ring Mom gave me. I'm going to propose to Angie today. I almost lost her and my son. I'm not wasting any more time."

"Good for you. Your mother will be very happy to hear that." His glance shifted to his wife, a few feet away, tapping on the glass and looking on at Baby Blue.

Uncle Billy's voice spoke over everyone and claimed the attention that his announcement deserved. Marcus and his dad rejoined the group.

"Well, family, believe it or not, we did it. That little boy will not want for anything. We finally hit the lottery." Uncle Billy told the story of their big win as he stroked his salt-and-pepper mustache. The Blue family was in the green.

Marcus slipped the buzzing phone from his pant pocket. An unknown number was calling for the third time that day. Maybe it was a family member or friend concerned about Angie. He stepped a couple of feet away.

"Hello."

"Is this Marcus Blue?"

"Yes, this is Marcus. Who is this?"

"You don't know me, Marcus, but that's not important. I thought I should inform you that you didn't get away with murder when you killed my sister and her unborn child. I know exactly where you are, and I will even the score in time. For now, enjoy the celebration of the birth of your son. When you least expect it, expect it. BOOM! But for now, sleep on it!"

"I didn't kill anyone," said Marcus to a silent phone. He squeezed the cell tightly in his hand. "Cassie has a sister?" he said shoving the phone into his pocket. The sound of the caller's voice accompanied Marcus back to the group. The threat cradled in his mind. An unknown danger was lurking about his new family. What would happen next? Marcus scanned the hallway. His eyes darted from one face to the next. It could be someone nearby, anyone. The excitement he'd felt minutes ago escaped him like water spiraling down a drain. Fear infused his veins. He clenched both fists. I'll protect them with my last breath. Another thought pierced his mind. Is she safe? His heart rate rose like the red liquid in a glass thermometer. He turned and sprinted down the hallway back to room five twelve. Not again. Please, God! Not again.

The End

Made in the USA
Coppell, TX
21 June 2026

82764453R00194